The Eternal Engagement

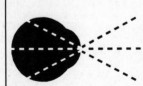

This Large Print Book carries the
Seal of Approval of N.A.V.H.

THE ETERNAL ENGAGEMENT

MARY B. MORRISON

THORNDIKE PRESS

A part of Gale, Cengage Learning

GALE
CENGAGE Learning·

Detroit • New York • San Francisco • New Haven, Conn • Waterville, Maine • London

GALE
CENGAGE Learning

LIBRARY OF CONGRESS CATALOGING-IN-PUBLICATION DATA

Morrison, Mary B.
  The eternal engagement / by Mary B. Morrison. — Large print ed.
    p. cm. — (Thorndike Press large print African-American)
  ISBN-13: 978-1-4104-4185-0 (hardcover)
  ISBN-10: 1-4104-4185-7 (hardcover)
  1. African-Americans—Fiction. 2. Betrothal—Fiction. 3. Domestic
fiction. 4. Large type books. I. Title.
PS3563.O87477E84 2011
813'.54—dc23   2011032897

Published in 2011 by arrangement with Dafina Books, an imprint of Kensington Publishing Corp.

Printed in Mexico
1 2 3 4 5 6 7 15 14 13 12 11

Leslie Small,
Dawn Mallory,
Richard C. Montgomery,
and (my son)
Jesse Byrd, Jr.,
Thanks

Special Dedication
With Loving Memories

Walter Zacharius

Eternally grateful that I'm a part of the empire you built and legacy you've left.

Decisions

influenced by thought
or the lack thereof
manifest in melancholy
or marinate in the magnificent
dictate direction that
makes one's life better
or bitter
but for better or for worse
each decision one deliberates
will become either
a compliment
or a catastrophe

ACKNOWLEDGMENTS

Thanks to my wonderful fans, I'm enjoying a double tenth anniversary. Some of you have journeyed with me from my self-publishing debut of *Soulmates Dissipate* in June 2000. The year 2010 marked my tenth anniversary as an author, and 2011 is my tenth anniversary being published by Kensington Publishing Corporation. I refuse to celebrate my success without you, because you are the reason that I continue to write.

Due to your loyalty, Jada, Wellington, Darius, and Fancy are headed to the big screen for seven films based on each novel in the *Soulmates Dissipate* series. Be sure to buy the re-release of *Soulmates Dissipate* and *Never Again Once More* with their new sexy covers and re-read the entire series before the movies are released in theaters.

Many of you started reading my novels out of order, not realizing I write in series. It didn't take long before you caught up on my SMD series, and then you immediately fell in love with the characters — Honey, Grant, Valentino, and Benito — in the Honey Diaries series. That's love I continue to feel.

November 5, 6, and 7, 2010, we showcased my first stage production, *Single Husbands,* based on my HoneyB novel. Packing the house for four spectacular shows, the turnout was the largest attendance at the Malonga Casquelourd Theater (in Oakland) in over a decade. We look forward to bringing *Single Husbands* to your hometown.

I have to give praise to my amazing son, Jesse Byrd, Jr. He's a playwright, film producer, entrepreneur, and, most importantly, a man with great character. I love you. You're the best. I'm inviting my fans to visit Jesse's website at www.OiseauChateau .com.

My mother and father, Elester Noel and Joseph Henry Morrison, are my guardian angels. It takes a lot to rear other people's children. I didn't live with my parents, so I give thanks to my great-aunt, Ella Beatrice Turner, and her husband, Willie Frinkle, for welcoming me into their home. And I'm grateful for my earthly mother, Barbara Cooper.

My brothers and sisters mean the world

to me. Wayne, Andrea, Derrick, and Regina Morrison, Margie Rickerson, Debra Noel, and Bryan Turner.

With all my heart, I thank each of the independent bookstore owners who have supported my career over the years. And I'm blessed to have friends whom I consider family: Felicia Polk, Vyllorya A. Evans, Marilyn Edge, Michaela Burnett, Carment Polk, Onie Simpson, Vanessa Ibanitoru, Brenda Clark, and Malissa Walton.

I love, love, love all of my Facebook friends and fans, my Twitter peeps, My-Space crew, and my McDonough 35 Senior High fam.

To my author friends Gloria Mallette, Marissa Monteilh aka Pynk, Kimberla Lawson Roby, and Victor McGlothlin, I wish you the best of everything.

Selena James, my editor, is simply the best. Looking forward to our next three books with Kensington Publishing Corporation. Adeola Saul, it was so wonderful getting to know you during the tour in Atlanta. To the entire Kensington family, I love you!

I miss and thank my career-long editor, Karen R. Thomas. Looking forward to working with you on future projects. To my new editor at Grand Central Publishing, LaToya Smith; my publicist, Linda A. Duggins; and to Jamie Raab, I appreciate all you do to make HoneyB a growing success.

I have two of the best agents in the literary business, Andrew Stuart and Claudia Menza. Thanks for all you do.

In loving memory of Manie Barron, you are truly missed.

Wishing each of you peace and prosperity. Feel free to hit me up at:

Website: www.MaryMorrison.com

Facebook Fan Page: Mary Honey B Morrison

Twitter: marybmorrison

AUTHOR'S NOTE

As promised, I'm still going to write the pre-
quel to *Soulmates Dissipate* entitled *Our
Little Story.*

FYI, in *Darius Jones,* I've brought together
the main characters from both series.

Below I number both of my series in reading order:

Soulmates Dissipate Series

1. *Soulmates Dissipate*
2. *Never Again Once More*
3. *He's Just a Friend*
4. *Somebody's Gotta Be on Top*
5. *Nothing Has Ever Felt Like This*
6. *When Somebody Loves You Back*
7. *She Ain't the One*
8. *Darius Jones*

Honey Diaries Series

1. *Sweeter than Honey*
2. *Who's Loving You*
3. *Unconditionally Single*
4. *Darius Jones*

MONA
PROLOGUE

May 2000

"Promise me you won't get upset."

Why did he have to say that, knowing she'd ask, "Upset about what?"

"I'll tell you in a minute, but first you have to promise me," he insisted.

Graduation day they sat in the empty stadium at their high school. The two of them. Alone. Surrounded by the morning's humidity and sunshine, they were draped in their royal blue gowns and caps with dangling golden tassels. The plastic-plated 2000 charm symbolized the end of their preadult years.

Batting her long lashes, she stood and gazed out over the field. Football season was over for him. Dating him was over for her. There were no new beginnings for them. Just old memories.

Licking the same soft, drizzling vanilla, their tongues would circle the sugar cone until their lips met. His kisses were sweeter than the melted yogurt she'd suck from his mouth. As they talked all night on the phone, his voice comforted her. Making love for the first time to Usher's "Nice and Slow" made the little girl inside her feel all grown up. The way Lincoln had moved his body — teasing, grinding, pleasing, winding, thrusting, easing his way inside of her — made her cry.

When you're a teenager, you think all there is to love is a feeling. A feeling that'll never end. You believe your world is perfect and you're invincible. No worries about having your heart broken. No cares about partying all night, where your next meal would come from, gas money to cruise around town in your bucket with your friends, or how your college tuition is going to get paid. Those worries were for parents, not children.

Their relationship had ended when he'd started showing interest in another girl. She knew there was someone else when he began looking through her, not at her. His walk was a little taller. Smile was a lot wider. He laughed louder than usual at things that weren't meant to be funny. Wow, there was another girl that excited him more than she had. She'd never imagined that happening. But it had. That's when they'd become friendly. The first day of eleventh grade, her friendship with him was never the same.

"Lincoln, how do I know if I'll be upset if you won't tell me?"

"Mona Lisa, please," he begged. "Just promise me."

If only he knew how many times she fantasized about walking down the aisle with him. She'd have the whitest white wedding dress with a train so long, two people would have to carry it. Going to his college football games would make her beam brighter than the panels of lights illuminating the field. She pictured what their babies would look like with his eyes and her nose. His hair and her smile. He was the only boy, soon to be a man, who had made her feel pretty inside and out. He was her first love, first lover, first real boyfriend. Steven Cunningham from the second grade didn't count.

Funny how the first could never be anything except. No one came inside of her before him. No one made her daydream in class, cut class, or have sex in an empty classroom, locker room, or backseat of her bucket, before him. She still loved him. Probably would always be in love with him.

He kissed her, then said, "If I don't tell you now, I won't be able to tell you after we walk across the stage."

His large, light brown eyes pleaded more than his words. His dark, short curly hair was twisted into perfect coils. One stood out atop his head. Gently she fingered it into place.

Standing before his six-foot-four-inch, one hundred ninety pounds, she held the back of his head, pressed his cheek against her stomach. She held his face there, this moment she'd cherish forever. She tried to sense if his news was good or bad. Not really sure, she opened her eyes, and whispered, "Then don't tell me."

His grandparents were well known throughout their community. They had raised him well. He was a true gentleman. She hated that he'd broken up with her two years ago, but she had to respect the way he'd done it. He hadn't embarrassed her after a game, in front of his teammates, or at a gathering with their friends. Hadn't called her out of her name or acted as though their breakup was her fault. One Sunday afternoon he'd come to her house, sat on the front porch with her, held her hands, looked into her eyes, then told her, "I'm going to ask Katherine Clinton to be my girlfriend. And if she says, 'Yes,' then our relationship has to end."

Lincoln grabbed her hand, the same way he'd done two years ago. He scooted back on the shiny metal bleachers, pulled her toward him. "Mona Lisa, please." He sat her down beside him. "I wanted to say I'm sorry for breaking up with you, man. You were nothing but good to me. I was stupid for that. Kather—"

Removing her cap, she placed it in her lap, then lamented, "Do not mention her name to me. You've been with her for two years. I've moved on. You got who you wanted."

Her pride said she'd move on. Her heart begged to differ. Lincoln was different from the other football players. He was the starting running back. He held the school's record for the most yards and the most touchdowns. He could've scored with any girl in Selma, and a few moms too, if he wanted. But he didn't. He stayed faithful to her until Katherine accepted his offer. Then he came back to her house, sat on her porch, and let her know his new relationship was official.

Squeezing her hands, he said, "But that's just it. I don't have who I need. I need you. I need you to pray for me. Pray for me every day. Pray I don't get killed. Pray I return home safe. I love you, Mona Lisa. I really do."

His kiss on her cheek was warm. He gently stroked his thumb over the spot he'd kissed. Like when they were a couple, everything Lincoln had done was passionate and deliberate.

"Why do you love me so much?" she asked him for the first time.

She knew her unique beauty wasn't what the girls consider commercially appealing. The bridge of her nose aligned with her forehead. No dip between the eyes like most people. Her nostrils, so close to the bridge they almost blended. Her upper lip was full and wide with a tiny V that pointed to a small bubble centered in her top lip. Her mother had told her, "That was no accident. God made you that way." He also divided her lower lip with an indentation, making it seem like two halves instead of one whole. Her cheeks were flat. Nothing a little blush couldn't redefine. Ears flat as though fading into the sides of her head instead of standing out. Nothing her hair couldn't conceal when she wanted.

Individually, her features could have made her appear freakish. But Lincoln loved kissing her succulent mouth. She didn't have a curvaceous ass, big breasts, or thick legs. She deemed herself a goddess worthy of royal treatment by all guys, but Lincoln was the one who mattered the most.

Tears dampened the cap covering her thighs. She fingered his gold tassel. Somewhat understanding what he meant by not getting killed and returning home safe, silently she said a little prayer for him. Prayed he hadn't done what some of the other graduates had done.

"I turned down all my D-1 football scholarships. I signed up for the Marines. My recruiter is coming to get me right after I accept my diploma."

Suddenly, her tears were accompanied by a downpour and an outburst. "Why, Lincoln? Why did you join the military without checking with me?" she cried. "Oh, my gosh, they brainwashed you into not taking a full ride? I would've begged you, told you to wait. Wait until we graduated from college, got married, had a few babies. That way you wouldn't be leaving me alone." She smothered his face with kisses.

"What am I going to do without you? It's not too late to change your mind. Take one of those scholarship offers and go to college with me like we'd planned. That way we can be . . ." Her Southern drawl faded with sadness as her words trailed off.

For a moment she'd forgotten he wasn't hers.

The dream she'd dreamt for them ended two years ago. But it still felt like their breakup was yesterday. She tightened her lips, blinked to force back new tears.

Lincoln shoved his hand in his pocket, pulled out a silver band. "I won't be gone for long. I'll be back in four years. I'm sorry I didn't tell you I want to serve my country. My grandfather said enlisting means more than football. And you mean more to me than her. This here is an engagement ring. Promise me no matter what happens, we'll be friends forever. Promise me, Mona Lisa Ellington, that when I come back from the military —" He paused, held her hand in his as he slid the silver band on her left ring finger and asked, "Mona Lisa, will you marry me?"

This was a good time to exercise the fifth amendment. Not answering him wasn't the same as lying. Mona kissed him. Unzipped his robe, turned it inside out, laid it between the bleachers.

"Make love to me, Lincoln. Right here. Right now."

"I didn't ask you to marry me so I can have sex with you. I —"

"Hush," she whispered. She unbuckled his pants, lowered them to his thighs. "Lay down for me."

Raising her dress, she pulled her panties to the side, straddled him. She held his beautiful, rock-hard dick in her hand, then guided him inside her. The second his head entered her vagina, she felt all grown up again. This was her first time having unprotected sex, and it made her feel like a woman.

"You need to get up," Lincoln said. "I'm about to cum."

She knew she should've done as he'd asked, but her body tingled with pleasure she'd never experienced. Rotating her hips deeper into his pelvis, she trembled uncontrollably.

"So that's what all the excitement is about," she said, standing over him. Her panties were wet. "I came too. That's another first for me, for us."

She'd never cheated on her new boyfriend, Steven Cunningham, until now. Steven had never given her an orgasm. Mona had to know if she could experience that again, but she couldn't tell Steven the truth. That would give him one more reason to hate Lincoln.

Lincoln stood, buckled his pants, put on his robe. "You didn't answer my question."

Mona kissed him. Her body burst with energy. They were both in relationships with other people. What he'd asked wasn't realistic.

"If this is good-bye, if going to the military is what you truly want, and I don't believe it is, especially after what just happened between us, I'll just say, I hope that works out for you. I'll keep your ring. And when you get back, we'll see."

As much as she loved Lincoln, there was no way she'd place her life on hold for four years waiting for him.

LINCOLN
CHAPTER 1

May 2000

"Promise me you won't get upset."

"Upset? About what?" she asked.

"I'll tell you in a minute, but first you have to promise me," he insisted.

Lincoln was in love with Katherine Clinton. When she strutted into his eleventh-grade homeroom class wearing a sleeveless dress and high heels, she instantly became the hottest girl in all of Selma, Alabama. He had to make her his girlfriend before any of his teammates got to her. His breakup with Mona Lisa was fast and to the point. He respected Mona too much to use her or string her along. Besides, two years of dating one girl in high school was not only commendable, but highly remarkable for an athlete with his stats.

Sitting on the sideline at the fifty-yard mark with Katherine brought tears to his eyes. Unlike being alone with Mona a half hour ago, Lincoln really felt like he and Katherine were the only two in the football stadium.

"Okay, I promise. Now tell me," she said.

Lincoln removed a gold band from his pocket, held it in his hand. He knew she expected a proposal and she was right. But first he had to tell her the bad news for her, good news for him.

"Katherine, I've joined the Marines."

Katherine hugged him tight. Her arms clamped around his shoulders as she cried uncontrollably. "Say it isn't so, William Lincoln. When did you decide this? What happened to all your scholarship offers? What about your going to USF in Tampa and my going to UFL in Miami? I was excited about us being in Florida together. That's all I've dreamt about since I got my acceptance letter. You know this."

That was one of the differences between Katherine and Mona that he really loved about Katherine. She always made him feel manly. As though he was the only guy in her world. Everything he did excited her. Nothing he'd done excited his parents. Not much of what he'd accomplished thrilled his grandparents until he agreed to enlist. His family's apathy was the main reason he refused to sign a letter of intent.

Lincoln stared over the field. He was trading a football field to fight in the field, as his sergeant called it. Truth be told, going into the military terrified him. The money he'd make excited him. He never had a steady income. His grandfather told him, "Football players come a dime a dozen, son. Only the few and proud can serve the greatest country on earth. What you gon' do if one of the big ole linebackers break your leg? When I was your age, I fought in World War II."

Grandpa was right about the potential injury. Several of his teammates had had offers, but once they were injured, the colleges didn't want them. Grandpa said, "The university will use you up, make money off of your talent, and not put a dime in your pocket for all your hard labor." But if the decision were Lincoln's alone, he'd take the full ride, go to college, and be the first in his family to graduate from a university.

Since joining "the few" would make his grandfather proud, he'd sacrifice his dreams. He doubted his mother and father would keep in touch with him after he walked across the stage. It might appear selfish on his part, but having the two women who loved him the most wait for him was better than returning home to no one who cared. He'd given up on going pro.

"I'm leaving today. Right after I get my diploma."

Tears drenched more tears as Katherine cried out loud. "What am I going to do without you?"

He was Katherine's first lover, first real boyfriend. With Mona, she said he was her first boyfriend, but it was hard to tell. He'd heard in the locker room that some loser name Steven Cunningham hit it first. Dude was a loner, a nerd, a weirdo.

Right now, Lincoln's priority was Katherine.

Handing her his high school championship jersey, he said, "You're going to go to UFL, major in journalism like you've always wanted to, and then you'll get that job anchoring the news. That way if there's cable TV where I'm stationed, hopefully I can see your beautiful face on the regular."

Katherine was ultrafeminine. Mona Lisa was a lady when she had to be, but mostly Mona was more of a mystery than the mysteries she loved solving. He understood why she'd started dating Steven after their breakup. They were both odd, but in different ways. Lincoln couldn't lie, Mona's spice and enthusiasm to explore the unknown excited him. If he could marry both Mona

Lisa and Katherine, he would.

Sliding the gold band on Katherine's left ring finger, Lincoln said, "I need you to pray for me. Pray for me every day. Pray I don't get killed. Pray I return home safe. I love you, Katherine. I really do. And when I get out, promise you'll marry me."

He pressed his warm lips to hers. Gently dried her tears.

"I promise, William Lincoln. No matter how long it takes, I'll wait for you," Katherine said, then hesitated. Her voice trembled. "I was going to tell you after we got our diplomas . . . I think I'm pregnant."

That was not what he wanted to hear. Instantly, her words made him regret having sexed Mona without protection. Lincoln held her tighter than he'd held Mona. Katherine made his leaving easier. Mona Lisa could keep the ring, but not answering his question gave him the answer he needed.

Katherine could keep her ring too. *I think I'm pregnant?* He thought she was different. Wrong. Katherine was a manipulator. Mona Lisa too. As long as they got what they wanted, they didn't care about him. Nobody cared about him.

To his parents in Chicago — who had come to his graduation as though they were visitors — he'd always be the thug/drug dealer/dummy kid they wished they'd never had. He wasn't any of those things. He was simply trying to fit in on the South Side of Chitown. The dealers and thugs in middle school loved and protected him because he was a great athlete. Plus, with a 4.0 GPA, how could his parents call him a dummy? He never understood why they'd sent him to Selma to live with his grandparents. Maybe he was his parents' insurance for them to remain his grandparents' beneficiaries.

To his grandparents in Selma, he'd given them a reason to get out of their house. They'd come to his football games. His grandfather would stand on his prosthetic legs and cheer each time he touched the ball. His grandmother's shaking hands spilled more popcorn than she ate each time she stood. They instilled in him a sense of pride. But his pride was not his passion. Maybe he could change his mind and go to college.

Neither his parents nor his grandparents cared about his scholarship offers or how he'd earned a slice of the American pie before it was done baking. If he stayed healthy, he could write his own ticket to the pros. That's what Katherine wanted. Not him. She wanted his money.

He stood, stared down at Katherine. "Let me know how that works out for you."

Lincoln trotted across the fifty-yard line, broke to the left, exited his high school stadium for the last time, and never looked back.

KATHERINE
CHAPTER 2

February 2001

"Owwww! I can't push again, Mama. It hurts too much," she cried.

Sweat rolled from her eighteen-year-old forehead down her neck. The hospital gown, soaked throughout, stuck to her body like a wet rag. She collapsed onto the mattress that supported her back in an almost sitting position.

Until now, losing her virginity to Lincoln was the worst vaginal pain she'd experienced. Eight hours of sporadic stomach cramping made her feel as though she were dying. How could any teenager survive childbirth?

"I can't do this anymore. Get it out of me! Cut it out! Pull it . . ." Her words faded into a sobbing cry.

"You're doing great, Katherine," the doctor said. "I can see the crown of your baby's head. Don't push until I tell you."

Three minutes later, Katherine snatched the sheet, balled it between her fingers, and hurled herself forward as far as her huge, round belly allowed.

"Owwww! This is awful," she said, flopping backward. "I need to push."

She didn't know which was worse, her labor pains or her not hearing from Lincoln in nine months. She needed him at the birth of their baby. Holding his hand would've eased the pain in her heart.

Abandonment. Dejection. Betrayal. Why?

All the times she'd been there for him. What was on his mind that made him not want to be there for her? What made him treat her this way? Her cell number and her mom's home phone number and address were the same. She wasn't mad at him for trying to please his grandfather, but why hadn't he called to find out whether she was pregnant with his baby? Didn't he care about her? About them? Did his grandfather tell him she was pregnant? Was his grandfather to blame for Lincoln's not calling?

"Ow . . . oh, God, help me." Tears rolled into sweat that soaked the gown that clung to her tender breasts. Every part of her body ached.

Holding her hand, her mother said, "Nothing hurts more than making a bad decision that you have to live with the rest of your life. Unless you're married, Katherine, do not, I repeat, do not birth any more babies into this world."

Katherine prayed for a boy. Maybe her baby would give her the love Lincoln used to. The ring Lincoln gave her was in her dorm room. She didn't want to risk losing track of it at the hospital, so she'd taken it off. Soon as she was released, and back in the family dormitory, she was putting it back on.

"I'm engaged to be marri—" Katherine held her stomach. "Mama! I wanna push."

Calmly the doctor said, "Not yet. But we're close. I need you to dilate two more centimeters first. Hang in there. You're doing great, Katherine."

No, she wasn't doing great. She was doing horribly.

In two years, she'd had sex with Lincoln only twenty-three times because he abstained during football season. They'd started out using protection. Toward the end of their senior year, she'd gone to Planned Parenthood to get on the pill. College was a few months after their graduation, and the last thing they needed was a baby. She protected them by taking birth control.

"Owwww!" Leaning forward, then flopping backward — her movements became redundant.

Didn't take long for her to realize she should've listened to the counselor and still used condoms. Maybe their baby was God's way of giving her a piece of Lincoln. Wasn't the jersey he'd worn in the championship game, then gave to her on graduation day, good enough? Or the ring? Or his love?

"Mama isn't saying your baby is the bad decision. Your mistake was not using protection. And honey, that's a bad decision for more than one reason," her mother said, then kissed her forehead. "I wanted better for you, Katherine. That's why I moved us from Hollywood to Selma. I didn't want you to end up a single teenage mother like me."

"Owwww!" Katherine screamed, leaned back, then exhaled holding her stomach.

Her mother was her biggest advocate. Her mom made her go to UFL. Finish her first freshman semester, start her second. Katherine should've been studying with her group of new friends. Instead, she was in the delivery room in Gainesville, her friends were in the waiting room, and Lincoln was only God knew where, doing what. She feared he'd fallen in love with someone else. If he hadn't, why hadn't he called?

Tears for him blanketed her eyes. "I'm

sorry, Mama. I'm so sorry I disappointed you. I promise I won't do this again."

At least she could make a promise she'd keep.

"Hush, honey. Having a baby is no reason for you to be sorry about anything. I'm going to stay here with you and watch our baby while you get your education. This baby is going to see its mother on television anchoring the news. That's always been your dream, Katherine. Don't ever let anyone take away your dream. We Clintons do not give up on anything, you hear me?"

Did that anything include Lincoln? He was a good man. An honest man. What made him tell her, "I hope that works out for you."

"Now look at me, baby." Her mother placed her palm against her cheek, then continued, "Your crown is crooked. Straighten it up."

Was her crown crooked because of Mona Lisa? Katherine hadn't seen Mona since last August, right before both of them left for college. Few people in Selma knew about her pregnancy. She'd hoped Mona was one of them.

"Owwww! This time might take a little longer, Ma. I can't help it. I love Lincoln."

Her mother had taught her, she was a

queen, and a queen with a crooked crown was a wannabe. She'd say, "Katherine, always know your self-worth, baby. And for that, you don't need a man or anybody else cosigning for you."

"Forget about him," her mother said.

The doctor said, "Okay, it's time. Come on. One more strong push for us, Katherine. You're almost done."

She prayed that wasn't true. Being done with Lincoln. Her school break was three months away. He should use his leave and come home for a summer vacation.

Katherine screamed, cried, squeezed her mom's hand, then curled into the fetal position again. She squealed, then pushed with love and disappointment. Happy her mom was there. But she was still sad that Lincoln was not.

No address to send him a letter and pictures. She'd make sure Lincoln's grandparents got to see their baby often. She'd take lots of photos and videos, and when Lincoln did come back to them, he'd see what he'd missed.

Maybe Lincoln never wanted to have kids because his parents didn't want him. A Chicago kid born on the South Side, Lincoln didn't get the choice to live in Selma. Their meeting must've been fate because it

37

wasn't her decision to move to Selma either. His parents sent him to Selma to keep him out of trouble. At least that was what he'd said. Maybe Lincoln hadn't joined the military. Maybe he had a girlfriend in Chicago.

Her mama shouted with joy, "It's a boy! I got myself a grandson."

And on February 14th, at eighteen years of age, Katherine Clinton had herself a beautiful baby. Her ability to do what she wanted would never be the same.

"Look at this bundle of joy," her mom said.

The doctor handed her mom the scissors. "Would you like to cut the cord?"

"Katherine?"

"Yes, Mama. It's okay."

"Thank you, Jesus, he's got all his fingers and all his toes."

"Let me see him, Mama."

Not caring about the slimy coating on his body, Katherine kissed her baby's big hands and feet. She uncurled one of his legs. He was really long. Dark curly hair framed his face. His large, light brown eyes were halfway open, full of love. He looked just like his daddy.

She might make the jersey Lincoln gave her into a receiving blanket for their baby if she could stop sleeping in it every night. Maybe one day their child would get a lot of scholarship offers like his dad. But unlike Lincoln, their son would get his college degree first. Then he could decide what he wanted to do.

"Mama, do you like the name Jeremiah?"

"Baby, Mama doesn't like it. Mama loves it. Hey, little Jeremiah Clinton. Grandmommy loves you. Yes, I do."

Katherine cried. What would she ever do without her mom? Her mother could call him whatever she wanted, but her baby's birth certificate would read Jeremiah Lincoln.

LINCOLN
CHAPTER 3

May 2001

One year in, three to go.

Being in the military wasn't that bad. He'd been promoted from private to private first class, soon to become lance corporal. Physical workouts were easier than football practices. He'd packed on a few extra pounds, all muscle. Mostly his biceps and thighs were bigger. He liked his new body, but not more than the females he met when draped in his dress blue uniform. Being a Marine had its perks.

Lincoln became fascinated with all the weaponry in the Marine Corps arsenal, especially the M16 rifle. His quickness and precision on the football field — running, dropping, rolling — aided his ability to hit a moving target five hundred yards away while kneeling, crawling, or standing, in daylight and in darkness. During his basic training, he'd scored 220; that qualified him as an expert shooter. In some instances, he was more skilled at shooting than the E4 and E5 Marine gunners.

The sergeant major entered the room. They immediately stood, slapped their hands to their sides, and saluted. Sergeant Major held a stack of papers in his hands. He called out one name after another, then said, "Men, it's almost time for you to show what you're made of. In three weeks, you're all going to Saudi Arabia. I'm approving a one-week leave so each of you can go home and say good-bye to your families."

The way he'd said good-bye sounded permanent. In many ways, Lincoln's leaving Selma after graduation was his good-bye.

A year had already ticked away. This would be his second deployment. Glancing at his orders, he read six months. Being in Saudi Arabia would be new and hopefully more fun than when he was in Okinawa. With the exception of confiding in his friend, Randy Thomas, Lincoln kept his personal life private. He'd hit it off with Randy during BT because they both played football in high school and they were the only two shooters in their unit who ranked above the marksmen and the sharpshooters.

"You going home, Lincoln?" Randy asked,

then started singing "Sweet Home Alabama."

Where was home for William Lincoln?

Chicago, where his I-don't-give-a-damn-about-that-boy parents lived? Or Selma where his know-it-all grandfather was born and raised. All his life, someone told him what to do or what not to do. Being in the military gave Lincoln a solid foundation and a new group of dictators.

"Nah, man. I'm good. I'ma stay here," Lincoln said.

"Man, this here entire section on base is going to be a ghost town. Why don't you call your grandparents? Go to Selma. See those two females you keep talking about all the time. Get your spill on, you feel me. Drop some seeds. Fertilize those fields," Randy said, bobbing his head. "And take some pictures, dude, because Randy don't believe you telling the truth about having fam in Alabama."

Sometimes, Randy called him William or Lincoln, but most of the time he called him Alabama. That was cool. Long as he never called him Bama.

There were lots of truths that Lincoln had shared with Randy. But he'd never said, "Man, the longer it takes me to call or write

42

Mona Lisa and Katherine, the easier it gets not to."

He wanted to know if Katherine had had his baby, but at the same time he didn't. What good would it do for him to be away from his child for years? Holding pictures instead of holding his kid and the woman who should be his wife? His mind wouldn't be on destroying the enemy. He'd be consumed with the enemy annihilating him. Worse, what if he died and his family became a gold star family before he ever laid eyes on his baby?

"I'll go home when I get out." Maybe.

"Then in the meantime and in between time, Alabama, you're going home with me. Ever been to New Orleans, my brother?" Randy asked. Not waiting for an answer, he continued, "You're in for a real treat."

Lincoln laughed. "There's a first time for everything."

Mona
Chapter 4

July 2001

"Why can't I go to New York and hang with my college friends?" Mona stood at the island, picked an egg from the paper carton, held it in her hand. After tapping the shell on the edge, she plopped the yolk and egg white into a bowl, then picked up another egg. She'd cracked two more eggs before her mother responded.

"I'll give you three good reasons why. Because you don't have a job, your father won't supplement it, and I can't afford it."

She watched her mom sit at the kitchen table thumbing through the Saturday morning paper. "Can you believe those pro-choice activists are planning to rally next weekend in favor of a woman's right to have an abortion? If these little fast girls weren't so quick to open their legs and mouths at the same time, they'd have a husband to take care of the baby instead of mutilating their bodies by having an abortion."

Her mother believed a woman's job was to procreate. Maybe her mom was right, but Mona was a free spirit and didn't want anything or anyone holding her down.

This might be the perfect time to confess. Detaching the tiny white embryo from the yolk, Mona reflected on the day she'd aborted Lincoln's baby. His leaving and not calling within two weeks made her decision easier. She didn't want kids, she wasn't prepared to be a mother, and she refused to be a single mom.

"Ma, times have changed. Women have the right to choose when they want to start a family. And if no one can make a man be a dad, then no one has the right to force a woman to be a mom."

Slapping the newspaper shut, her mother scolded, "Don't speak crazy in my house. Only God reserves that right. We're Christians. And true Christians don't kill. The Bible says, 'Thou shalt not kill.'"

True Christians? Mona was convinced she'd take her secret to her grave. Being away from Selma for a year was great. Gave her time to mature. Discover what she liked most about herself. Spontaneity. Spunk. Suspense intrigued her.

Studying a little. Partying a lot. Getting

drunk. Having tons of sex. The independence she had at Clark Atlanta was awesome. Selma was still her home base, but Mona wanted to booze it up in the Big Apple.

"Mama, I have to see Times Square, go to plays on Broadway, tour Brooklyn, get —"

"Brooklyn?"

"Yes, Mama. It can't be bad to visit a place where people live. I know you can afford it. Come on." Mona poured grits into the boiling water, layered bacon into a pan, beat the eggs, then poured them into a hot cast-iron skillet.

Her mother married at twenty, worked ten years, gave birth to her at the age of thirty, and never spent a penny of her money for anything. Mona's mom told her that story enough times for Mona to know that neither her dad nor her mother was broke. Her mom was what her dad referred to as penny-wise and dollar-smart.

"Little girl, who do you think has to pay your tuition for the next three years? And your dorm fees? And for your meals? Your clothes? And who puts money in your pocket and gas in your car? Money does not grow on trees."

Mona mumbled, "You do." But a couple of hundred dollars wasn't much.

Digging her cell phone from inside her bra, Mona answered, "Hi, Steven. What you doin' tonight?" She'd broken up with him right before leaving for college. No need in lying to herself. She had zero intentions on being faithful.

Steven called every day during her summer break. She wished he'd gone to college instead of bumming around town. Mona wasn't sure what he did to earn money, but Steven was never broke.

"Whatever you want. Where you wanna go? I can pick you up whatever time you say."

A wide smile crossed Mona's face. "I wanna go to New York!"

"Then let's go. Pack your bags. You can stay at my house tonight and we can head out first thing in the morning."

Mona flipped the bacon, put grits and eggs on her mama's plate, then hers. "Mama, Steven is taking me to the Big Apple." Her smile disappeared. "Oh, wait, Steven. I forgot to tell you I don't have any money."

In his country accent, he said, "That's what you've got me for. I've got you covered."

"Mona, hang up the phone. You're not going anywhere with him. I said no, and that's final."

Final was relative. "Steven, let me call you back. Bye."

She stared at her mother, placed her mom's breakfast on the table, then said, "I see this has nothing to do with money. Be grateful, Mama. I'm not pregnant. I'm in college. I have good grades. I'm grown, and like it or not, I am going to New York. You don't tell Daddy where not to go and you're not going to tell me."

Mona had lost her appetite. She went into her bedroom, slammed the door. She'd made up her mind. What was her mother going to do?

She couldn't stop her from leaving.

KATHERINE
CHAPTER 5

August 2001

A blessing and a curse.

Bouncing her baby in one arm and holding a book in her hand wasn't fun. Her attention was continuously divided. A social life was virtually nonexistent. Not being invited to go to UFL games, Greek shows, parties, and movies, and not being able to readily accept offers to go out on dates made Katherine feel her college experience was passing her by. Loving her son was easy. Being a single teenage mother should not have been her destiny. But it was her reality.

Her baby was already six months old, twenty-two pounds, twenty-eight inches long, and still breast-feeding. Placing the book on the end table, she moved from the sofa to the rocking chair and lifted her blouse. His small hands held her breast on both sides, then he latched onto her areola with his eyes closed.

Seated on the sofa, her mother surfed through television channels while keeping watch over a toddler in the playpen in front of her. "It's time to stop letting that baby drain you dry, Katherine. Feeding him five times a day is too much. I don't know if he's nursing or nestling. We can squeeze a few extra cans of formula out of the budget."

"Mama, Jeremiah is not out of the woods yet. We don't know if the formula, the diet, the vaccines, immunizations, or a combination of it all causes autism, but I'm not taking any chances. I'll feed my baby until I dry up. That's the way nature intended."

The modest two-bedroom unit was cozy. Her mother earned a few extra dollars by keeping other students' kids throughout the week and occasionally on weekends. The kitchen table doubled as Katherine's desk when she studied for midterms and finals.

"There's no proof of what causes autism, but I'm sure sticking your tittie in that boy's mouth all day isn't preventative," her mother said. She picked up the little girl from the playpen and fed her a bottle of water.

Maybe her mother was right. Katherine asked, "What about the fact that feeding honey to infants and toddlers can cause irreversible nerve damage or even death? All

I'm saying is, breast-feeding can't hurt him."

If Katherine would have secretly aborted her baby when she first found out she was expecting, would her life undoubtedly be easier? And she wouldn't be having this conversation or living on campus with her mother and son. Katherine wasn't sure that the guilt of killing her unborn wouldn't have haunted her forever.

She couldn't ignore what her mom told her. "God doesn't make mistakes. People do."

Getting pregnant was a huge mistake, but why was it that Lincoln could go on with life? Had he made a mistake? He could have another girlfriend or girlfriends if he wanted. Have sex whenever he wanted to be pleased. The simple joy of being alone was a decision he could easily make. He could freely do all the things that she had to make arrangements for.

"Mama, it's time for us to go home to Selma. I'm not ashamed of my baby or my situation. I like being in Florida, but I miss home. I want my friends to see my son."

Friends. Her friends who were at the hospital when she'd had her baby had moved on with their lives. She couldn't blame them. What college student wanted to be trapped in an apartment playing auntie to an infant? Katherine was anxious for Lincoln's grandparents to see their great-grandson. Hopefully when she saw them they'd give her an address or phone number for Lincoln.

She erased all of her thoughts about having intercourse when hearing the doctor say, "No sex for six weeks." Six weeks had snowballed into six months of celibacy. Not intentionally. With the horror stories of condoms slipping, breaking, or being no guarantee she wouldn't get pregnant again, she was afraid to disappoint her mother again. Becoming a born-again virgin wasn't the solution. She had to be wiser about what man she opened her legs for and under what circumstances.

Trumping not having sex was her nonstop expenses when she had no job and no independent source of income. Diapers. Clothes. Baby wash, shampoo, and lotion. Medical expenses for her follow-up visits. Payments for her son's shots and checkups. And she prayed neither of them got sick and needed medication. Baby food. Blankets. Baby bed. Stroller. Car seat. Diaper bag. Wipes for his butt. Ointment. Baby powder. Wipes for his face. Teething rings. Pacifiers. And the older he'd become, the more expensive he'd get.

"I know you want to go home, baby. Me too. But timing is important. My grandson has to build up his immune system. You know all my friends will want to kiss him, hold him, and feed him food he shouldn't eat. I don't want him getting sick, and I don't want you traveling right now. We'll go home for Christmas. That way both of you will get lots of gifts."

At times she felt depressed. Everything was about and for her son. It would be nice for someone to give her something. Even her educational expenses were a financial burden on her mom.

There wasn't extra time for her to join a group or support any campus organizations or causes. No discretionary money for her to do anything for herself or with her friends. Going to the matinee had become a sacrifice or a treat from someone. Having her hair, nails, or feet professionally done was out of the question. The things she'd taken for granted were no longer an option.

She was a dependent with a dependent. That wasn't fair to her mother, but thank God her mom was willing and able to help watch Jeremiah and financially provide for them.

"Mama, you can't protect us from everything. He's a baby. He has to build up his immune system and he's not going to do that staying inside."

Christmas might not be bad. Gifts would be nice. Gift cards for her to buy clothes would be great.

No one warned Katherine her homecoming queen figure — thirty-six, twenty-four, thirty-six — would drastically change during her pregnancy. Her breasts were two sizes larger, her butt five pounds bigger, and her waist was four inches wider. Thanks to her mother telling her to saturate her stomach and buttocks with cocoa butter oil twice a day, she didn't get a single stretch mark.

The upside of having her baby young, Katherine had lots of energy to play with him. The downside was Jeremiah wanted to play at two in the afternoon and two in the morning.

A jewelry commercial came on. Her mother looked at her and Jeremiah with what Katherine thought was love until she said, "When are you going to stop wearing that so-called engagement ring? Take that thing off."

"No, Mama. I keep telling you, I'm not. One day Lincoln will come home, and when he does, he's going to marry me just like he promised.

"Remember, Mama. You were the one who said, 'Never give up on your dream.' "

LINCOLN
CHAPTER 6

September 2001

From Saudi Arabia to Afghanistan in less than ninety days, 9/11 changed his life overnight.

"Get down! Hit the ground!" Lincoln shouted.

The enemy troop charged toward them. Bullets flew over his head.

Crawling on his elbows and belly, Lincoln fired back with expert precision. One down. Two down. Three down. Four. Like a pack of wolves with the determination to devour its prey, the more enemies Lincoln and Randy killed, the more the madness multiplied. The opposition relentlessly charged at them. Combat was no life for a twenty-year-old. He didn't know what to expect when he joined the military, but shooting every day to kill the enemy or risk dying wasn't it.

"Ahhh!!!! I've been hit!"

He wanted to cry out for his mother, but

that would make him the next target and probably not be worth the effort. Would his mother ever hear his cry? Did it matter?

Yes, it did.

He was tired of seeing and smelling death. Like an oxygen mask permanently strapped over his nose and mouth, the stench of corroded and burning flesh was lodged in his nostrils. The scent of the fresh air at Grist State Park, where he used to hang out with Katherine, was a memory exhaled over a year ago.

He was man enough to kill but wasn't man enough to care if he had a kid. *God bless America,* he thought, firing another round.

Lincoln looked to his left. Another one of his friends was injured. Blood spilled from her head; her body went limp. She was a wife and mother of a two-year-old boy. All she ever prayed for was to hold her husband and her son in her arms again. She was his age. Lincoln often wondered if he too had a baby living in America. If so, was it a girl? A boy? A daughter would make him more compassionate. A son would force him to be a man.

He pulled out a grenade, pulled the plug, then hurled it as far as he could. Fifty feet away . . . *boom!* He prayed he'd taken out enough enemies for them to cease firing.

Lincoln crawled to her, pulled her body into their hideout. "Do not die on me," he told her, then shouted, "Hurry! I need help! She's still alive. We've got to get her to the hospital."

The enemy retreated, but his work wasn't done. He ripped his sleeve, wrapped the material around her head to stop the bleeding. He never wanted to see another bleeding heart or zip another body bag. The closest military hospital was twenty miles away. They'd hike the distance, praying not to get shot at again before arriving at the infirmary. Then they'd hike back, for what? To fight another day? Or wait for an American plane or helicopter to fly over their heads, drop their food, water, and mail, then fly away or risk getting shot down from the sky.

The words his football coach shouted at him, "Don't you set down on the steps 'cause you finds it's kinder hard," when they were down by six in the championship game, were those of Langston Hughes. Coach's encouragement led them to the big W. War was a bigger W. The battlefield was no playground. Kill or be killed. The difference between sports and war was, at least in the game, he knew what he was fighting for.

The stretcher wasn't nearly as heavy as

carrying the guilt of having taken so many lives. All in the name of Operation Enduring Freedom? *I'm actually over here sacrificing my life every day for selfish-ass Americans who don't give a damn about me. My parents included.*

They trampled through the desert. Lincoln thought about his history teacher, recalled how she'd taught him about the Selma to Montgomery march. How the movement that Dr. King led from Selma over the Edmund Pettus Bridge into Montgomery ended with over twenty-five thousand marchers standing strong. In the end, their 1965 mission for coloreds to have voting rights was accomplished.

What was Lincoln fighting for again? Wasn't like he didn't remember. He was clueless. If he knew for certain, he might feel better about living 24-7 with an M16 by one side and a handgun by his other. Was his commitment in the name of, or in vain of, the continued freedom for his country?

Who in America felt that their safety was threatened? Americans didn't need to be afraid of foreign countries invading their space. Their greatest threat was being killed by another American. Drive-bys. Driving while texting. Driving under the influence.

Right place, wrong time. At least that's the way he felt when he lived on the South Side of Chicago.

Pow! Lincoln released his grip on the stretcher, aimed his weapon, hit the ground, and started shooting.

"Dude, get your ass up! You can't keep doing this shit. You keep this up, hearing sounds in your head, and I'm going to have to tell Major to send your ass home. You're going to get us killed. Save those football workout skills for a pickup game. Now pick up the damn stretcher, youngster, and get your shit together!"

Lincoln protested, "I'm not a quitter. I'm not going anywhere until my assignment is over." If he were dishonorably discharged and sent to the States, where would he go? Definitely not to his grandfather's house.

"That's right. As long as we're at war, I can keep your ass as long as I want. You're not leaving until I say so," his captain said.

Signing up to serve shouldn't have been the same as signing away his right to live, but it was. If he made it out of Afghanistan alive, he'd never tell a soul what really happened to them.

MONA
CHAPTER 7

May 2004

Military life must've agreed with William Lincoln. Mona hadn't heard from him since he'd slipped the silver band on her left ring finger, then shared her first orgasm.

She knelt beside her bed, put her hands together, then said, "Lord, please keep Lincoln safe. I pray he hasn't been killed. Keep him out of harm's way. If he's deployed, bring him home soon."

In the beginning her prayers were heartfelt; now her words were like the chorus in a song. She could recite them from memory, repeat them without forethought or afterthought.

Did Lincoln know his grandparents missed him dearly? Did he care? When she ran into them at the local grocery store, all they talked about was how proud they were of Lincoln and how they wished he'd call or write. No one had showed up at their front door with a folded American flag, so they presumed Lincoln was alive. With his new family in Selma, Mona knew he had a reason to return to Alabama, but word around town was that Katherine hadn't heard from him either.

For the first time, the words to her prayer had changed. Mona didn't pray for God to bring Lincoln home to her. She removed the silver band, placed it in her jewelry box.

"Enough," she whispered. Four years still not knowing if Lincoln was dead or alive was too long.

She was in her prime and ready to have a real relationship. Maybe she was ready for marriage. She realized she was a planner, not a dreamer. But having kids was not part of her plans.

"Mona Lisa," her mother called out, "Steven is here to pick you up."

Good ole Steven Cunningham from second grade had never given up hope on being hers again. She hadn't dated him since graduation, but his determination to reunite grew after their whirlwind trip to New York. She wasn't interested in having sex with him, cuddling with him, or kissing him in the Big Apple, but she appreciated the unforgettable all-expense-paid vacation. Thanks to Steven she'd experienced Los

Angeles, New Orleans, and Lincoln's hometown of Chicago.

With Lincoln out of her life, Mona reverted to familiarity. In a way, she was dating Steven. The guys in college were fun, some exciting, but none replaced Lincoln. All of her lovers had moved on with their lives. Time had come for her to do the same.

She never understood why Steven had opted not to go to college. He'd said higher education wasn't for him. He liked roaming the streets. Said, "The streets are an extension of who I really am." Whatever that meant. Said he'd done some things he wasn't proud of. But who hadn't.

Although she didn't know where his money came from, Steven was sort of a cash blanket and he kept her financially comfortable. Maybe he was a catalyst to get her back to the man she should marry.

"I'm coming, Mama!" she yelled from her bedroom.

There was no place like her home. Her mom had finally given up on trying to dictate who Mona dated, and Mona had decided to stop inviting unfamiliar male company to their house without her mother's prior permission. She would've asked her dad, but he was never home long enough. Word around town was her dad had a second family in Mobile. But he still paid all the bills and her mom never questioned him.

"Hey, you," Mona said with a smile. When Steven leaned in to kiss her, she gave him a hug, then nodded toward her mom.

"I've got a surprise for you," Steven said.

Mona's mother commented, "Just make sure your surprise doesn't entail Mona taking off her shoes."

"Mama, I haven't taken off my shoes in —" Mona paused. Her mother still believed she was a virgin. Her father didn't seem to care what she did as long as she didn't get pregnant. Mona's sexual relations were nobody's business but her own. Mona loved living her life one thrill after another, and she was way overdue to take off her shoes.

"Steven, have her back by midnight."

"Yes, Mrs. Ellington."

"Mama, I'm twenty-two and —"

Her mother interrupted, "And still living under my roof. I'm not taking care of you and no baby. So don't have any until you can take care of yourself and your child." Her mother looked at Steven, then continued, "Any man that wants to keep you all night has got to make you his wife first. Then he can take off your shoes as much as he'd like."

What? "It's not like I don't have a part-time job, Mama. And a license to carry a gun." She'd secured a good job at the police department as a forensic specialist. Mona loved her job. "Besides, we've been knowing Steven since I was seven."

Mona made enough money to rent a small house in Selma, but she enjoyed the comfort of having someone to come home to after work. And her mom wouldn't admit it, but Mona knew she liked having her there at night.

"Don't make me no never-mind how long we been knowing him. He's a man now. Midnight, Steven," Mama said, then walked away.

Steven was available during the day but wouldn't tell her what he did most nights and weekends. Being the Christian man his parents reared him to be, all Mona cared about was that Steven was the perfect gentleman.

STEVEN
CHAPTER 8

May 2004

"When you gon' let me hit it, Mona?" Steven asked.

"I was wondering when you were going to make a go for it," she said. "We haven't had sex since high school."

"Well, it's not because *I* didn't want to."

He'd tried to make love to her in New York, but she refused him. Turned her back each night, hugged her pillow tight. He'd tried again in Los Angeles and Chicago, and she turned him down both times. Enjoying her company was more exciting than forcing himself on her. Mona was his best friend.

She wasn't easy like some of the girls in Selma. Mona always knew what she wanted, had to have things her way. That was okay with him because there was nothing that she wanted that he couldn't give her. So far. Mona was the one woman he was patient with. He knew one day she'd be Mona Lisa Cunningham.

He even told his mom and dad that he was going to ask for Mona's hand in marriage. They gave him their blessings. Mona's mother would be the hardest to convince. But seeing how Mona wanted to get from under her mother's rules, sweeping Mona into his arms might be easier than he'd thought.

"Women around this town are nice, but you know I've been crazy about you since second grade. And even when we dated in high school, I could tell you were still in love with Lincoln. You haven't mentioned him in years. Hope you've gotten him out of your system, because I've got plans for you."

All the girls at Selma High were attracted to Lincoln. He'd handpicked two. Mona and Katherine Clinton. The same two Steven had chosen. But Steven was no second-time loser standing downfield waiting for Lincoln to throw him the ball so he could try to score. Mona was no easy win.

Steven had met her first and known her longer than Lincoln. And if Mister Loverboy Lincoln was so supposedly well endowed, why was Mona still a virgin in the eleventh grade? Steven was happy when

Mona had told him, "I saved myself for you."

Mona bounced in her seat. "Let's do it right now. Go in there," she said, pointing toward Grist State Park.

He frowned. This wasn't what he'd had in mind. Actually, after holding out for so long he hadn't imagined her immediately agreeing to have sex with him.

"No, not now. We're on our way to breakfast. We can go back to my house afterward. Relax. No pressure," he said, admiring her cocoa complexion.

Fumbling to unbuckle his belt while he drove, she said, "Breakfast isn't going anywhere," then slid his black leather belt from his waist. She tried unbuttoning his jeans.

"Stop. You can't be serious. A lot of people are in the park."

"I'll show you where to go. You'll see."

As Mona navigated their destination, his dick pressed hard against his jeans. He drove into the state park, paid the entrance fee, followed her directions to a secluded area, then turned off his engine.

Mona slid her panties from underneath her sundress, placed them over his face, then asked, "So tell me what your job is."

Should've figured there was something she

wanted or wanted to know, he thought, sniffing her sweet underwear. "I can show you better than I can tell you. You can go with me tomorrow," he said, lowering his zipper.

"You really gon' take me with you?" she asked, sliding between his front seats onto the backseat of his big, black Chevy SUV. "Well, what are you waiting for?" She removed her dress, hung it on the handle above the window like a curtain.

He hesitated, climbed in the back after her. "Um, I don't have any protection."

He was eager to hit it, but he wasn't trying to get Mona pregnant the way Lincoln had done Katherine. But Katherine had faired well. He'd heard that she was looking for an anchor position doing the morning news. If she got the job, he'd definitely tune in. He always thought Katherine was prettier than Mona, but he wasn't pursuing another woman who was attached to William Lincoln. If Katherine hadn't had Lincoln's baby, she might be on the backseat of his SUV. Nah, Katherine was too classy for that.

"Well, you're going to have to go down there and lick it, Steven. Next time you ask to hit it, make sure you're prepared to do just that," Mona said, spreading her legs. "You got to hunt for the pearl."

The what? This wasn't a game. His dick was hard and he was excited about sticking it inside of Mona for the first time in four years.

"I ain't hunting for nothing. I'll wait 'til we get to my house. I've got condoms at home," he said. "I'll take you with me tomorrow. But I have to warn you, it can be dangerous, and you have to promise never to tell my parents what I do for a living."

"Dangerous? Oh, yes, that's got me all wet. I promise I won't tell them." Mona shoved his head toward her vagina. "Now go on and get it, Steven. You ain't gonna get full staring at it."

He'd never tasted a girl's private before. "You gon' do me next?"

"If you eat me and make me cum, I'll spit shine your trophy real good."

Damn! That was all he needed to hear. Steven pushed Mona's knees to her shoulders, placed her buttery smooth ass in his palms, and didn't stop licking until Mona screamed "Steven" repeatedly.

Wiping his mouth he noticed the windows were foggy. He couldn't see out.

"Steven, that was incredible. Do that again. This time suck it."

He stretched his neck side to side. He'd already been down there a long time. Ten minutes at least. Now he had to suck it. For how long?

Steven exhaled. "Let's do this the right way. You know I've been in love with you since the second grade, and I've given this some thought for years. Mona, will you marry me?"

"Yes, as soon as we're done, we can go straight to the courthouse. That way I won't change my mind," she said, spreading her thighs.

"We're done?"

"Yes," she said, pushing his head back down. "Me first."

MONA
CHAPTER 9

May 2004

Today was filled with exciting things.

Mona was moving out of her mother's house, going with Steven for him to buy her wedding ring. She didn't need the whitest white gown. She wasn't marrying the man she'd planned. But she was equally thrilled that tonight she'd finally find out what Steven did to earn so much money.

"Mona Lisa, where on earth are you going?" her mother asked, standing in the doorway.

The red Samsonite suitcase was on her bed. Six boxes filled with her clothes, shoes, and favorite possessions were stacked outside her bedroom. Her dolls were neatly propped on her queen-sized bed.

"Steven is picking me up, Mama. We got married yesterday and he's taking me to get my ring today, then I'm moving in with him." Mona paused, double-checked. The silver band Lincoln gave her was hidden in the inside zipper pocket of her purse. "I know things are somewhat out of sequence, Mother. I'll always be your daughter, but now I'm Mona Lisa Cunningham."

Mona hugged her mom. Her mother broke their bond.

"So you just threw away our family's last name?" Her mother balled her fist, braced it on her hip, stepped her foot forward, then shook her head. "You've done a lot of dumb things, little girl, but this by far is the dumbest. You don't love him. Marriage isn't some sort of joke."

It appeared that way to Mona. Her father did whatever he wanted, and her mother did whatever her father said. She never questioned his whereabouts. At least Mona knew how to get Steven to do whatever she wanted him to.

"I promise, Mother, I'll do better with Steven than you did with Daddy."

Slap! The sting burned Mona's jaw. That was the quickest her mother had moved in a long time.

Holding her cheek, Mona said, "I apologize, Mama. But I'm ready to make my own mistakes."

"Knock! Knock!" Steven said, entering the bedroom. "Hi, Mrs. Ellington."

"Don't you *hi* me. How dare you not ask my husband and me for Mona's hand."

Steven's lips curved downward. His eyes widened.

"It's okay, Mama. It's done now and I'm not divorcing him. Put my boxes in the car, Steven. I'll be out in a minute," Mona said.

Before closing her suitcase she placed her favorite doll on top. It wasn't Barbie or Ken. She picked up her Magic Genie Troll Doll, kissed it. Fingering the pink spiked hair, she straightened the tiny pink short shorts, then placed her genie in her purse for good luck.

"Steven, wait," her mother said. "You hear me and you hear me good. You take my Mona Lisa out of our house, you pay for her every need down to the drawers on her behind. You'd better make sure she doesn't want for anything."

"I can do that, Mrs. Ellington," Steven said, leaving the house.

Mona's mother's approach differed from her dad's, but she knew they both had her best interest at heart. "Mama, I'll be fine. I'm not dying, I simply got —"

Slap! Her mother hit her again.

This time Mona wanted to hit her mother back. But she didn't. Why was her mother so angry at her?

"Stop sassing me, little girl. You grown?

74

I'm not telling him to take care of you because I care about what's on your ass! I'm telling him to take care of you because no matter what you do, you can't come back here. Ever!" Her mother walked away, left Mona standing alone.

Holding back her tears, Mona grabbed her suitcase, put it in the trunk of her new red convertible sports car, and followed Steven to his house.

Mona's only regret was that her dad wasn't around for her to kiss and tell him good-bye. She'd call him later.

As Mona parked her car in Steven's garage, it dawned on her. With her father gone weeks, sometimes months at a time, this would be the first time her mother would truly be alone.

Why should Mona choose her mother's happiness over her own?

KATHERINE
CHAPTER 10

September 2004

Lights! Camera! Almost time for action!

"Thanks for everything, Mama!" she said, kissing her mom, then her son.

Her assistant Tyler opened the door to the green room, peeped inside. "Ms. Clinton, it's time for your hair and makeup."

"Go, baby. I'm so proud of you. Jeremiah, tell your mommy you're proud of her."

Running toward her, Jeremiah clung to her skirt, then started crying. "I wanna go with you, Mommy."

"Ms. Clinton, I really have to get you to hair and makeup now," Tyler insisted.

Her mom picked up Jeremiah. "He'll be all right, baby. You go get ready for your debut."

Following Tyler, Katherine strutted through the hallway as though it were her own private runway. She was the first in her family to earn a college degree. One of her dreams had come true, to anchor the local news in Selma, the other she'd hold on to until Lincoln came back to her.

Tyler opened the dressing room door. "Amber and Nichelle will take care of you. I'll be back in fifteen minutes to escort you to your station."

My station. Wow! Was every workday going to start the same?

Katherine removed her jacket, handed it to Nichelle, then sat in the black stylist chair facing the mirror. From tiaras to crowns, she was accustomed to the spotlight, but she didn't want to come across as a diva on her first day. Being a newscaster officially made her a local celebrity.

"Okay, Mz. Undercover Diva extraordinaire," Nichelle said, "My best advice to you is to take advantage of your health benefits and get yourself a psychotherapist."

"Excuse me," Katherine retorted.

Amber chimed in. "Nichelle means no disrespect, girl."

Girl?

Amber continued, "We know you're all excited. Eager to be in front of the camera. And trust me, when we're done with your hair and makeup, you'll be ready for the red carpet. But by next week, after you've covered all the homicides, suicides, kidnappings, rapes, babies being abused, casualties, police shootings, gang shootings, drug wars, and how many soldiers are dying in the war each day, you won't feel like a diva."

"But you will look like one," Nichelle repeated. "Get yourself a damn good therapist. Because even if it's not your story to report, if you want to stay on top around here, you still have to know what's happening. Now turn around and let me make you look even more fabulous."

Katherine slid her fingers from her eyes, up an inch to her temples, then pressed hard. She closed her eyes, exhaled, then looked at them. "That's better. I'll be fine."

Amber held the makeup brush in front of Katherine's face. "And what's that supposed to mean?"

"My crown was a little crooked. But I've straightened it. Thanks for the advice, ladies," Katherine said, easing out of the chair.

Tyler stepped in. "You look fantastic!"

Katherine reached for her jacket. Tyler got to it first. "Let's go," he said, holding the door open. She followed Tyler to her station. He looked her up, down, then back up. "You'd better showcase that diva strut you had a few minutes ago. Look, the news is depressing enough, don't make me put you on that list too."

Stopping outside the door to the news-room, Tyler said, "Katherine, you're a fresh face, you're young, you're beautiful. Selma needs to see your face in the morning. Delivering the news is a job. Don't take it personal and don't take it home. You'll be just fine."

"Thanks, Tyler."

He placed his pointing fingers at the corners of his mouth, curved his lips up. "If your energy drops, this'll be my signal to you to pep up."

Katherine entered the newsroom, sat at her station. The visual and audio techni-cians made sure her seating, posture, posi-tion, and voice were perfect. "Would you like me to get anything for you, Ms. Clin-ton?" Tyler asked in a more professional voice than when they were alone a moment ago.

Ms. Clinton sounded so formal and made her feel older than twenty-two. Wow. It hit her that she was the youngest reporter ever to have a prime morning spot. More impor-tant than her position was being in a posi-tion to financially support herself and her son. If the balance on her student loans weren't so high, she could take care of her mother.

"No, thanks. I'm good for now, Tyler. And please, call me Katherine."

Glad she'd skipped breakfast, Katherine felt her stomach cramp with the anticipation of going live on television. Katherine was proud of what she considered a major accomplishment. With the help of her mom petitioning their community, she'd gotten overwhelming support to be hired.

I'm actually living my dream. She screamed on the inside, *Ahhh!*

Coanchoring the seven o'clock morning news; today her crown was straight. She felt Amber and Nichelle's advice was genuine, but it was too early to get comfortable with women she didn't know.

Katherine was ecstatic that her mom and Jeremiah were in the green room cheering her on. In a few minutes, all of Selma might be watching her. Katherine held a mirror in front of her face, checked her hair and makeup one last time. She took a deep breath. Her fitted sleeveless blue dress was layered with a rich lavender jacket. The neckline scooped slightly above her collarbone. She wore the pea-sized pearl earrings her mom had given her for graduation.

If she delivered the news half as good as she looked, she'd do fine. Or if she screwed up maybe no one would complain because she looked good. All she had to do was read the teleprompter without appearing as though she was reading the teleprompter. Look into the camera and connect with her viewers. Maybe she could put a little Hollywood spin on her delivery by smiling, raising her brows, and touching her hair. A few signature moves would set her apart from the others.

Katherine twisted the gold band on her ring finger, thankful that her mom had finally accepted that her engagement to Lincoln was serious. She desperately wanted them to be a family, live together, raise their child together. Their baby was now three years, seven months and had never had a hug from his father.

She prayed wearing the ring would keep viewers from judging her. Calling into the station questioning how a single mom got the job. Then there were those true Christians she'd have to worry about. During her interview, she'd told the panel, "My fiancé is stationed overseas in the military," but she never mentioned Lincoln by name.

The studio was cold. Her counterpart, who was a ten-year veteran in the business and twice her age, sat beside her. His charcoal gray suit complemented his blue shirt and lavender tie.

Katherine smiled at Warren Golf. "We're coordinated. That's a good thing, right?"

Glancing up from his notes, Warren said, "You look nice. Relax. You'll do well."

The cameraman said, "We're going live in five, four, three, two," then pointed at her.

Maybe she should've reviewed her notes instead of worrying about her appearance. Katherine looked directly into the camera as she read, "Today, America, we remember nine eleven. Three years ago the World Trade Center bombing sparked a renewed and continued search to capture Osama bin Laden."

Katherine continued reading the teleprompter as footage of U.S. troops played for the viewers.

"American troops are on the ground in Afghanistan, and Operation Enduring Freedom is stronger than ever. More American troops are being deployed in support of Operation Iraqi Freedom to find the weapons of mass destruction."

Fading out the troops, the camera focused back on her. "I'm Katherine Clinton, and we take you live to Ground Zero where we have Serena Henry with the story. Serena."

In that moment, while Serena was in New York reporting, Katherine had the brightest idea of her one-day career. She no longer wanted to be anchored behind a desk delivering the news. Katherine wanted the flexibility to occasionally have assignments that would allow her to travel the country and cover major breaking stories like Serena. She'd get a few years of experience before pursuing her new dream.

Maybe during her travels, she'd gather enough information to find her man.

MONA
CHAPTER 11

May 2005

"You sure you want to go with me again tonight?"

"Ready when you are," Mona said, slipping her firearm into her black purse. She hung her bag over her shoulder, tucked it under her arm.

To minimize the time sitting at home with Steven during the day watching the news — especially the morning news — she accepted a forty-hour-week schedule at the police department. And although he made more than enough money to let her quit her day job, her access to confidential data made his apprehensions easier.

"You know, we deserve a reality television show for what we do," she said, watching Steven load his gun.

Working at the police station full-time during the day and going with Steven at night was exhilarating. Secretly, Mona hated watching Katherine on television. Katherine always seemed to have a bigger spotlight. Mona wasn't stupid. She saw the way Steven stared, not at the news but at Katherine, the entire time she delivered the news.

"Baby, we should leave Selma and move to LA. Get our own show for real." Just getting out of Selma would be good enough for Mona.

"Have you ever had to shoot anyone? Have you ever killed a man?" Mona asked, closing the wooden shutters on each window.

During the day, Mona worked linking criminals to crime scenes. She could get a job doing that in California. After dark, she helped protect Steven from criminals. And he could get a job bounty hunting in California. They were two country folks from Alabama that could make a huge Hollywood splash . . . bigger and more entertaining than *The Beverly Hillbillies*!

"No," he said. "But tonight might be a first. Can you handle that?"

Mona had proudly become her husband's sidekick, in and out of bed. The chance that she could get caught by the police helping her husband bring in fugitives gave her a rush. At times, his job excited her more than he did. She fumbled through her purse to make sure she had her flip video camera. Tonight she'd start capturing footage, save it for the right time to submit to the right person. Mona was determined to become famous.

Their reality show would top everything on TV, including the news. She wasn't afraid to shoot in self-defense if she had to. Firing rounds at the range twice a week kept her skills intact. Plus, she had a badge and a CCW license to carry a concealed weapon wherever she traveled. Each time she accompanied Steven, he'd apprehend the person. She was there to slap on the handcuffs and back him up in case something went wrong.

He'd call the bail bonds agent, take the person to the local jailhouse near the station where she worked, then collect his money. Not that he had to, but he always cashed her out twenty percent of his earnings.

Steven kissed her, then said, "I think you should stay home tonight. I don't want you to get hurt."

She couldn't tape if she wasn't there. "I'm going and that's final. What if I don't go and I could've kept you from getting hurt?"

"Mona, sit down for a moment," he said, sitting on the sofa.

She sat beside him, remained quiet trying not to reveal her excitement.

Their two-bedroom house was modestly furnished. The home was suitable for a bachelor, and Steven hadn't added much since she moved in. The living room had one recliner, the love seat didn't match the area rug, and the rug didn't match the recliner. He hadn't bothered to repaint the white shutters or replace the wooden wall panels with Sheetrock. He'd bought the large sofa so she'd have someplace to sit or lie when they watched television together.

Mona waited for Steven to speak. Maybe he was going to say, "I shouldn't have married you." It was too late for an annulment. Didn't matter. Long as he bought her out, Mona was prepared to move on.

"Tonight is different. Things might get dangerous," he warned her.

"That's more of a reason for me to be there," she said, looking at everything except him.

Their bedroom had a queen-sized bed, two dressers, one night-stand. He'd bought the second dresser for her clothes. The kitchen had a table with two chairs. One of the cabinets was filled top to bottom with bottles of his favorite whiskey.

Before moving into his house, she had no

idea he drank all the time. Ruining his liver was his mistake, not hers. If he took ill, she'd put him in rehab. He wouldn't become her burden. No man would.

Steven held her face, made her look at him. "We went to high school with this guy. You know him."

Great. That would help boost ratings. Mona knew that look on Steven's face. He stared straight through her. He was up to something, but she had her own hidden agenda.

"Don't tell me who it is. I'm going with you. That's final."

"Fine. Since you insist, here's what you have to do," he said, scooting to the edge of the sofa.

He made an unusual request — that everything they wore had to be destroyed immediately afterward. Tonight's fugitive was also a neighbor.

"No matter what happens, stay behind me," he demanded, then said, "Let's go." The drive was only a few blocks down the road.

When they arrived, Steven walked three feet ahead of her, making it easy for her to record. He stood in front of her, then banged on Calvin's door. Calvin opened the door.

"You know why I'm here. Don't make this complicated," Steven said.

Calvin shoved Steven. Steven stumbled backward; Mona pushed him forward into the living room. Zoomed in. Calvin ran toward the back of his house, and Steven was right behind him.

Mona held her camera in one hand, drew her gun with the other, followed them into the bedroom. Calvin opened a drawer, reached for his gun. Before he turned around, *bam!* Steven punched Calvin in the back of the head so hard, Calvin hit his temple on the sharp edge of the dresser. Steven pulled a pair of latex gloves from his pocket, put them on, then placed Calvin's gun in Calvin's hand. He bent Calvin's elbow, positioned the barrel at Calvin's temple, then pulled the trigger.

Steven checked for a pulse, then said, "He's dead."

The only thing Mona knew for sure that night was her marriage to Steven was her biggest mistake. Quickly she turned off the video camera and dropped it into her purse.

What had she gotten herself into? Even if she turned in the footage, how could she prove she was innocent?

STEVEN
CHAPTER 12

May 2005

"Ma, Pa — Mona and I are headed West," Steven said, entering his parents' home. He sat a yellow gift bag on the coffee table. "It's that time. I've got to show up for that lucrative job I told you about working for the oil company in California." He told the truth about the lucrative job, then lied about working for the oil company.

"What happened to you? You cut yourself," his mother said, reaching for his hand.

"I'm fine, Ma. It's not that bad."

His dad chimed in, "Leave him alone, Regina. He's not a kid anymore."

Steven didn't know his own strength. He'd split the skin on his knuckle when he bashed Calvin in the back of his head. It was time to leave Selma.

The suitcases he'd packed — one for Mona, the other for him — were in the back of his black Chevy SUV parked outside in his parents' driveway. Mona's red convertible was locked in the garage at his house. The clothes he should've destroyed were in a garbage bag in the trunk of her car.

"Buttercup, that's too far away. You waited until you're leaving to tell us," his mother said, then asked, "Why? How much are they paying you?" His mother picked up the gift bag, peeped inside.

Relocating was Mona's idea. He had no objections but refused to reside in Los Angeles. "Ma, I told you and Dad that we were moving to Bakersfield a week ago because I knew you guys would try and talk me into staying. My mind is made up." He'd told the truth. "They offered me six figures." Then lied again.

Truth was he was about to make a fast 1.5 million. He had two more hit jobs — Macon and Kansas City — and since Mona had insisted on going to Calvin's, she might as well go with him on the road. He was in no hurry to get to California. Settling in Bakersfield would take getting used to for both of them.

"Where's Mona?" his mom asked.

"I'm on my way to get her."

Staying in the same town where they'd washed their hands with blood wasn't wise. He'd spoken with a few bail bonds business owners and had lined up some legitimate bounty-hunting work in Bakersfield.

After Calvin's murder, Mona turned in her resignation. Today was her last day on the job. She'd applied for a job as a California correctional officer and as a forensic specialist at a toxicology laboratory in Bakersfield. Mona insisted on working but said she didn't want to work for another police department.

"I love you, Ma, Pa," he said, kissing his dad first. "I'll call you soon as we get there. The pink-wrapped box is for you, Ma. Don't open the other one."

"Well, who's the other one for, Buttercup?"

"Katherine Clinton. It's a gift. I like how she delivers the news. Make sure she gets it, please." He hoped she didn't think the diamond princess-cut earrings were too much.

"I always thought you should've dated her," his dad said.

Me too, Steven thought. But he didn't. "I'll call you guys when I get to California."

Steven didn't want his cell phone to register at any of the towers while he was in transit to handle his business, so he'd powered it off. Mona could use her phone whenever she wanted.

"Is Mona going to come say bye to us?" his mother asked, still hugging his neck.

"No, Ma," he said. "I'm headed to pick her up and then we've got to get on the road."

His parents followed him outside. His dad yelled from the porch, "Don't forget to call us, son! We love you."

"If you need any money, baby, call me," his mother said.

"Love you guys too," Steven said, waving from the driver's window.

En route to pick up Mona, Steven called her. "I'll be there in ten minutes."

"Did you remember to pack my troll doll?"

"Of course. You called your mom?"

"See you when you get here," she said, ending the call.

He'd packed all the things Mona requested, including her troll doll. Mona had her registered gun in her purse. Being so close to his parents, he felt bad that Mona hadn't spoken to her mother in over a year. When Mona and her mom held a grudge, they were two of the most unforgiving persons he knew.

En route to pick up Mona, Steven wondered whatever happened to that loser William Lincoln.

LINCOLN
CHAPTER 13

May 2006

Whatever happened to voluntarily reenlisting?

Two years ago, Lincoln demanded his release. If he hadn't returned they would've considered him AWOL. Absent without leave was an offense that could've gotten him arrested. Wasn't his government supposed to be a democracy and not a dictatorship? Hadn't he fulfilled his commitment? Lincoln still wanted out of the hellhole madness!

"This is bullshit!" he shouted at his superior. "How you gon' tell me I can't be discharged?"

"You didn't read the fine print, solider? When our country is at war, we keep you as long as we need you. And I need you here in Iraq."

The daily desert heat was unbearable. Visible waves floated through the air commingling with the stench of death, suffocating him. Lincoln hated walking around all day with layers upon layers of clothing with a metal helmet strapped to his head. Camouflage jacket layered with heavy body armor. Trousers with side, back, and thigh pockets. An M16 strapped across his shoulder, a semiautomatic in his hand, combat boots laced tightly to his feet.

He missed wearing basketball shorts, a cutoff T-shirt, and slip-on shoes. The days of enjoying a shower — what he wouldn't give to take a bath — were long gone. Being prepared to fight every moment of his life was mandatory. His handgun was strapped to his side. No grenade in his pocket. Needed to get one.

From Saudi Arabia, to Afghanistan, to Iraq, Lincoln walked away shaking his head. "Fuck you, man!" What was his superior going to do? Send him home? Lincoln felt more defeated by his country than by his enemy. Who was the real enemy?

Six years in when he'd only signed up for four was insane. There were many times he regretted making the decision not to follow his dream. If he could roll back time and change his mind about having joined the military, he'd be playing professional football. And if football hadn't been his destiny, he'd be on American soil like the rest, not caring much, if at all, about the soldiers fighting the war. He could be living comfortably in a big house with Katherine. If he had a kid, his child would be five years old now. Maybe he should write Katherine and Mona letters.

Randy patted him on the shoulder. "Let's hang in there, man. We'll get discharged together and go home together. This war can't last forever."

Randy was right. But the war could last their lifetime. Thank God he had Randy Thomas. He didn't need any other friends. Every time he tried befriending a soldier, they were either wounded or killed. Being in the war didn't differ much from being in a gang. Neither gave the man fighting the cause — not his cause — freedom.

"I love you, man," Lincoln said, patting Randy's back.

Before the war, Lincoln hadn't spoken the L word to anyone. Not his parents, grandparents, Mona Lisa, or Katherine. Didn't know what it truly meant until now. Caring about someone who could be taken away from you in a heartbeat, now he understood the meaning of love. Had a few more people he needed to say that to face-to-face.

"Randy, man, I've been thinking about

writing my girls. What you think?"

"Okay, that's it," Randy said, smiling. "Your ass is going to do that today and I'ma seal the envelopes and slap the postage on for you."

Lincoln playfully nudged the side of Randy's head with his fist. "Man, if I die over here, how do I make sure Uncle Sam doesn't get the money I've saved up?"

"Why you dwelling on death? We can't worry about that, dude."

"But seriously. I don't want the government to keep what I've earned."

Randy looked in his eyes. "Who do you trust?"

"You."

"Now you talking crazy, man. You ain't leaving me nothing 'cause you ain't leaving me. Who else you got? What about that kid you might have? Find out if it's true. If you really have one, leave it to 'em."

Lincoln coughed. Randy coughed. Dust filled the hot air.

Pointing at an eighteen-wheeler driving toward them on the dirt road, Lincoln said, "Man, we're on the wrong side. Those dudes work for American companies. They come through here every day to transport oil. They get paid seventy-five thousand dollars a year. We get thirty thou. They don't have to risk their lives every day. And we have to deal with real threats of terrorism every fuckin' minute. At least now we know what we're protecting. The rich man's future!" Lincoln yelled, running toward the truck. He chased the truck at least five hundred feet down the road. He stopped, picked up a huge rock, hurled it at the company's name on the side of the truck.

Boom!

Lincoln looked behind him. It wasn't the rock he'd thrown that caused the blast. Just like that, a bomb exploded.

"Randy!" The attack came from out of nowhere, and Lincoln's life went from bad to worst. He retraced his steps to his troops. Everyone except him was dead.

"Fuck this shit! I hate being here!" Why did he have to chase the truck? He could've died with his best friend, and the nightmare of having to live with what was in front of him would be someone else's reality.

"Randy," he cried, holding his best friend in his arms.

Splattered on the dusty desert next to Randy's body was what was left of the suicide bomber, a little kid. Lincoln leaned Randy's bleeding body against him, drew his weapon. If he saw another kid within five hundred yards, he'd shoot 'em dead.

He'd shoot 'em all dead.

"Why!!!!!" he cried to heaven. Randy was his best and only white friend. The racial tension he'd occasionally experienced in Selma didn't matter when you were fighting each day to save your life. Angrily glancing around, he saw one, two, three . . . ten, eleven . . . thirteen more soldiers were dead.

Lincoln closed Randy's eyes, then removed his combat boots. Lincoln unlaced his own boots, and put them on Randy. "I will walk in your shoes, my brother, until it's my turn to die."

That could be a few minutes, a few days, a few months, a few years, or a few decades, but Lincoln wished that day would've been today. He prayed God had a purpose for sparing his life.

KATHERINE
CHAPTER 14

September 2008

Another breaking news flash scrolled across her computer screen. *Twelve American soldiers were bombed today in Iraq. Half were killed instantly. Two lost limbs. Four survived with minor injuries.*

Katherine refused to lose hope that Lincoln was alive out there somewhere. "God, please keep Lincoln safe. Keep all of our soldiers safe and bring them home soon."

In between reporting events that made local and national news, Katherine continued to pray for the troops and campaigned heavily for Barack Obama to become the next president of the United States. She needed hope more than ever before. Hope that Jeremiah's dad was still alive. Hope that one day she'd find him. Hope that one day soon the war would end.

She stood in front of her local grocery store. A two-by-six rectangular table was covered with applications and pens. "Register to vote today. Ma'am, are you a registered voter?" Katherine asked, handing her an application before the elderly woman answered. "If you are, take this application and pass it along to a person who hasn't signed up. Perhaps a family member, church member, or friend."

The woman stopped, balanced herself on a cane, then proudly articulated, "Honey, I mights not be ables to write and speak a lotta fanzy words, but I've been registered to vote for over forty years. Give me a few of those applications. We've gots to encourage these young peoples to get out and vote for Obama."

Glad the woman had made her efforts easier, Katherine gave her a hug and a stack of voter applications.

"Mommy, what about her?" Jeremiah asked, pointing at a young girl in tight denim short shorts and a white tank top.

"Ask her to come over here," Katherine said.

Though the girl was dressed extremely provocative, had a sassy swing in her hips, and oversized breasts, it wasn't Katherine's position to judge the girl's character. The same as Amber, Nichelle, and Tyler had become her newest friends and biggest advocates at the station, Katherine allowed people to show her who they were.

Jeremiah ran about twelve feet, grabbed the girl's hand. "My mommy wants to talk to you." He smiled. Didn't let go of the girl's hand until she was at the table.

Initiating the introduction, Katherine extended her hand. "Hi, I'm —"

The girl interrupted, "I know exactly who you are. 'Good morning to you, America, I'm Katherine Clinton.' My name is Makeda. I see you on the news all the time."

Depending on the girl's perception and projection, that may be good or bad, Katherine thought, then asked, "What's your age?"

"I just turned eighteen, just graduated from high school this summer. I want to be just like you."

Wow, she was face-to-face with a girl who considered her a role model. How many other young people saw her that way? Handing out applications wasn't enough. Katherine was going to start publicly speaking at high schools and universities.

Jeremiah handed the girl an application. "Here." His eyes appeared fixated on her breasts.

Katherine laughed. "Good job, Jeremiah." She always complimented him when he did well. Never wanted him to think liking girls was a bad thing, so she didn't give the situation undue attention.

"Thanks, Mom. What about him?" he asked, pointing at a young man a short distance away.

"Go get him," Katherine said.

The girl smiled a wide and inquisitive smile. "I see how this operation is running. Send the irresistible kid to reel us in, huh?"

"Are you a registered voter?" Katherine asked her.

"I will be as soon as I complete this application." She looked at the young man Jeremiah led to the table, picked up a pen. "Here, fill this out," she told him, handing the guy a pen and an application. "If you need help, let *me* know."

He placed his grocery bag beside a chair. "Hey, thanks. I've been meaning to do this so I can vote for Obama."

By the end of the day, Jeremiah and Makeda had become inseparable. Or more like her son had become attached to Makeda. Together they'd registered over a hundred people. Their persistence to make sure the applications were processed timely and the people showed up at the polls on Election Day was Katherine's next battle.

"Thanks, Makeda. You were a tremendous help. Whatever I can do to help you, you just let me know. Here's my card."

Makeda hugged her, then kissed Jeremiah on the cheek. He jumped up and down. She clenched the card in her hand. "My mom is not going to believe this! Ms. Clinton, thank you so much! And if you and your husband," she said, eyeing the ring on Katherine's finger, "ever need somebody to babysit this handsome fella, I'll come to your house and watch him for you. Bye!" she yelled, running off.

Katherine smiled at Jeremiah grinning at her. "Yes, she can come over sometimes to chaperone you and your friends. But only on weekends. Grandma could use a break."

Truth be told, Katherine could use a break too, but she didn't want to make her son feel she was tired of him. Single parenting was arduous. Taking care of Jeremiah and working all the time consumed her. If she wasn't cooking, cleaning, or shopping, she was helping with homework, volunteering, at PTA meetings, working, or going to what they called pre-football practice preparedness.

The exercise was great for her son. She didn't want him sitting inside obsessing over video games and not caring about taking care of his mind and body. The hour that he'd practice, she'd run laps around the track and keep an eye on him with his team-mates in the middle of the field.

"Hey, champ. Great job," she said, giving him a high five. "What do you want to eat tonight?"

He yelled, "McDonald's!"

"You sure you want to use your last Fast Pass today? You know your friends are coming over tomorrow."

Katherine never wanted Jeremiah to feel he couldn't have what he wanted, so she taught him moderation. He was allowed to eat twice a month at a fast-food restaurant of his choice. Giving him the option helped him to make better decisions. His Fast Passes were use or lose, because he couldn't use more than two per month. But she'd let him hold on to the unused tickets because somehow he thought saving them was a good thing.

"I'll wait. Let's go home, Mama. Can Makeda come over tomorrow? I want my friends to meet my new girlfriend."

Whoa. New girlfriend? "Jeremiah, you can't decide she's your girlfriend without asking her first. Besides, she's almost twice your age and she might already have a boyfriend. Let's continue this conversation over dinner with Grandma. See what she thinks."

Katherine was going to have to start an

open dialogue with her son about girls and sex soon. Real soon.

MONA
CHAPTER 15

May 2010

Five years in Bakersfield. Mona wasn't homesick, but she did miss Lincoln. The only guy who had ever made her feel pretty was William Lincoln. But she didn't marry Lincoln; she'd married Steven. Each day she was married to Steven, she regretted he was never the man she was in love with. But no one had taught her what marriage meant, so she'd have to continue this journey on her own.

Working two jobs in Bakersfield kept her preoccupied. She had no incentive to go back to Selma. In some ways she'd become better at bounty hunting than Steven. Utilizing her forensic skills and intuition, she was more efficient at locating bail jumpers. Her day job had just gotten started with the ritual of listening to other people's problems.

No matter what time of the day, the news

was depressing. On television and in her adult life, she'd grown to expect more bad than good. Things weren't always that way for her. All her life she'd been a free spirit secretly in search of the fairy-tale love and happiness most girls dreamt of. She wasn't there yet.

Mona put on her protective eyewear and a latex glove. The lab was quiet. Like most days, she'd come in early. She had fifteen specimens to sample for drugs before noon. If a positive change were to come, the decision had to start with her.

Thanksgiving was six months gone and six months away, and this was her fifth year living in Bakersfield. Last year she'd promised herself this year would be different. She'd file for divorce, move out, and get her own place. Again she'd lied.

She exhaled. "Every time I blink or breathe is an opportunity to leave him. God, please give me the courage to just do it. What am I afraid of? I'm tired of making mistakes. Next time I go home, just push me back out of his door and out of his arms forever."

A welcomed interruption of her mental monologue came when she heard a familiar voice say, "Good morning to you, America. I'm Warren Golf with breaking news. An

Alabama woman was arrested at her home minutes ago on charges of first-degree murder of her husband. We take you live to Katherine Clinton, who has the story. Katherine."

The digital clock in front of Mona displayed 8:17 — Pacific time. The dialogue from the reporter was background noise to keep Mona company while she worked in the toxicology lab. She put on her other glove, picked up the tweezers, then carefully placed one strand of hair on the rectangular glass slide.

The position paid a decent seventy-two thousand a year, but drug testing was illogical to her. Functioning alcoholics, like the man she lived with, could be gainfully employed. The Food and Drug Administration approved pharmaceutical companies to dispense drugs that caused heart attacks or meds that disclosed suicidal thoughts as a side effect, but companies wouldn't hire individuals with traces of cannabinoid in their system.

Mona chuckled. She'd rather take her chances working with someone who was high than to be around a depressed co-worker who was mentally unstable. She wondered what would employers drug test for next.

Katherine's voice faded out the rhetoric in Mona's head. "Thanks, Warren, I'm in front of the police station here in Selma with Detective Daniel Davenport where the time is approximately six-twenty a.m. Detective, tell us, how was this forgotten case miraculously solved?"

The detective cleared his throat, then boasted, "I'd never forgotten this case. I simply didn't have sufficient evidence for a conviction."

Mona refused to look at the television. She refused to give Katherine the acknowledgment of a job well done in landing the lead anchor position for reporting national news, for stealing her first love while they were in high school, and for having Lincoln's baby. Passively listening, Mona imagined the detective was her height, five four, barely a hundred and fifty pounds with an ego ten times his size.

He continued, "That was until I received a lead. The lead provided me the missing link that cracked this case wide open. Now the McKenny family can be at peace knowing who killed their loved one."

"What the hell?" Mona swiftly turned to face the flat screen attached to the wall. Knocking over several flasks, she watched urine spill onto the table, then cascade to the floor. She'd clean up the mess beneath her feet later. The conversation, once boring, instantly commanded her attention.

"That murder occurred five years ago." *That case made national headlines? How? Why?* More important, what lead did he receive? Mona hadn't seen Sarah in five years nor had she contacted Daniel, and Steven had better not have . . .

"Thanks, Detective Davenport," Katherine said as the camera faded him out and zoomed in on her.

That cutthroat-boyfriend-thief-trick Katherine was still as gorgeous as the day she was crowned homecoming queen. Her long, dark hair highlighted her standout cheekbones, slender nose, and plump lips. Her buttery brown skin, amazingly flawless. But that was okay. That finders-keepers-losers-weepers bitch got what she deserved. Right after graduation, Lincoln dumped Katherine's ass and left her with baggage.

"It's called karma, bitch," Mona said to the television. "You ain't all that, and your seemingly glamorous lifestyle probably sucks."

Katherine continued her story. "Sarah McKenny was taken into custody moments ago and is now being escorted inside the jail you see behind me."

Mona stared at the flat screen. Her body stiffened with numbness. Her eyes and heart overflowed with sadness when she saw sweet little Sarah in handcuffs.

Tossing her straight hair over her shoulder, Katherine thrust her 36DDs forward — those titties must've been a bonus for having a baby or implants. She straightened her five feet eight inches, then articulated, "The twenty-seven-year-old woman is a lifelong resident of Selma. Her bail is set at one million dollars. If Sarah McKenny is found guilty of killing Calvin McKenny, she could get life without the possibility of parole or worse, Sarah could face the death penalty. I'm Katherine Clinton with *Morning to You, America.* Back to you, Warren."

Mona mouthed, "Sarah McKenny is innocent." But to prove her so would bring unwanted attention to Mona and probably joy to Katherine.

That case was not worthy of national attention. Katherine probably elevated the case hoping Lincoln would be watching her. But how could Katherine have that much power? Mona never liked Katherine, and the feeling was mutual. They never had a catfight or called one another names, but if looks could kill, they'd both be dead.

Calvin's homicide, Mona's mother, and

Katherine Clinton were the three reasons Mona agreed to move over two thousand miles from Selma. She'd abandoned her family, that didn't matter. Her mother still wasn't speaking to her. Left the few friends she had. And she hadn't heard from her first love. But she still had the silver ring Lincoln gave her in her purse, along with her troll genie.

She wasn't going to get hard-core answers about the McKennys standing in a puddle of piss. She tossed a handful of paper towels to the floor, then tramped outside the lab to her desk.

One call after another registered on Mona's cell. First, her mother. *So, now she's calling.* Then her dad. Students that attended Selma High with her called back to back. *Damn!* Why were they calling her? Had they heard something she hadn't? Forget all of them. Mona prayed the tragedy would somehow reunite her with her first and only true love. Maybe Katherine had done her a favor.

There was hope in her heart. Perhaps he'd call. She prayed Lincoln wasn't gawking over Katherine if he'd seen her on the news. Mona hadn't seen or heard from Lincoln since graduation, ten years ago.

Removing her white lab coat, Mona flung

it on the chair, hurried to her boss's office, stuck her head through the door, then said, "I have an emergency. I'm leaving. I'll be back in tomorrow." Maybe.

Oh, my God, she thought. Mona prayed the video of Calvin's murder was still in her safety deposit box at the bank.

If not, maybe she wouldn't be back at all.

LINCOLN
CHAPTER 16

May 2010

He had no place to get help.

When he was fortunate to get a job, he couldn't keep it. Not sleeping at night. Falling asleep at home when he should be in transit to work. Sounds and smells triggered bad memories, made him do things that weren't considered normal by those who hadn't spent a day of their lives fighting for their country. He was on a few lists for housing assistance, but no one had contacted him. Refusing to give up on what he deserved, again today he'd seek help from his government.

He slipped on a T-shirt, jeans, then laced up his combat boots. Not a day went by since his best friend was killed that he didn't walk in Randy's shoes.

Lincoln opened his apartment door. Another piece of paper was taped to the front. He read the embarrassing headline — NO-

TICE TO COMPLY OR VACATE. This time instead of having three days to pay, he had ten days to move out.

After snatching the paper, he ripped it in half, balled it up, threw the notice on his living room floor, then slammed his door.

"This is bullshit!" he said, making his way to the VA Prime Care clinic to see his Prime Care doctor.

Damn government trying to operate like HMOs and PPOs. Constantly blindsided by what they didn't know, the government needed to stay in their lane and focus on viably helping war vets.

Lincoln sat in the waiting area hoping today he'd get a positive response. He placed his elbows on his knees, spread his feet six inches apart, stared at his combat boots. He concealed his sniffles as tears streamed down his face. Wiping his nose with his palm, he whimpered like a baby. That wasn't the manly thing to do, but his best friend was dead and that shit hurt more than all the enemies he'd killed.

"William Lincoln."

Somberly, he responded, "Yeah," rising to his feet.

The routine visit hadn't changed much over the last two years. But he fought to remain optimistic. He followed the assistant through the door.

"How are you feeling today, William?" she asked.

Biting his bottom lip, anger looming in his eyes, he stared at her without blinking. "How the fuck you think I'm feeling? You tell me."

She wrapped the pouch around his biceps. "I'm going to take your blood pressure."

"Why?" he asked. "So my doctor can prescribe more medications that keep making me feel worse than when I come up in here? Y'all trying to kill me so you don't have to help me get better? What? What! Am I a burden to my country now? Being a fucking war vet don't mean shit!"

She jumped when he yelled.

He snatched the pouch from his arm, threw it on the floor.

Calmly she said, "Why don't I take you to the doctor's office," leading the way.

Her soothing voice subsided his anger. He didn't mean to yell at her. "Look, I apologize." His mental instability, nightmares, and paranoia weren't her fault.

"It's okay, William."

He hoped she didn't say, "I understand." If she did, he was going to lose it for real. He followed her down the hall.

She entered the doctor's office before him,

then turned. "My husband was in Iraq too. Have a good day, William," she said as she left.

His doctor greeted him. "Hey, William. How's it going today? How are you managing your PTSD?"

What the fuck is he so cheery about? This isn't some damn joke. Bet if I kicked him in the head with this boot, I'd knock that stupid grin off his face.

"Look, man, they put a notice on my front door this morning. I've depleted all the money I saved while in the military. I've got my last eight hundred in my pocket. It ain't enough to pay my cell phone, electric, rent, and still eat this month. I have no place to go. I don't have any friends here in Seattle. Man, I'm telling you, I'm a few days away from being homeless. I need a housing voucher or something from the VA 'cause none of those places I've applied to have called me back."

The doctor stared at his laptop computer. "So for today your contact information, cell phone, and address are the same. Right?"

For today? "Yeah, man, but what about tomorrow?"

Still staring at his damn computer, the doctor said, "Well, we have to house the homeless vets first." He scribbled on a blank sheet of paper. "Here, call this number. They might be able to partially pay your rent for this month. I can refer you to the housing authority too, but let me warn you now," he said, stretching his arms wide, "their waiting list is extremely long."

Lincoln felt as though every place he called or went to had some sort of pecking order that placed him at the bottom. The media made it seem like all you had to do to get a spot in the apartment complexes built to house veterans was be a veteran. Then when he showed up to apply, veterans who were homeless with families or just homeless had priority over him.

"Why can't *you* just get me a housing voucher, man?"

The doctor looked at him for three seconds, then back at his screen. "It doesn't work that way, William. There's a process. You see, one federal government agency can't give money to another federal agency. HUD gets all the federal funding for housing. Then HUD allocates a set number of vouchers — say, twenty thousand — that go to participating PHAs, that's public housing agencies. Those vouchers are specifically for *homeless* veterans. And once the county or the city gets the money, they can issue through HUD-VASH a housing choice voucher. That's Housing and Urban Development and Veterans Affairs Supportive Housing. But you're not homeless yet, so you wouldn't qualify."

This is the bullshit I'm talking about! Lincoln was not impressed with how much the dude knew. If there wasn't a voucher with his name on it, none of what he'd said would keep Lincoln from being homeless before the end of the month.

His government took care of women choosing to have baby after baby by different dudes, giving them housing vouchers, food cards, WIC, and all kinds of shit. Their babies' daddies didn't have to give them a dime. But his government couldn't keep a roof over his head, let alone food in his stomach.

That doctor had better be thankful. The one thing the military taught Lincoln was self-discipline. Through all of his anger, he killed to protect, never to prove his point.

Glancing at his watch, the doctor said, "William, it's time that I refer you to the Trauma Recovery Program." He scribbled on a piece of paper, then continued, "Are you able to sleep at night? Do I need to prescribe you more sleeping medication? Do you have a preference? If the Ambien I prescribed isn't working for you, I can put you on Desyrel. What about pain meds? You need more of those?"

Lincoln sarcastically said, "How about a prescription for cocaine?"

Some vets were self-medicating with street drugs like cocaine and marijuana just to cope with the madness. Others had become alcoholics. He didn't want to take that route, but for the vets that did, he understood.

Lincoln also understood the new recruits' reasons for taking cocaine and smoking marijuana. Failing their drug test during boot camp meant they could get discharged. What was worse? Getting kicked out of the military with a dishonorable discharge and having a hard time finding a job or risking going to war, being killed, or coming back mentally fucked up for the rest of your life? The new recruits weren't dumb. They were actually smarter than him. Look at what eight years of service had done for him. And the second four years his government held him hostage.

The doctor shook his head. "William, I am not the enemy. I'm on your side," he said, handing him three prescriptions.

Lincoln stood, took the prescriptions, said, "You, sure? I can't tell. 'America! America! God shed His grace on thee. And crown thy good with . . .' yeah, right. What the fuck ever, man," Lincoln said, walking out of the doctor's office.

He'd drop back in tomorrow praying for better results. He had faith in the Obama administration. One day his government would give him the help he deserved.

That day just wasn't today.

Mona
Chapter 17

May 2010

Among her peers, Mona Lisa was best known for finding that one speck of blood that linked murders to the scene of the crime. But she'd stopped investigating crime scenes when they'd left Selma.

If the forensic specialist assigned to Calvin's case had collected and tested blood samples from the base of Calvin's head, they might've found two types. Calvin's and the man she was headed home to. When Steven punched Calvin in the back of the head, Steven's knuckle bled. She knew because she saw the cut on his hand and there was blood inside one of the plastic gloves Steven put on after hitting Calvin but before shooting him.

Working at the lab in Bakersfield was less stressful than working for the police department in Selma. Mona was skillfully trained in identifying fingerprints and palm prints, photographing and videotaping crime scenes, collecting evidence, attending autopsies, and testifying as an expert on many court cases. Depending on what lead was allegedly sent, it could attach her to the crime. If it was tangible and submitted as an exhibit in court, she could ultimately end up being an accessory to three murders.

Halfway home Mona realized she hadn't completed the drug tests. Sure the remaining hairs were floating on the table or scattered on the floor, she knew by now all of the affected samples were tainted.

Errors and omissions were inevitable in laboratories and in courtrooms. Specialists never wanted to appear incompetent, but like with the OJ trial, experts were fallible too. Whomever those potential employees were, they might get a needed break, as the test results would be labeled inconclusive.

En route to her home, she stopped at her bank, checked the contents of her safety deposit box. The video camera was there. She was partially relieved.

One block from home, she heard her phone chime two times, signifying she'd received a text message. The cell was inside her purse; she'd check it later. Mona zipped into their driveway, turned off her engine, left her key in the ignition, then hurried into their bedroom. She shoved panties, bras, socks, shirts, a pair of jeans, a sweat suit, and a pair of tennis shoes into a black overnight bag, then hurled the bag onto her shoulder with no intentions of ever coming back to him. No note. No good-byes warranted.

After swiftly turning to exit the bedroom, she screamed "Ahhh!" In the blink of her eyes, she felt like she'd collided face-first into a brick wall. Mouth wide open, she held her breath. Her heartbeat tripled.

"Leaving without telling me?" he asked, blocking her exit. "It's because of Sarah McKenny, isn't it?"

Tears streamed down Mona's cheeks as she exhaled. "I can't do this anymore, Steven. I just can't. You sent Davenport that lead, didn't you? But why frame Sarah? You know she doesn't deserve this. And what was the lead that you sent? I know you. I know you did it. But I can't believe you sent something without my knowledge and consent."

Pounding on his chest, Mona yelled, "Why didn't you talk to me first? Tell me! Why?" She fell to her knees. "Oh, Jesus, what have I gotten myself into?"

She'd always followed Steven's lead. She wasn't in love with him, but she did trust him. Until now. He used to tell her everything first. Not anymore. Now he held secrets? Tears filled her eyes. "So now you're hiding shit from me, Steven? Things that could send me to prison!"

He pulled her up. "You weren't crying when I gave you that hundred grand six years ago. Or when I gave you another hundred Gs or that last hundred thou six years ago. Besides, I told you to stop watching the damn news at work, but no, you won't listen!" he scolded, removing the bag from her shoulder.

He'd changed. She'd changed because of him. Mona buried her face in her palms so she wouldn't have to search his eyes for lies or the truth.

"Baby, this new guy Daniel was put on the case and came calling, questioning me about my whereabouts the night of Calvin's murder. Said someone reported seeing my SUV parked in Calvin's yard. Wasn't hard for him to single me out, being I was the bounty hunter looking for Calvin. You saw the whole thing. You were there too. You saw Calvin get his gun."

And she had proof of who pulled the trigger. What was the lead he'd given? That she was there? Mona uncovered her face, narrowed her eyes at him. "And Katherine?

How is she involved? She just happened to be the reporter on this?"

"What? I don't know; it's her job. She's still the lead anchorwoman in Selma, isn't she? She reports all of their big cases. You're not still bitter about her taking that Lincoln dude from you, are you? Is that what this is about? Katherine?" he asked, facing his palms up and at her. "Lincoln?"

"Fuck you, Steven!" she yelled, slapping his hands away from her. "You've always been jealous of my relationship with Lincoln. This here conversation is about you giving that detective only God knows what. I demand to know what it was!"

His lips tightened, eyes narrowed. "What, what was?"

"You bastard. Don't play mind games with me. After all I've witnessed because of you, I have to live with myself. But I don't have to live with you." *How dare his ass try to hide shit from me.*

Steven dropped her bag to the floor, embraced her. "Baby, what was I supposed to do? Let him shoot me, shoot you? You're just as guilty as I am. A simple-ass failure to appear for a DUI, Mona. Granted it was his fourth time driving under the influence. But Calvin should've taken his ass to court. Sarah should've left Calvin behind bars instead of putting their house up as collateral. Now his stupid ass is dead and this is what his wife gets for bailing him out. You can't feel sorry for people like that. So, yes, I had to give Daniel information that would take the focus off of us."

Us?

STEVEN
CHAPTER 18

May 2010

Talking wasn't going to make things better between them. He knew what she needed and exactly when to give it to her good. Right now.

Sex was a sedative for Mona, especially her favorite, oral. No man could make love to her better than him. He'd learned all of her erogenous zones. Could polish her pearl to perfection. Make her come fast or slow. Hard or soft. He controlled her pussy.

Steven pressed his lips to Mona's forehead. Trailing kisses to her nose, he moved to her lips, sucked tenderly before gently luring her tongue into his mouth. "Everything's gonna be all right, baby." The tip of his tongue danced along her cheek, outlined the perimeter of her ear, then slowly penetrated her ear.

Mona grunted, then moaned.

The welcoming sounds resonating in his

ear made his dick grow tight in his pants. He squatted to align his mouth with her breasts. Opening every button on her white blouse, he lowered her lace bra beneath her titty, then clenched her nipple between his teeth. Firmly, he cupped her pussy into his palm, lightly scratched his middle finger along her shaft.

Mona whispered, "Steven, don't," as she squirmed in his hand.

The moisture from her excitement soaked his palm. "That's my girl. Let it flow for your husband. I got you."

Steven kneeled before Mona, unzipped her pants. Lowering her thong to her thighs, he teased her clit with his tongue, allowing her juices to saturate his palate. "Relax, baby. Let go," he said, laying her on the bed.

After removing her pants, he released his manhood, tossed their clothes to the floor beside the bed. Burying his face in her pubic hairs, he inhaled, filling his lungs to capacity. He held his breath, savoring her sweet fresh scent of cocoa, then blew cool air on her clit. Mona Lisa smelled and tasted just like chocolate. The only taste he preferred more than hers was whiskey.

Steven figured if he got her undressed, made her cum hard, she wouldn't go anywhere. At least not for a few hours. By then he could convince her to stay by her own will.

He stroked his long, stiff erection, rubbed the tip inside her vaginal lips, then slid the head in. He didn't stop sliding until his entire shaft was inside her, then he pressed deep, applying the pressure Mona loved. He held his dick in position, awaiting her flood of fluids.

When Mona came to him, thrusting herself harder and harder against his erection, she repeatedly screamed, "Steven, I hate you!" Her body couldn't stop trembling as she soaked the mattress.

Showering his seeds, he came with her. "I need you, Mona. You don't hate me. You love me," he whispered. "And I love you too, baby. We're in this together. I got you. Trust me. Thanks for staying with me."

MONA
CHAPTER 19

May 2010

What just happened had nothing to do with their staying together.

Sex was Steven's way of reminding her what she'd be missing if she ever left his ass. His big dick was good; actually, it was fucking fantastic. But his dick was no magic stick, had no superpowers, and no matter how hard, his dick would never make her feel the incredible connection she'd felt when Lincoln was inside of her. If she hadn't aborted Lincoln's baby, her life would be different.

There were many times when Steven was sucking her clit that she held the back of his head and came hard in his mouth while fantasizing about graduation day when she'd sexed Lincoln between the bleachers. Like the first time Steven went down on her at Grist Park in the back of his SUV.

Based on what Steven had done, Mona's

decision to leave him remained the same. An innocent woman was in jail, and Mona's name might be in Calvin's file.

Steven unzipped her black bag, emptied the contents, tossed her bag on the bed, wrapped his arms around her, then pressed her head to his strong chest. "You have my word. I promise it won't happen again. Now put those things away."

New tears streamed down her face. He dried them with the back of his hand. But it had already happened again. Two more not-so-accidental deaths had occurred during their road trip from Selma to Bakersfield. One was in Macon, Georgia, while Steven was taking Brian Norris into custody. The other, Terrence Vince, an inmate on the run, was gunned down by Steven in Kansas City, Kansas.

"Your random acts of violence aren't exciting. Not knowing when or if you're going to kill another person is driving me insane. This is not what I signed up for. Bounty hunters are not the same as assassins. You're wearing two hats. I'm not taking any more chances that you'll randomly murder innocent people. What happened to you? You used to be the nice guy. You used to make me feel safe. You kill the wrong person and sooner or later someone will kill us! That's if you don't drink yourself into an early grave. Stop it! We've got more than enough money. Quit, go back to making a decent living working nine to five, and I'll stay."

She'd stay as long as Lincoln didn't resurface and ask her to be with him. Nothing or no one could keep her from loving Lincoln. Not Katherine or her son Jeremiah.

Steven laughed. "Decent doesn't cut it, Mona! I've never worked a decent nine-to-five job, whatever that is. I'd die living paycheck to paycheck trying to get rich working for the man or one of these oil companies here in Bakersfield! I've been on the streets all my life. Hunting is what I live and breathe. I don't like working indoors. I'm not like you. I can't sit at a desk or stand in a lab for eight hours. I hate wearing ties, I hate punching clocks, and I refuse to call anyone 'boss.' "

Mona shook her head. "You don't get it, Steven. I don't care about your not wanting to work inside. I cannot, will not, live like this another day. Go on. Kill everybody in Bakersfield if you want to. But do it without me. Murder is wrong! I'm done!"

She stood naked in front of him, hoping, whether she stayed or not, he'd make the right decision.

"You're the one who doesn't get it. Sit down," he said, backing her up to the bed. Sitting beside her, Steven explained. "I said I wasn't going to tell you because you already know too damn much. But those three murders," he said as though someone else had committed the crimes, "had nothing to do with bounty hunting. They were all a work for hire."

Frantically, Mona shook her head, remained silent, scooted to the edge of the bed farthest from him. Her lips tightened with anger.

Staring at her, he confessed, "We received a half million dollars . . . a head. But you know this here isn't about money. We've been together practically all our lives. I'm *not* letting you leave me."

Now that she knew the truth, leaving was her only option.

He was *paid 1.5 million* because somebody wanted all three of those men dead. What Mona didn't know was who or why.

Steven moved so close to her she had to straddle the corner of the bed, then firmly plant her feet on the floor to keep from falling off. "When my clients are paying that kind of money, they become my pimp and I'm their whore, baby. I'm in too deep, Mona. If they say, 'jump,' I don't even ask,

'How high?' I just do it."

That was the dumbest thing she'd heard him say. Was he serious? What clients? Was he working for the mafia? Drug dealers? Mona tapped her foot, became silent. She nodded, then shook her head. She knew what she had to do.

"Greed is what gets most people caught. I'm not selfish, you know that. I anonymously sent each of the widows a cashier's check for a hundred thousand. I admit I didn't tell you that I sent Sarah money when I knew she was in jeopardy of losing her house. She was desperate. Each widow was strapped for cash. They chose to deposit the checks I sent them, and they were foolish to spend the money. That was on them."

Mona sprang to her feet, stared down at Steven. "So you blackmailed them as insurance to cover your ass."

Holding up his pointing finger, he interrupted, "Our asses. I knew if they were ever questioned, they couldn't prove to authorities where the windfall money came from."

A question for every dollar he'd given those women was in her head. How could they not know where the money came from? Whose name was on those cashier's checks? The answers didn't matter right now. Mona thought about the three six-figure deposits

Steven had wired to her account. She didn't know the legal name on the account. Six years was a long time ago. Constantly gasping for air, she paced in front of him.

"I love you, Mona. I gave you my word. Calm down." He stood, hugged her.

"I'm okay," Mona lied, then kissed him. "I just need something cold to drink."

"I'll draw your bubbly bath water," he said, releasing her. "That always helps to relax you."

Steven shouted from the bathroom, "We've got a big job tomorrow. Another FTA. Thirty Gs."

That meant he'd give her six grand, the same amount she'd earn in a month working at the lab. *I can't. I just can't do this again.* She knew his name — Steven Cunningham, Incorporated — was on all of the paper checks he'd given her. Money was not going to be her pimp, and she wasn't going to be her husband's whore.

Mona quietly entered the bedroom, dressed from the clothes he'd scattered on the floor. Panties, bra, blouse, and pants were on in less than a minute. She opened the bottom drawer, wrapped her other gun along with the box of bullets in a T-shirt. She left her black bag and jeans on the scrambled sheets, bypassed their kitchen, ran out the front door, got in her car. Her purse was still on the passenger seat. Opening then closing her armrest compartment, her registered gun was there. She stuffed the wrapped T-shirt and its contents into the glove box.

She mumbled toward the sky, "Thanks for giving me that push."

The next-door neighbor, Mama V, waved. Mona backed out of the driveway, fanned her hand in front of the windshield, then sped off, leaving a cloud of smoke behind. Never again would she return to his house. This would be the last time she'd exercise her right to remain silent and let an innocent person like Sarah McKenny go to jail.

What if Sarah got the death penalty?

STEVEN
CHAPTER 20

May 2010

"Mona, baby!" Steven called out from the bathroom. "Your water is almost ready."

Turning off the cold water, he noticed the house was quiet. She was probably sitting in the living room in his recliner. That was her preferred place to unwind. It was his favorite place to watch *Maury, Family Feud,* or sports when she wasn't sitting there. Damn, he loved some Mona Lisa. There was no way he'd let her abandon him.

Steven was glad Mona's mother ostracized her. Made it easy for him to isolate his wife, keep their private life private.

He didn't have any sob stories about not being loved as a kid. His childhood was awesome. His father hadn't walked out on his mother. His parents were happily married for thirty years, living in the same Selma house he grew up in. He was never bullied as a kid, straight-A student. Voted most likely to succeed in high school. Being successful and making lots of money weren't the same. Steven had learned that on the streets watching drug dealers. They made him smart about making money the legal way.

Bounty hunting made him debt free. The right assassination contract could afford him an early retirement in three years at the age of thirty, but was the money worth risking losing Mona?

Was he remorseful for the murders he'd committed? It wasn't personal. It was business. If he hadn't pulled the trigger, someone else would've. Would he kill again? For two reasons. If his or Mona's life or livelihood was threatened, and if the price was right.

"Mona, baby," he called out. Again, there was no answer.

Her wanting out of his life was a reasonable request. Had it been any other woman, he would've packed her things for her, took or sent her any place she wanted to go. Steven smiled, picturing Mona in their second-grade class blowing big pink bubbles with her gum. When the bubble burst and covered her mouth, oh, how he wanted to be that piece of gum. Her head had a dozen long, pretty plaits with twice as many bows and barrettes. From that day and eight consecutive years after, at the beginning of class he gave her a piece of Hubba Bubba. The day he stopped was when he saw her bite his gum in the middle, then mouth-feed William Lincoln the other half.

"Mona!" he yelled, entering their bedroom. Her black bag was still on the bed where he'd tossed it, but most of its contents were gone.

He searched the kitchen and living room, but no Mona. After opening the front door, he stepped onto the porch, stared at the driveway. Her car was gone. "What the fuck? She can't be serious," he muttered between his teeth. "I should've followed my first mind and blocked her car in."

"Hey, Steven," Ms. Velma, or Mama V as others called her, yelled from her neighboring porch.

"Hey, Ms. Velma. You seen Mona?" He called her Ms. Velma out of respect, but the only person he addressed as Mama was his mother.

"She left. Drove away from here as though her life depended on her getting to or from something. Either that or she broke a nail." Ms. Velma laughed. "You know how these young girls are. Always in a hurry," she said, then pointed. "See the tire marks in the

141

street? That there's hers. If y'all don't feel like cooking tonight, I got some ribs smokin' on my grill. Come get a slab."

"Thanks, Ms. Velma. I might take you up on that offer," he said, going inside.

He opened the liquor cabinet, gripped a bottle of 101 proof Wild Turkey whiskey by the neck, yanked off the top, pressed the opening to his lips, then turned his liquid lunch upside down. With each gulp his throat burned like fire. He didn't stop gulping until the bottle was near empty and his head was on full.

He made his way to his recliner, flopped down on the cold black leather, sat the bottle beside the lever, then propped his feet up. A slab of ribs wasn't what Steven needed. He needed his rib. Mona Lisa.

MONA
CHAPTER 21

May 2010

A woman should know what her man is thinking well before he thinks it. Most men are predictable, and Steven Cunningham was no exception. Most of the time Mona was right about her husband. The one thing she hadn't foreseen or detected was his motivation to kill.

When did he get caught up? Why didn't the cowards who'd paid Steven do their own damn dirty work? Her Steven wasn't perfect, but he didn't grow up gang banging either. Intentionally taking a person's life was out of character for the sensitive guy that gave her bubble gum in school for eight years straight. He definitely wasn't raised in a thugish way. His parents took him to church almost every Sunday. If Steven could sing, he would've been a choirboy.

Steven knew now that she was gone, his first recourse would be to sit in his recliner, then gobble a bottle of Wild Turkey, not necessarily in that order. The more he drank, the clearer his thoughts would become, or so he'd imagine. There were three times that he consumed to the point of almost passing out, and each time he'd taken a life. Tonight wasn't that kind of night for him.

He'd probably wait until he was functionally sober, drive around town looking for her car, then show up at her job tomorrow. If he didn't find her, he'd think she was running out of fear, long gone, headed up or down Interstate 5. Mona didn't have to run. She wasn't afraid of him killing or hurting her. If he did, it would be a first. She was surprised he hadn't called yet but was certain he would before midnight.

The drive from Steven's house to her first destination was less than twenty minutes with traffic. En route she stopped at the Bank of America on Chester Avenue, went inside, opened her purse, presented her California driver's license, and withdrew five thousand dollars from her account. That was the first time, since saying, "I do," to Steven that she'd touched any of her two point five million dollar savings.

Her cell phone chimed, rang, chimed, rang. Dang. Sarah wasn't dead, she was in custody. Mona silenced her phone. She'd check it later.

She carelessly married Steven at the Selma courthouse when they were both twenty-two. What in the hell was she thinking? Her mother was right. Mona hadn't given much thought to being Steven's wife.

Most of her friends had gotten hitched right after high school and had babies. When she hadn't received a phone call or letter from Lincoln, Mona had momentarily lost hope of their getting back together. No one had heard from Lincoln, not even his grandparents, so he had to have reenlisted, gotten out, or was dead.

Liking the way Steven had his own house, and enough money to take her on vacations and take care of her, Mona didn't think marrying Steven seemed like a bad decision. She would've gotten an annulment if Lincoln had come home or had she not witnessed Calvin's murder. Lincoln should be out by now. Maybe he was already discharged. She'd give Lincoln time to come around. Holding on to false hope was her way of escaping reality. Mona could wait a few years to get pregnant by Lincoln, again. Having kids with Steven was not happening, ever.

"I'd also like to apply for a credit card as

well as a Visa debit card," Mona said.

"Sure thing, Ms. Ellington," the teller said.

Mona didn't have to request that the teller remove Steven's last name because she'd never put his name on either — the Selma or Bakersfield — bank account or any of her stocks, bonds, and certificates of deposit.

Her father had told her, "Mona, there's nothing worse than wanting to leave and not having enough money to go." Now she understood what her dad had meant. He'd be proud that she'd taken his advice. Though her mom's advice differed, her mom should be happy too. Mona had enough money to stay gone.

"Oh, I'm in between residences so hold my cards here. Call me at the number on file when they're ready to be picked up," Mona insisted, then wrote her cell phone number on a deposit slip. "Is this the number you have?"

"Yes, it is, Ms. Ellington," the teller said, placing her cash in the money counter. She checked, double-checked, then ran her five thousand dollars through the machine a final time before putting the cash in front of Mona along with an envelope.

Stuffing the money into the envelope, then inside her purse, Mona left.

There were no worries about her bank statements going to Steven's house. Soon as they settled in Bakersfield, she got a post office box near her job at the lab and a safety deposit box at the bank. But she'd thought it more efficient to pick up her cards than to have them mailed.

Steven had paid for her every need and want, while her desire to be with Lincoln remained unfulfilled. What made people hold on to first loves forever? Since she believed that her desires dictated her happiness, it was time for Mona to accept responsibility for her daily sorrow and move on.

The ache in her chest, the worry lines that had developed on her twenty-seven-year-old forehead, and the heaviness of a once outrageously joyful spirit were coaxing her into a life of depression. Sex with Steven was great. He knew how to satisfy her in bed, but even while enjoying climaxing, she was no longer excited about him.

After driving a few blocks to the hotel, she parked her car in the rear of the open lot, entered the back door, then approached the receptionist. "I'd like a room for a week."

"What name is your reservation under?" the girl asked. She appeared younger than Mona.

"I don't have a reservation. I said I'd like

a room, for a week."

"No problem. Let me check." She tapped on her keyboard, then said, "Great, we have availability. Would you like a king or two double beds?"

"A king," Mona said, scanning the lobby, front entrance, and the bar area. She turned around each time the elevator doors behind her opened or closed.

"Are you okay, ma'am?" the receptionist asked.

"I'm fine. Just expecting someone," Mona said, not knowing if she was lying or not.

"Certainly. May I see your credit card and ID?" the girl asked.

Mona observed her name tag, then handed the receptionist her driver's license. "Tiffany, I don't have a credit card that I care to give you. I'm paying cash."

"Sorry, ma'am," Tiffany replied. "We need a credit card for your incidentals."

Sternly, Mona replied, "There won't be any incidentals. And cash is legal tender everywhere in the U.S." Mona paid for her room, got her key, then headed to the bar for a much-needed drink.

She wasn't running from Steven; her decision was to leave him. There was a difference. Leaving her new hometown, she'd do in her own time, not his. And no matter what he said, regardless of what he did, and she didn't care how amazing his mind-blowing orgasms were, she was never going back to him.

STEVEN
CHAPTER 22

May 2010

When all failed and he felt there was no way out, he'd call his mother.

Tempted to phone Mona first, he sat in his recliner contemplating how he could make her life hell until she'd come home where she belonged. A wife's place was beside her husband. What man would want her if he knew what she'd done?

For better or worse was what Mona had legally agreed to at the courthouse. One option was to frame her like he'd done Sarah. That would be extreme yet effective, but Mona wouldn't go down without a knock-down, rake-his-ass-over-the-coals-and-drag-him-into-the-quicksand-pit-too kinda fight. He hated to admit it, but Mona had become better than him at his own job. His wife was one step ahead of brilliant.

Mona was many things, but she wasn't a passive woman. Trying to frame her would no doubt eventually backfire on him. Cutting off her credit cards and cell phone wouldn't equate to cutting her off. He didn't make enough money to make her wealthy, but in addition to making her financially independent, Steven let Mona keep all the money she made on her nine-to-five jobs. Steven never wanted Mona Lisa to want for anything except him.

"This is fucked up!" he cried out loud, then turned the whiskey bottle upside down.

Steven held his phone, retrieved his list of favorites, then dialed the first number.

"Hey, Buttercup. I was just thinking about you. Everything okay?" his mom asked.

"I guess, Ma."

"Well, if you have to guess, tell me what's wrong. You haven't lost that good job at the oil company, have you?"

Any job paying over fifty thousand dollars was considered good to most people in the South. If his mother knew how much he made bounty hunting, she'd swear he was working for the godfather himself. If that were her guess, she'd be close to being right.

"No, Ma." He wasn't lying. They didn't have a chance to fire him because they'd never hired him. Suit. Tie. Meetings. Sitting behind a desk in an office with a dreary view of downtown Bakersfield wouldn't have lasted three minutes.

The upside was Bakersfield was a bounty hunter's paradise. Probation offenders, drug dealers ditching court while out on bail, and the long list of everyday citizens with unknown warrants were one step away from having to post bail. One step away from skipping out on bail. They put him one step away from getting another contract. With a population of almost three hundred forty thousand, the residents made his job easy because most offenders in Bakersfield never left Bakersfield.

"Then what's the problem? Is it one of those guy things? I can put your daddy on the phone. You don't have men hitting on you, do you?"

Steven laughed. He didn't have anything against same-sex relationships. Business was profitable and he didn't discriminate. When it came to slapping on the handcuffs, he didn't care about gender or sexual preferences.

"No, Ma. I'd rather talk to you. Mona left me and I'm not sure when or if she's coming back."

"Aw, Buttercup, is that all? I knew this was coming," his mom said. "I'm surprised it took her so long."

What did she mean by that? How could

she have known? Why hadn't his mother warned him?

Steven frowned, sat on the edge of the recliner, stared at Mona's picture on the wall. Looking at his wife's picture made him hate her more. But he wasn't angry with Katherine Clinton. In a way, they were aiding one another. Katherine could use the money and he needed her assistance. He owed Katherine ten grand for using her influence to personally interview Detective Davenport, but he never wanted the Mc-Kenny story to make national news. He had to find out why she'd done that. Had to make sure Davenport hadn't linked Calvin's murder to the other two. Maybe he should've used a different bank account for each of the cashier's checks.

"But, Ma. I'm a good husband. I've been nothing but good to Mona. You know that. I don't deserve this." He wanted to add the word *shit*, but Steven never cursed while speaking to or in the presence of his parents.

"You men are all alike. This isn't about you. Sometimes a woman needs to find herself. Mona went from her mother's house to yours. She married you the same day you proposed. Except for when she was in college, she's never lived on her own, and even then you said she had a roommate.

I'm surprised it took her this long. Y'all been knowing each other since second grade. And then you go and drag her all the way cross country where she doesn't have friends. Give her space to find out who she is. And you need to take advantage of her time away and do the same."

Maybe his mother had been drinking too. Steven eyed Mona's 24 × 36 framed picture on the living room wall. "How much time?" He feared the longer Mona stayed gone, she'd get comfortable being away from him and never come back.

"Six months tops."

Six what? To find out who she was? For real? And he should do the same? He'd never taken time to figure himself out. Didn't see the point in doing that. "Mona needs to come home now, Ma."

"How long she been gone?"

Steven checked the time on his cell, then answered, "An hour."

His mother laughed. "Buttercup, you're funny. Mona loves you. She'll come back to you. You didn't hit her, did you? We raised you better than that. Please tell me you didn't —"

He interrupted, "No, Ma. You know I'd never do that."

Steven never saw his parents fight. They

154

never argued, at least not around him. His parents weren't the norm in Selma. A lot of the Southern men abuse their women and their wives. He loved Mona too much to physically hurt her. But if she didn't come back, he would not have mercy on her soul.

Six months? His mother never gave him bad advice. He could give Mona that much space hoping she'd be back in a week. One hundred and eighty-two days from today — he counted the days on his phone, then calendared the exact date and time. If she hadn't come back by 12:00 a.m. Thanksgiving Day, her time was up.

No matter where she was, he'd find her. In six months, she might not matter.

"You want me and your dad to come visit you?" his mom asked, not waiting for his answer. "We'll be there Memorial Day. Your daddy needs to get out the house anyway. We need to do something with all this money you keep sending us besides adding on rooms to the house. And you need to keep a clear head. Now, don't get so upset you lose that good job with the oil company. If you do, Mona will leave you for sure. You know how her mama raised her not to be with a man that can't take care of her. And you're not gonna embarrass us. No, siree. Give that girl six months to be on her own.

Be patient. She'll come back to you, Buttercup. I love your daddy to death, but I sure wish I hadn't gone straight from my parents' house to his. Speaking of death, you saw the news today? I can't believe that Sarah McKenny girl was arrested for killing her —"

"Ma, I've gotta go find Mona. See y'all Memorial Day. Love you. Tell Dad I love him too. Bye."

MONA
CHAPTER 23

May 2010

The bar inside the hotel was fairly quiet. One bartender, one patron. Her arrival doubled the customer count. Mona sat at the end farthest from the entrance. The bar stool with a high back appeared to have a firm cushion until her ass sunk deep into the seat. "Whoa," she said, gripping the edge of the bar.

The bartender laughed. "Be careful there."

"Don't bother changing seats. They're all like that. Mind if I sit next to you?" a tall and handsome guy asked. "Give this lady whatever she'd like," he told the bartender.

His friendly demeanor and dazzling smile made her smile, a little. He was as tall as Steven. His haircut was a bit military, reminding her of Lincoln. Mona wished she had Lincoln's number. She'd gotten so sidetracked getting away from Steven, she hadn't checked her phone since this morning. Maybe Lincoln had called.

"What would you like?" the bartender asked.

Lincoln, she thought, then answered, "I'll have a Long Island iced tea." She thanked the guy seated next to her as she retrieved her cell. Was it fair she wanted her ex to emotionally rescue her from her husband?

"My pleasure. Make that two Long Islands. My name is Davis. And you are?" he asked, extending his long thick fingers.

Didn't he see both of her hands holding her phone? "Mona Lisa," she said, pressing the on button. Gasping, she mouthed, "A hundred and three missed calls and more texts than that. Wow." She had to find out what Steven had done, but she wasn't going to call anyone tonight so she might as well drink and try to relax.

"Yes, wow. What a beautiful name. Please to meet you, Mona Lisa." Davis placed his elbows on the bar, interlocked his fingers. "You live around here, passing through, visiting, or on business?"

Shaking her head, she wished he'd *"Shut the hell up!"* for a moment. Did he think his one-sided conversation would command her attention? Mona scrolled through her list of missed calls. "Not sure yet," she said, briefly eyeing the entrance to the hotel.

Damn, only fifty-two missed calls registered on her phone. What happened to the other fifty-one calls? The ones she could see, half of them were from her mom. She guessed Sarah's arrest gave her mother an excuse to call until she'd spoken with her. What if Lincoln had called but there were too many numbers for his to show up? Disgusted, Mona placed her phone on the bar. She had nothing to say to her mom.

At the moment, Mona was unsure of a lot of things. Going to work tomorrow would mean a trip to the local Walmart on Highway 178 for clothes to wear. She could go to the airport, take the next flight to wherever the plane was going. Sleeping in all week and ordering room service for breakfast, lunch, and dinner was another option.

"Well, you don't have to tell me anything. I respect that," Davis said. "Have you eaten? Would you like to join me for dinner? Here at the hotel, that is."

Mona was consumed with the monologue in her head. Was Steven looking for her? Did he care? She hadn't missed a single call from him. And although she wasn't going back to him, she wanted him to fight for her return.

"We can order from the bar menu if you'd like."

"Huh? What?" she replied. "Do what?" Mona snapped. "What are you talking about?"

"Never mind," Davis said, picking up his drink. "I can see you have a lot on your mind. Granted this is a public place, but I'll just move to the other end of the bar so you can be alone."

That made her laugh a little. Mona touched his arm. "No, please stay. You're right. I do have a lot on my mind," she said, eyeing the entrance again.

She needed his company more than he wanted hers. She didn't want to be alone tonight. Sex wasn't on her mind. Having a man to protect her was what she desired.

Happy he'd asked again, "Would you like to have dinner with me?" she firmly replied, "Only if it's serviced in my room."

Davis smiled, tossed thirty dollars on the bar. "Ready when you are. We can take our drinks to your room. I got 'em."

Mona felt safe at the hotel, safer with a big, strong man like Davis by her side. She prayed he'd stay the night, and she knew exactly how to entice him. She should've requested two double beds. Hadn't planned on meeting a man, a fine one at that, so quickly. Sexing him could take a lot off her mind, but sex wasn't on her agenda, and she didn't want to give him the wrong idea.

As they entered her room, her cell phone rang. It was Steven. Mona declined his call and locked her door.

"You must be a popular person to have your phone constantly chiming. Now it's ringing," Davis said, then asked, "Was that your husband? 'Cause I don't sleep with married women. In case you don't know, the men in this town are crazy and possessive, in that order."

"I don't have a husband anymore. Make yourself comfortable. You're welcome to stay but you have to shower before getting in the bed. And, so there's no confusion, we're not having sex."

Davis sat the drinks, his wallet, and keys on the nightstand, then headed to the bathroom. Sticking his head out the door, he said, "I'm a complete gentleman. If you want to see my California's driver's license, it's in my wallet on the nightstand." He closed the door.

Mona took him up on his offer. Snapped a photo of his license with her camera phone, then powered off her cell. She'd need to preserve the battery until she could buy a charger in the morning. A new car was also on her list of things to buy, but she'd wait until she left Bakersfield. Steven wouldn't vandalize his own car, and if he did she wouldn't care.

The bathroom door opened. Davis stepped out with a white bath towel wrapped at his waist. His chest was bare, smooth. Nipples, erect, tight. Stomach, flat. Pubic hairs, partially exposed. The imprint of his dick molded the towel like a twelve-inch lollicock.

Damn! Her eyes widened, mouth opened. *Nice package,* she thought.

"Thanks for letting me use your shower. I feel great. Your turn," he said, flashing his dazzling smile.

Mona wasn't as trusting as Davis. She took all she had with her — purse, gun, and cell — into the bathroom. She left the door open so she could hear what was happening in the room.

Her reflection in the mirror was pretty, but she felt like shit thinking about Sarah sleeping in a jail cell while she was staying in a hotel. Mona could go anywhere in the world if she wanted. Sarah could not.

The shower cap neatly covered Mona's hair. She closed her eyes. The hot, steamy beads of water bounced on her face, then flowed to her feet. Massaging her breasts, her body tingled with pleasure as she visualized Davis's dick. She thoroughly cleansed between her inner and outer labia, then touched her clit with the tip of her middle finger trying to have an orgasm. Struggling to let go of the mounted tension consuming her, she stroked herself.

"You okay in there?"

Almost forgetting Davis was in the room, she exhaled. "Yeah." Didn't know he heard her.

Mona washed herself, scrubbed her underwear, hung her panties and bra on the hook behind the door. She wrapped her naked body in the towel.

"Wow, you always take almost an hour to shower?" he asked, leaning against the leather headboard.

"Yes and no."

Mona peeled back the comforter and sheet, exposed his feet, sat at the foot of the bed. Placing his legs over her lap, she saturated his shins with lotion. With long, graceful strokes, she massaged everything below his knees. She took her time kneading his toes, arches, and the ball of his feet until Davis fell asleep. Massaging him helped take her mind off the things she couldn't control.

Curling in a fetal position, Mona secured

her body at the edge of the bed far away from him, placed two pillows between them. Tomorrow she'd resign from her job and take time to decide whom and what she really wanted.

LINCOLN
CHAPTER 24

May 2010

Whatever happened to the Homes for Heroes Act that was never voted on under the Bush administration?

Lincoln had to decide whether to use the last eight hundred dollars he had to pay his cell phone bill, eat for another thirty days, and live on the street, or to bring his rent current for the last time, have no cell phone service, and starve the rest of the month. Or last, ask his family for help. The decision was difficult.

Memorial Day he awoke in a park, wrapped in an American flag. He wasn't proud that he'd stolen the flag from a pole on someone's lawn. If someone thought about robbing him while he was asleep, he prayed the flag would change their mind. If he died being homeless, maybe whoever found his body would automatically assume the red, white, and blue meant he was a vet.

Neatly aligning the stripes and stars, he shoved the flag into his backpack, then headed to the park's public restroom to wash his face and brush his teeth. Later he'd try to sneak into a hotel or low-star restaurant, lock the door or stall, and charge up his cell phone while taking what his grandmother called "a ho bath."

He tossed his backpack atop a picnic table, pulled out his cell phone. Mom, Dad, Grandma, Grandpa, Katherine, or Mona? In a few hours the park would be flooded with people celebrating . . . what? A day off from work with pay? He couldn't believe his government actually paid millions of dollars to workers and gave just about every employee the day off to celebrate and he just woke up in a park.

After scrolling through his numbers, he dialed his grandparents.

"Hello," a sleepy voice answered.

"Hey, Grandpa."

His voice escalated. "William, is that you, son?"

"Yeah, it's me."

"We thought you were dead, but we hadn't heard anything from the military so we figured they might not be able to identify your body." His grandfather sounded excited, confused, and inquisitive. "Where are you? When are you coming home? Your grandma and I want to hear about all your adventures. Honey! William is on the phone, pick up the other end!"

There was no way he could ask them for money. He ended the call soon after his grandma said, "William, baby, is that you?"

Barbeque pits were being set up near picnic areas, families were unloading foil pans that he assumed were filled with baked beans, potato salad, ribs, chicken, hot links, hamburger patties, and more trimmings. He was sure if he stayed close by, someone would give him a plate if he asked, but he doubted anyone would offer. Maybe a kid would. They seemed to have more compassion for him than adults. But he prayed no kids came near him, fearing they'd trigger a flashback of the day Randy was bombed. Having kids too close to him made him nervous. Kids triggered horrible homicidal thoughts.

Exhaling, he knew he'd prolonged the inevitable long enough. He prayed Katherine's home phone number was the same. There was no need to contact Mona, unless Katherine didn't answer.

"Hello, Clinton residence." That wasn't the voice of the Clinton he wanted to speak with.

He cleared his throat. "Good morning, may I speak with Katherine Clinton, please?"

"Good morning to you. Hold for a moment while I get her," Katherine's mother said.

Good. She must not have recognized his voice. He tapped the toe of his combat boot in the dirt, started to end the call as he heard, "This is Katherine."

A lump the size of a golf ball choked him. "Katherine, it's Lincoln. William Lincoln."

Silence filled the airways between them. Then he heard, "Ahhhh! Oh, my gosh!" She started crying.

From the freaked-out tone of her voice, he wasn't sure if she was happy to hear from him or just shocked. He figured he'd wait until she said something else.

"You're alive. Thank God. Thank you, Jesus. Are you in Selma?" she asked, gasping. Sounded like she was hyperventilating.

He imagined her doing a praise dance. "Not yet. I need your help, Katherine. I need to know if you can wire me five thousand dollars. I promise I'll pay you back when I get on my feet." The military made him a sharpshooter, so he always got straight to the point. He expected her to hang up, but she didn't.

"Are you coming to Selma?"

He hated when women answered questions with questions. "Eventually. I'm not doing too good. I don't want you to see me like this. I promise when I get better, I'll come see you."

"Me and your son, Jeremiah, Lincoln. He's nine years old. Give me your address, I'll send you some pictures. He looks exactly like you."

Tears streamed down his face. He wanted to hurl his phone like a football across the park. He knew he should've called her sooner, like years sooner. Pictures might help him mentally prepare to see Jeremiah. What a nice name.

"What's his last name?"

"Lincoln?"

He couldn't tell if that was another question or the answer. All this time she's been raising their son alone while . . . "Did you get married?" he asked, praying she hadn't.

"No, I promised you, remember? I'm still waiting. Stupid, huh? But now that I know you're alive, I'm pissed."

That song, "Still Waiting on Your Love" by LaKai, resonated. Katherine could never stay mad at him. "You have no idea what I've been through," he cried, unable to hold back his tears. He wished her arms were around him.

Katherine angrily countered, "No, you have no idea what we've been through."

He didn't want to start an argument during their first conversation in ten years or make her upset to the point where she'd hang up. "You're right. So can you help me?"

"It might not be five thousand, but I'll see what I can do. Where should I wire the money?"

Was she trying to track him down? If he wanted the money, he had to tell her. "I'm in Seattle, Washington. Here's my cell phone number. Write this down . . . area code 206 . . . Once you send the money, text me when I can pick it up."

The little furniture that he had he'd left in his apartment. He had no new place to put his things. His Prime Care doctor told him the landlord was required to put his things in storage. But for how long? Depending on how much money Katherine sent, he'd decide whether to pay the cost to get his things back or start over. At least he'd be able to sleep in a hotel tonight.

"Katherine, who's that on the phone?" he heard her mother ask.

"Mama, it's Lincoln."

"Is he in Selma? Is he coming over to meet

his son? Does he have the fifty thousand dollars he owe you in back child support? If not, hang up the phone right now, Katherine, and I don't want no mess about being engaged."

"He needs help, Mama. I'm going to send him a few dollars to help him get on his feet."

The last words Lincoln heard before the call ended was Katherine's mother saying, "You ain't sending his ass shit!"

STEVEN
CHAPTER 25

May 2010

"Hey, Steven. Who's that with cha?" Ms. Velma asked, waving from her porch.

If retirement meant staying home, he'd work the streets for an eternity. That woman had too much free time. No one had to impose a neighborhood watch on Ms. Velma's street. No break-ins, stolen cars, drug dealing, or shooting happened on their block. The surrounding neighborhoods weren't as fortunate. Steven was lucky to have her next door. She was tough. Long as she didn't cross his property line trying to get into his business, her constant daily greetings were fine.

His mom waved back. "Hi, I'm Steven's mother, and this here is his dad."

"Where y'all from?" Ms. Velma asked, leaning on her pink column.

Pink and purple must be Ms. Velma's favorite colors. Her entire house stucco exterior was pink with purple trimmings. His house was white with red borders. He didn't like the red but didn't hate it enough to repaint.

Ms. Velma was the first African-American to buy on that block. She'd seen families come and go, but she refused to move, telling him, "Everybody has the right to own themselves a piece of property, and I don't see no sense in doing what y'all youngsters call upgrading 'cause that don't do nothing but keep you in debt. Take care of what you got, Steven. That way you keeps more of your money in your pockets."

He couldn't take it with him, so he used his money to make others happy. Steven wanted to buy Mona a mini-mansion in one of those new developments in Bakersfield — five bedrooms, four baths, split level, backyard with a pool. Mona had chosen their area and their cozy two-bedroom house. Said it reminded her of her mother's home in Selma.

His mom proudly said, "We're all the way from the historical Selma, Alabama."

Ms. Velma stopped leaning on the column, stood straight. "Well, we got our own piece of history nearby. It's called Allensworth. Ever heard of it?"

"Can't say I have. I'm Regina, and this

173

here is my husband, Richard Cunningham."

"Well, Regina and Richard, you're welcome to my house for dinner anytime. Open invite. Your son calls me Ms. Velma, but y'all call me plain ole Velma. I'm cooking later, so if you hungry, no need to call. Come on by and I'll tell you all about Allensworth. It's the only California town to be founded, financed, and governed by African-Americans, and it's the only town of its kind in all of America. If you're here long enough, I'll take you there and on the way you can tell me all about Selma."

"Nice meeting you, Velma," his dad said, entering the house.

Velma knew his parents' names, where they were from . . . he was surprised she didn't ask how long they'd be there. Or where Mona was. It was probably on Ms. Velma's list of questions she hadn't gotten to yet.

"Make yourself comfortable," Steven said, carrying his parents' suitcases to the extra bedroom. Couldn't call it a guest bedroom 'cause they were family and he never had overnight company.

"Your daddy needs to eat. And we're not going to that lady's house next door," his mother insisted. "She's nice and all, but we can take her up on her offer another day.

We got two weeks to be here."

Two what? "Fine, Ma. What would you like to eat?"

"Breakfast sounds good to me, son. And Regina, I would like to see Allensworth before we go back to Selma."

"Me too, Richard, but it's two o'clock in the day. It's too late for pancakes."

His dad protested, "But it's never too late for pancakes."

"I wanna go to that Tina Marie's Café we passed on the way here."

Steven said, "Let's go." He didn't bother telling his mother that was one of the best breakfast spots in Bakersfield. His dad lucked out this time.

"Look at the pretty table settings in the display window," his mother said. "Richard, take a picture. I like the way the pink tablecloth is layered over the black one, and oh my, those two pink chairs are adorable."

Soon as his dad took the photo, Steven ushered his parents inside. The café was half full. Steven told the hostess, "We'd like a booth."

"I like the décor, Richard. Look up there at that pink and black ruffled waitress skirt on the wall. Remember when I used to be a cheerleader?"

His dad blushed. Yes, Steven was grown, but he did not want to know the details of that conversation.

"I like the pictures of those cars from the twenties," his dad said, then pointed. "Look at that red one with the chrome grille."

"The pink booths are nice," his mother said, sliding in before his dad.

"I'ma step outside and smoke," Steven said. He needed a cigarette more than the fresh air.

His dad said, "I didn't know you smoked, son."

"I don't. Not really. But since Mona left, I can't seem to stop smoking."

His dad frowned, looked at his mom. Steven could tell she hadn't told him, which clarified why his mom hadn't mentioned Mona yet.

Steven stood on the corner of Chester and Twentieth Street. He tightened his lips to the filter, flicked his lighter, then inhaled the smoke into his lungs. The only thing missing was a bottle of whiskey and . . . the cigarette fell from his lips, rolled off the curb.

He mumbled, "Is that Mona?"

A dingy pickup truck was stopped at the red light. He shook his head. "Couldn't be." Steven crossed the street, tapped on the window. The woman turned to him, stared him in the eyes.

Sure enough that was his wife. "Get your ass out of his car!"

The guy sped off. The SUV behind the truck blocked Steven's view of the truck's license plate. At least he knew Mona was still in town, but she'd probably leave now that he saw her.

Lighting another cigarette, he took one long drag, tossed it to the ground, stomped on it wishing it were Mona. He went inside the restaurant, sat across from his parents. Steven looked at his mom, then his dad.

"Your mom is right, son. Give Mona six months. If she's not back by then, divorce her and move on."

"Buttercup, did you hear your dad? Buttercup, answer me."

Steven's stomach boiled with anger. Dude's ass was riding around town with his wife. "Yeah, I hear you."

MONA
CHAPTER 26

November 2010

Months after quitting her job and leaving Steven, Mona was still with Davis. She'd planned on leaving Bakersfield but refused to go to Selma. Dating Davis made it hard for her to go anywhere. Why should she run from Steven? He was the one who'd messed up. Mona had the right to live her life the way she wanted.

Speaking from her heart, Mona told Davis, "I wish every day could be like this. Living in the moment, you know. Not caring about what happened minutes ago. Not worrying about what's going to happen in the next few seconds. You know, baby, an earthquake could happen right now and our lives could change forever."

She stared out his truck's window as he drove by the entrance to a dilapidated trailer park near the house she rented. Mona could've bought a new house in an upscale gated development. Leasing was a better decision, since she still wasn't sure how much longer she'd stay in Bakersfield. Living in a poverty-stricken hood had its benefits. She didn't have neighbors anxious to meet her. People mind their own business, but not much happened that someone didn't see or hear about.

"Yeah, I know what you mean," Davis said, driving with one hand atop the steering wheel. "But answer this. If you knew you had twenty-four hours to live, honey, what would you do?"

Thinking about Sarah McKenny, Mona prayed Sarah's upcoming sentencing wouldn't be the death penalty. Alabama's method was by lethal injection. Alabama had executed fewer inmates than Texas or Virginia, and although those two states ranked first and second, respectively, in the nation, Alabama was in the top ten.

Mona interlocked her fingers with his, closed her eyes, kissed the back of his right hand, held her lips there momentarily. Opening her eyes, she beamed from the inside out. The corners of her mouth curved wide across her face.

"Oh, Davis, that's a fantastic idea! Let's do it. Let's *pretend* we only have twenty-four hours to live! You take the first twenty-four and I'll do the next." Lowering their hands to the armrest, she leaned toward him, bit the corner of his bottom lip, then kissed his cheek.

Shaking his head, he kept his eyes on the road ahead. "That's crazy. I plan to live until I'm a hundred, so why would I live like today is my last?"

The question intrigued her. "Because we never know. But I would like to know what you would do," she said.

"I know how unpredictable you are, honey, and we're not going to do that . . . but if we were, I'd pack a picnic basket and cruise south along the Pacific coast with you by my side. We'd never step foot indoors. I'd feed you in the sunlight. The moon would glow around us as I held you in my arms. We'd meet all of my family and friends at Disneyland at sunrise. I'd ride the fastest rides with you by my side. And for my farewell I'd take the stage and co-star with you in a romantic comedy. I'd dance with you in my arms, and we'd make the audience laugh like children. As the curtains were closing a ray of light would beam us up to the sky. Everyone in heaven would welcome us with a standing ovation."

The mention of children reminded her of aborting Lincoln's baby. Again, she wondered what path she would have traveled if she had a nine-year-old son or daughter.

Mona really liked Davis's mention of making people laugh. She didn't want to piggyback off of his idea, but she wanted people to smile when they remembered her. If that meant their saying, "That Mona Lisa was so crazy," that was okay with her. And though her relationship with her mother was strained, she'd always love her mama.

Silence stole some of their time before he continued, "I still don't know what you see in me. I'm just a simple country man with this here dingy white pickup, my two-bedroom house with one bed, and I have you. I'm so glad I stopped at the bar that night. You've changed my life. You make me so happy, Mona. I love you."

Love almost killed her, once.

She thought she'd die when Lincoln left her for Katherine. It's like that with your first. Love was a word she took seriously. She'd never said those three words to any man except Lincoln. Couldn't say it unless she'd meant it. Couldn't mean it unless she was sure. But she'd felt certain the first time with Lincoln. And in her own way the second time with Steven, but she was never in love with him. She loved the things her husband had done for and given to her, but she was never in love with him. Now that her heart knew the difference, she wasn't trying to love or fall in love with Davis. She was just trying to find happiness each time she breathed.

Smiling, he turned right on Dr. Martin Luther King Jr. Boulevard and drove by an empty lot, a pasty gray stucco building with boarded-up windows, an abandoned house with KING'S DREAM spray painted on the front, and a grocery store at the corner to their left. No two blocks in her neighborhood were the same.

"You don't realize how awesome you are," she told him. "You're a man. A manly man. You're a true gentleman. You're muscular. You're tall. You're handsome. Especially when you don't shave for a few days. I like that rugged look and scratchy feel of your beard. But what I see most in you, Davis, is your heart. Your heart beats more love for your family and friends than all the oil pumps pumping petroleum in this here li'l town. Now, let's head south, stop at the Walmart on 178, pick up what we need for our picnic, then head toward Anaheim. Give me your phone. I'll call your family and friends and tell them to meet us at Small World."

There'd be no need to call her family. She still hadn't spoken with her parents.

Davis laughed. "Mona Lisa, please forget I said that twenty-four-hour thing, will you? We're going to Knotty Pine Café as originally planned. No detours. We can be adventurous next year."

Kicking her feet in protest, she squeezed his hand. "Next year? Aw, come on. That's practically six weeks away! You got me all fired up! Okay, let's compromise. Let's do one thing that I want to do before I die. Just one. And let's do it now."

Shaking his head, he chuckled. "I'm not going to win this one. And I'm probably going to regret this, but that's why I love you."

Her stomach churned with anticipation. "So is that a yes?"

"That's a yes. But can we do it after we eat breakfast? I'm hungry, baby. I don't understand you sometimes. What makes you so spontaneous all the time?"

Her smile faded into melancholy. "Because I've seen people die. I can't say they were saints, but I don't know if they deserved to die either. Just 'cause somebody don't want you around doesn't give them the right to have you killed. We're all sinners. Who's to judge what we do? That's God's job. . . . I wonder if those people I saw die lived their lives to the fullest or if they wasted their lives trying to please others. If they had kids. Whether people care about you or not, everybody's got family. When you see a person take their last breath, there's no way that that can't change your life forever."

Mona said a silent prayer for Sarah.

He released her hand, held both sides of the steering wheel. "Are we talking natural causes here? Accidental? Homicide? Suicide?" he asked.

A tear fell from her left eye right before she turned her head to stare out the passenger window. She became quiet.

"Why won't you tell me what happens on your job? You can always get another job. A normal one like the rest of us. I can get you on at the farm where I work. I make a decent salary. It's physically demanding, but my mind is clear when I go home."

She had nothing against Davis packaging baby carrots all day. He made an honest living and he was a respectable man working for a company that shipped the vegetables to more than twenty-two countries around the world.

Mona had told him, "My background in forensic science and my job at the laboratory is classified. Top secret. All matters are confidential," to keep from doing what most women did. They shared too much and knew too little about the men in their lives.

People all over the United States lost their livelihood, their source of income because of what she did. Their positive test results weren't her fault. She didn't force anyone to take the drugs that showed up in their urine, hair, blood, sweat, or saliva.

She could tell Davis it was in the line of duty that she'd repeatedly come face-to-face with death. But it wasn't. Why had she asked to assist Steven? The less Davis knew about her not-so-distant past the better. He turned left on California Avenue, unknowingly drove past her place of employment, then took a right on Chester Avenue.

Deciding to change her dreary attitude, she cheered, "Turn right, right here, baby."

"Here?"

"Yes, now. Just do it."

"What the hell, woman. You win. But this is the only detour, because I told you, I'm starving."

A few blocks along Truxtun she said, "Pull over and park here."

"Here? You sure, here?"

Her lips curved high, causing her cheeks to rise. "Yes. Whenever I die, Davis, at least I can take this off my bucket list today."

Davis exhaled. Did as she'd requested.

Soon as he parked his truck, she got out

and waited for him. She held his hand and led him to the fountain in front of the Rabobank Arena. Clear running water streamed over a huge cluster of gray boulders. Five cement horse statues stood tall beside the rocks.

She removed her tennis shoes and socks. "Take yours off too."

He did as she'd asked, placing his shoes beside hers.

She removed her T-shirt, flung it to the ground. "Take yours off too."

"You do realize it's eleven . . . a.m.?"

"We're just going to skinny-dip, silly," she said, removing her jeans.

He looked west toward the superior courthouse and city hall. East was the convention center's hotel where they'd met. When he faced the fountain, she was completely nude standing atop the highest boulder.

"You are amazing," he said, removing his pants. Bypassing the blue sign that read, PLEASE STAY OUT OF THIS FOUNTAIN, he climbed the rocks, stood beside her, then asked, "Now what? We're done? Can you take this off your list? Can we get down before someone calls the police?"

Gingerly she gazed into his eyes, then whispered in his ear, "Make love to me, Davis. Right here. Right now."

STEVEN
CHAPTER 27

November 2010

For the first time his mom might be wrong.

After dragging a long stream of smoke into his throat, down to his lungs, he held his breath. Slowly he exhaled through his nostrils. He pinched the butt of the filtered cigarette, contemplating what to do next. White clouds escaped his mouth as he mumbled, "Took them long enough to get out of his raggedy truck and go into the café."

Should he storm into the café, snatch her by the arm, and wrap her hair around his fist or grab her legs, then drag her ass out. Nah, if he were going to do that, he would've done so fifteen minutes ago when Davis's windows were fogged up like the day he'd sexed Mona in the back of his SUV at Grist Park.

All Steven saw was Mona's footprints against the glass. He didn't want witnesses if he beat Davis's ass, then broke his neck for going down on his wife.

The nicotine calmed him as he took another drag. He crushed the tip of the cigarette into the ashtray. "Too many people with videophones and shit." He'd give her one last chance to do what was right.

An incoming call on his cell interrupted his intentions. "Hey, Katherine. What's up?"

"Hi, Steven. Is this a good time? I don't mean to bother you," she said. "But, well, this is out of character for me, but can you send the ten thousand dollars you promised me for helping you with the McKenny case? It's been six months, the holidays are coming up, and I could use the money for my son. I wouldn't ask if —"

Abruptly, he stopped her monologue. "You did catch me at a bad time. A very bad time," then ended the call. Until she told him how that case made national news, he wasn't giving her shit.

Whatever her desperation was, it was his money until he gave it to her. It was best to let Katherine find solutions to her financial situation. He had his own problems to worry about.

He entered the café, then slid onto the stool at the end of the counter farthest from them and watched Mona with Davis. She smiled, laughed, giggled like the little girl he remembered with plaits and barrettes. She tucked her hair behind her ear.

Mona's girlish mannerisms were the same as when he first saw her dangling from the monkey bars back in elementary school. She picked a strip of bacon from Davis's plate, sucked the pork instead of biting it.

A tall, heavyset woman wearing black denims and a black T-shirt almost blocked his view. "Hey, suga. My name is Sally. I'll be your waitress. What would you like to drink?"

Leaning to the left, not taking his eyes off Mona Lisa, Steven said, "I'll take a regular coffee, black."

"Sure thing, suga, anything else?"

"Yeah, a piece of paper and a pen."

Mona's back was to him. She was so into that bastard that she had no idea he was there. But she should've known, as promised, he'd resurface. Should've known it wasn't that easy to leave him for good. She should've gotten the hell up outta Bakersfield. How dare she sit in the booth where the black-and-white photo of Elvis hung on the wall between them. That was their table! That was his woman!

"You ain't nothin' but a hound dog," played in his head. The guy she was with was definitely more than a friend to Mona. A lot more. But not for much longer.

The waitress sat the pen, a blank sheet of paper from her receipt book, and the porcelain coffee cup on the counter in front of him. Still not taking his eyes off Mona, he sipped his coffee, then wrote, "If you don't want me to cause a scene up in here, meet me out back by the Dumpster in five minutes. If you're one second late, I'm coming back in to get your ass." He scribbled the time — 3:30 p.m.

"You know what you want to eat, suga?" Sally asked, holding her pen in one hand, pad in the other.

"I've lost my appetite. But you can do me a favor," he said, folding his note in half, then in half again.

"What's that, suga?"

Placing the paper in her hand, he said, "Give this to the lady over there with the honey-colored eyes," he said, pointing.

"Unless she's got eyes in the back of her head, how do you know that, handsome?"

Hmm. How did he know that? He'd gazed into her eyes many nights as they slept in the same bed. Even the nights they didn't have sex, he still held her in his arms. She was the first and only girl he loved. Why did she treat him so bad?

First Lincoln, now he had to deal with this dude, Davis. Once Steven found that truck and got the license plate number, it wasn't hard to find out who Davis Singletary was and where he lived.

Steven answered, "The one sitting beneath the king of rock and roll. That's the one. You'll see."

Whatever happened to William Lincoln — Mr. Starting Running Back with the tight ass, MVP, highly recruited nationwide by major Division I colleges — after he joined the military?

Today, Katherine would get the ten thousand he'd promised her. He was so pissed off with Mona that he'd directed his anger toward Katherine too. He'd wire her the funds, then find out what he needed to know.

One thing he knew, if Mona kept fucking up, Katherine wouldn't need to ask for another dime. He'd pay Katherine a lot more to help him frame Mona's ass. After all he'd done for Mona, she was bold enough to take off his ring.

"Whom should I say this note is from, suga?"

"She'll know." He handed Sally a ten-dollar bill for her trouble and the coffee, then walked outside.

If he hadn't moved to Bakersfield, if he hadn't made those phone calls to Daniel and Katherine, if he hadn't gotten caught up assassinating, if he hadn't confessed to Mona about the killings, if he hadn't made one bad decision after another, Mona would've never left him.

If he didn't have another assignment in this oil-pumping town, he'd leave and drag Mona with him, start all over. Steven was willing to work hard to mend his marriage. But would Mona give him the chance?

He paced beside the Dumpster waiting for Mona to arrive. The white pit bull caged inside a fence adjacent to the parking lot kept pace with him.

Steven rehearsed what he'd say to her when she got there. His voice echoed in his head. "Mona, let's go." That should be sufficient. Not really, knowing Mona. She was stubborn. Maybe he could ask her, "How long do you plan to continue this ridiculous affair?"

Scrolling through his list of favorites, he pressed the name at the top.

"Hey, Buttercup! I'm so glad you called. You still got that good job at the oil com—"

"Ma, I need for you to write a check for ten thousand dollars payable to Katherine

Clinton. Please don't ask me any questions. Just do it. I'll explain later. Katherine is going to stop by today and pick it up."

"Butter—"

"I love you, Ma. I'll call you tomorrow. Bye."

Steven ended the call, then phoned Katherine and told her to pick up the check from his parents' house. Actually having his mother write the check could prove helpful later.

Mona had done a lot of things to humiliate him, but this morning was the most despicable. Really. Fucking Davis in front of the Rabobank Arena. And as if that weren't enough, her footprints, still on his windshield, were wide enough for Davis to have been doing what Mona enjoyed most — having her pussy licked.

Steven didn't care that the sheriff's department was less than two hundred feet away. If he didn't love his freedom and Mona Lisa, he'd go back inside the café and shoot her in the head.

LINCOLN
CHAPTER 28

November 2010

Living with post-traumatic stress disorder was killing him slowly. He never got accustomed to living under bridges, on streets, or in parks, but he was trying to adjust to his new way of living. He refused to stand by the freeway with a sign that read "Homeless Vet Will Work for Food." His pride wouldn't allow that.

Dry skin covered his body, made him scratch like a crack addict. His hair matted into the neatest afro he could pat close to his head. Jeans, T-shirt, sweatshirt, smelly. He couldn't afford to wash his clothes. The folks at the mission occasionally gave him clean clothes and let him take a quick shower. But like with VA housing, the mission's beds were given to people with greater needs than his.

Today he had hope again that someone would hear his prayers. Lincoln sat waiting for his name to be called. He rocked back-and-forth in the cold, plastic armless orange chair. His fist rested in his palm, feet spread six inches apart. He leaned over his lap, his head aligned with the floor. He stared between his combat boots at the white square tile and kept rocking. His eyes shifted quickly, left right left right. From ear to ear, the enemy was always near.

Snap!

Lincoln hit the floor. "Don't nobody move!"

His fingers pointed at the patients in the waiting room. One turn after another, he rolled his body several times toward the door. A woman with a small baby in her arms moved to the opposite side of the room. He rolled back to his seat. Cautiously he balanced himself on his hands and knees, sprang to his feet, saluted the receptionist, then sat back in the cold orange chair.

He placed his fist in his palm, stared at the six-inch opening between his feet. He leaned forward. Left. Right. Left. Right. His eyes shifted.

The lady sitting next to him whispered, "I'm sorry. My eyeglass case always snaps loud like that when I close it. I won't do that again."

For a moment he was thankful. She seemingly understood his suffering. Perhaps because she was the wife or family member of a vet that also had PTSD.

"William Lincoln." Someone had called out his name.

He sprang to his feet, stood tall, saluted, then slapped his hands by his side. "Yes, sir!"

The nurse at the VA clinic in Seattle escorted him to the back. "I'm just going to check your blood pressure. I need to wrap the band around your biceps. You'll feel a little pressure, but this won't hurt a bit," she said.

Lincoln sat as the band tightened. More and more air filled the black pouch strapped to him. "That's enough!" he shouted. The prescribed medication he once resisted was now the main substance sustaining him. But he'd run out of pills yesterday.

He'd be the last to admit he was psychotic. Didn't want anyone to call him crazy. But when he didn't take his meds, his mental instability worsened. He deserved a decent paycheck from Uncle Sam.

He didn't have enough money to pay Katherine the back child support Katherine's mother had yelled about when he called their house six months ago, so he hadn't called back. Katherine and his son, the son he'd only heard about, were the main reasons he'd go back to Selma. He needed somebody to love and somebody to love him. But best to stay put in Seattle until he could provide for them.

"The doctor will see you now." The nurse escorted him to a small, cold office with a wooden desk and two plastic chairs, one on each side of the desk.

"Hey, William, how are you doing? Come on in and have a seat," the doctor said, not looking up from his laptop computer. "Thanksgiving is two days away. Got any plans?"

Lincoln sat in the chair, feet in his comfortable position, fist in palm. He scratched the back of his neck, twitched his head, then placed his fist back in his palm.

"I heard you had a mild anxiety attack out in the waiting area," the doctor said, still not looking at him. "I'll write you a prescription for a stronger antidepressant."

Bam! Lincoln pounded his fist on the desk.

"Look at me when you're talking to me! I deserve that much respect."

Calmly, the doctor looked him in his eyes. "William, I'm doing my best. I have almost a thousand patients to see. Look, don't you have someone who can financially sponsor a private doctor for you? Send you to a therapist?"

"Man, you asked me this the last time I was in here. And the answer is the same. I've given ten years of my life to the military to come back to this country for what? I can't provide for my fiancée or my son. I refuse to call my parents. They don't give a damn about me. And my grandparents are barely making it on their fixed income. Why should anyone other than my government take care of me?"

The doctor pressed his lips together, thought for a moment, then said, "Friends. You have any friends that could sponsor your medical needs through an HMO?" He handed Lincoln several prescriptions.

Friends? Lincoln thought for a moment. Maybe Mona would help him if she wasn't mad at him. He pressed a few buttons on his cell phone, accessed the Internet, located Mrs. Ellington's home phone number. It hadn't changed.

"Maybe I do have one person I consider a friend left," Lincoln said. "Let's see."

The phone rang. "Hello," a woman answered.

"Hi, may I speak with Mrs. Ellington."

"This is she. Who's speaking?" Her voice was firm.

"William Lincoln, ma'am. I was hoping I

could get Mona's cell number from you."

"I'm sure she'll take your call. When you talk to her, tell her her mother said hello," Mrs. Ellington sarcastically said, then recited Mona's number. "Lincoln, how are you doing?"

"Not good at all, ma'am. Joining the military was a bad decision for me. Well, thanks, and I'll give Mona your message," he said, ending the call.

The doctor was staring at his computer screen, clicking on keys. "Now, see, that wasn't so bad, was it? Glad I could help."

Lincoln stood, looked down at him, shook his head, then walked away. When he reached for the doorknob, the doctor said, "Wait, I think I overlooked something. Have a seat, William."

Think he overlooked something? Sitting on the edge of the chair, Lincoln spread his feet six inches apart, placed his fist in his palm.

Smack! The doctor clapped his hands. Lincoln remained calm.

"Hot damn, William! Your housing choice voucher is approved! You can pick it up Friday, day after tomorrow. You'll be in your new place well before Christmas. We did it, William! We did it!"

We? Right.

Lincoln sat listening to the doctor explain what to do next. His phone buzzed. It was a text message from Katherine.

Happy Thanksgiving Eve. I just wired you two thousand dollars. Hope this helps. Jeremiah and I love you.

MONA
CHAPTER 29

November 2010

Interrupting their laughter, Sally said, "Here you go, suga. This note here is for you," handing Mona a piece of paper.

Mona frowned, stared at the note, at Davis, at the waitress who wasn't theirs, then exhaled. "Who sent this?"

"Don't know his name, suga. Just doing what he asked."

Davis chimed in, "*His* name?"

"She doesn't have to read it, suga. It's not for you," Sally said, walking away.

Reaching for the note, Davis asked, "You want me to read it for you? Or is this 'top secret' too?"

Mona pulled the paper close to her breasts. "Davis, don't start." Her Southern drawl became gentle with compassion. "If my twenty-four hours ended right now, this day has been the best of my life in quite some time. The way you just teased my pussy with your tongue in your truck until I came in your mouth, still has me tremblin' inside."

He frowned, then smiled. Sat up straight, thrust his chest forward.

Men. Predictable.

She tucked her hair behind her ear. "I have no regrets for anything we've done over the past six months. I want to keep it that way. Forget the twenty-four hours to live thing. You deserve your own day for us to do whatever you want. At eleven o'clock in the morning, when my twenty-four hours are up, a tour bus is picking us up and we're picking up your family, and we're going to Disneyland."

Davis opened his mouth to speak. Mona shook her head. "No buts. That's final."

Mona unfolded the paper once. Her cell phone dinged twice like a butter knife against an empty crystal glass. "See, perfect timing. That's probably the bus driver confirming our trip."

Davis frowned but didn't speak.

She paused, picked up her cell phone. Smiled, giggled, then burst into a joyful laughter that permeated throughout the café as she silently read, Hey, princess. Hope you don't mind. Got your # from your mom. It's your knight in shining armor. I'm living in

Seattle now. Come see me. Wherever you are, get a ticket today and I'll reimburse you when you get here. Lincoln.

Princess? Was the text meant for her or Katherine? No, he'd said he called her mom for her number. And her mom gave it to him? That meant his message was definitely intended for her. If she left now, packed her suitcase, hit I-5, and drove north, she could be in Lincoln's arms by eleven o'clock tomorrow night.

The more she tried to contain her excitement, the more she felt joy expanding. Any moment she could burst, scream with anticipation. Maybe the note in her hand was from Lincoln too. Maybe he'd come to Bakersfield to sweep her off her feet the way he should've done graduation day. She'd prayed for him every day, but she'd stopped praying that one day they'd reunite. Maybe he really did love her more than he loved Katherine.

"You okay?" Davis asked.

Mona dug in her purse, pushed her gun aside, checked the side pocket. Her silver band and her genie troll with the pink hair were there. "Yeah." She beamed, kissed her doll, then shoved it back in the side pocket. "I'm real good. Give me a minute. I've gotta go pee," Mona said, clenching the note and her phone in the same hand as she stood. "Keep an eye on my purse."

She scurried to the back of the restaurant, entered the ladies' room, locked the door. "Ahh! Oh, my gosh! I can't believe it! William Lincoln texted me. Me!" she yelled, jumping high in the air. She settled herself, lined the toilet with two seat covers, pulled down her pants, sat, then opened the note.

A puff of air shot from her mouth. The momentum escaped her body as she read each word. Why was he determined to make her life miserable? He hadn't contacted her since the night she'd ignored his call at the hotel six months ago. His chasing Davis's truck like a fool that day in front of Tina Marie's Café didn't matter to her. She thought he'd moved on. She never should've married him, moved from Selma to Bakersfield with him. She should've filed for a divorce, but she still didn't know what he'd told the police. Mona never loved Steven the way he loved her. He was obsessed. Kinda like she was with Lincoln.

"Damnit, Steven!" She flushed the note down the toilet, marched to their table, told Davis, "Wait here, I'll be right back," then stormed outside.

Crunch. Crunch. The rubber soles of her tennis shoes — the same shoes she'd worn the day she'd left him — marched toward the Pepsi marquee with the words KNOTTY PINE CAFÉ. Cars zoomed by the two-way road. Houses with piles of stuff some would call junk were on the other side of the road. She did a one-eighty, hiked between rows of parked cars. The crunch beneath her feet echoed in her ears. There he stood, damn fool that he was, staring at her. A few feet from the restaurant's back door, Mona made her way to the Dumpster.

"What, Steven, what! What the hell do you want now?" she yelled.

"I want you to stop seeing him, that's what."

Mona looked around. Her gun was inside her purse. Her purse was with Davis. Probably best. In the heat of the moment she was positive she'd shoot Steven if she had her weapon.

She replied with the same demanding tone, "The hell I will. Even if it weren't him, it sure as hell will never be you again."

"If you're not coming back to me, I'm sending you back home to Selma and you're staying there! Your only other option . . . listen to me!" he yelled, grabbing her arm. He yanked her close to his chest, then whispered in her ear, "Your only other option is to room with Sarah McKenny."

Her first thought, knee him in the groin. Instead she pushed him away. Her fingers curled into fists, slammed atop each hip.

"I'm a grown-ass woman, Steven, and I have enough money to live any damn where I please and I don't need your permission! And I wish you would try to frame me."

An unknown man passing by said to Steven, "Let her go, man. Take it from me. You can't keep a woman that doesn't want to be kept. It's not always cheaper to keep her. If she's miserable, you're going to be miserable too," then got in his car and drove away.

"You heard the man," Mona said, raising her hands toward the sky.

Steven gripped her wrist. "Shut up and let's go." He pulled her toward him. "You've gone too far with this Davis guy. Get over him," he said, wrapping his lips around a cigarette.

Breaking his hold, Mona spat at his feet. "Even if I wasn't with Davis, I ain't never coming back to you."

Exhaling smoke in her face, he retorted, "I'm not asking you, Mona," then grabbed her biceps.

This time she slapped his face hard as she could to let him know she wasn't playing by his rules anymore. His cigarette fell to the ground. She jerked her arm away. Stepped back. "It's over between us. Over, you hear me. Accept it."

His broad shoulders squared back as he rubbed his jaw. His dark brown eyes narrowed. Six feet of once-upon-a-time, melt-in-her-mouth caramel stood before her. But the only man her appetite craved was Lincoln. The prayers she'd given up on had been answered.

Laughing, Steven lit another cigarette, then said, "Are you serious?" Swallowing his cynical laugh, inches from her face, he grunted. "It's not over until I say so. And I'm never going to say so. Understood? Go inside and get your purse from him. Or should I go get it for you?"

"Stay away from me, Steven. I'm not coming back to you. That's final."

His voice escalated with each word. "Don't tell me what's final! I say when things are final!" Then he whispered, "And don't forget what I do for a living. Don't make me choose which hat to wear for you." His lips locked around the filter. He inhaled long and hard, then blew smoke in her face again. He plucked the cigarette to the ground.

"I'm doing what's best for you," she said. "You really should thank me."

Steven wasn't her first, second, or third choice of man. He was most available and the best provider. Now that she had a second chance with the only man she'd ever loved, Steven didn't know he'd already lost this battle.

Steven leaned his head back, opened his mouth wide, then roared with laughter. His eyes narrowed, lips tightened. He stooped, stared at Mona. "Slut, you weren't thinking about what was best for me when you were fucking him. Earlier your ass was screwing him in public. Then you're so horny, you got your feet so high in the air pressed against his windshield, that neither of you noticed me. Guess you were too busy cuming, then putting your nasty-ass drawers back on," Steven lamented, shoving her. "I should kill him and you too!"

Stepping on the burning cigarette lying between them, she boldly told him, "And don't forget I'm better than you. I have evidence that could get you life without the pos-si-bi-li-ty of parole. That's right. I stashed away video footage that'll link you to every murder you've committed. Don't make me testify against you, Steven. I'm serious. Dead serious."

Steven lit another cigarette. "You've got exactly" — he glanced at his watch —

"seven hours. I'm not playing with you. Tonight. Midnight. The top of Thanksgiving Day. If you're not back in our house by midnight, Mona," he said, tossing the cigarette to the ground. "There you go. More evidence. Videotape that. I don't give a fuck what you claim to have!"

He smashed the burning tobacco into the gravel with the tip of his shoe, emptied the remaining cigarettes in the carton on her head. "Be grateful that I still love you. Because if I didn't —" He stopped mid-sentence, then slowly walked away.

"I hate you, Steven Cunningham! I hate you." She saw Davis headed her way, toting her purse. Mona shouted louder, "I love Davis! You hear me," she lied out loud again to piss Steven off more. "I love Davis!"

Mona stomped on the cigarettes repeatedly. Tobacco spilled between the gravel. Davis stood holding her purse.

Mona snatched her bag from Davis and said, "Let's go . . . I'm staying the night at your house."

By the time Davis would awaken, she'd be on a flight to Seattle.

STEVEN
CHAPTER 30

November 2010

Thanksgiving Eve and he didn't have a damn thing to be thankful for.

"Mona had better get her shit together or I'm going to get it together for her," he said aloud.

Talking to his mom on the phone and to himself at home had become the norm since Mona had left. His wife was his best and only friend. Mom was a few hours away from being wrong for the first time. He paced his living room floor, checked his gun. Made sure it was fully loaded.

"Nah, I got one better for her ass." Steven went to their bedroom, put his gun on the nightstand. He put on a pair of latex gloves, then opened Mona's bottom drawer.

Furiously, he scrambled through her clothes, shut the drawer, opened another, scrambled, slammed it shut. Slam. Shut. Slam. Shut. "Damn!" Her backup firearm wasn't there. Reverting to Plan A, he stuffed his gun into a yellow padded envelope. Put a bottle of whiskey in a brown paper bag, then stepped outside.

"Hey, Steven. When Mona coming back?" Velma asked.

"Tonight. I'm going to get her right now."

He put the envelope and alcohol on his passenger seat, then drove to Mona's house on the other side of town. He parked in front of her driveway and blocked her car. The lights were off, all of them. Opening his large pocketknife, he got out of his SUV, started to slash all the tires on the black-on-black 4Runner but changed his mind. He closed the knife, went to his SUV, grabbed a handful of flathead two-inch nails from his toolbox. He leaned several nails against each tire. The car he'd bought her five years ago was paid in full and in his name . . . not hers! But he didn't have the keys. She did.

All that they owned was purchased by him and in his name. Deed of Trust. Flat screens. Sofa, bed, pots, dishes. Cell phones. Mona's name was on the credit cards, but he paid the bills.

When Mona's mother insisted, "Steven, the only way you're going to take my daughter out of our house is if you can afford to provide for her. And by provide I mean be a

211

man and pay for all of her needs down to the drawers on her ass," he had no problem with that.

His problem was, Mona thought she was hot shit. If necessary, he could go home to his parents. What the fuck was she gon' do? That's probably why she hadn't left Bakersfield.

Now she threatened to use whatever she had to bring him down. That wasn't happening. Mona wouldn't have shit if it weren't for him! No more being nice to her ass.

"I'm done letting my wife make a fool outta me!" he shouted with his back to her front door. "What the hell you lookin' at, dude? That's right, I said it."

Steven got in his SUV. *Slam!* His door rattled.

He drove along East Brundage Lane, passed the Assembly Hall of Jehovah's Witnesses. Maybe that's what he needed to do, pray, go to church, something. His woman was probably at *his* house riding or sucking *his* dick. Steven knew where Davis lived. On the other side of town, off of Airport Boulevard in a single-family homes subdivision. Two miles from the café. In a few, he'd be there.

Cruising along Brundage, he turned right

on Chester Avenue, then right on Truxtun. The detour wasn't in his plan, but he found himself there. Steven stopped in front of the Rabobank Arena. A snapshot flashed before his eyes of Mona and Davis having sex in broad daylight only hours ago. Now he imagined they were at Davis's house having sex for at least the third time today.

Fuck! He punched the steering wheel.

No matter how many orgasms Davis gave Mona, they weren't making love. Steven saw in Mona's mannerisms when she was sexing Davis in public that she wasn't in love with him. She was fucking that guy like it was her last orgasm. And it might be close to her last if she kept fucking up.

What man wouldn't lose his mind knowing another man was sexing his woman?

He made an illegal U-turn, arrived at Mona's house for the second time. All of the lights were off. It was eight o'clock, too dark to see if the nails were still leaning against her tires. He used his flashlight to confirm what he suspected. The nails were still there.

"Damnit, Mona!" he grunted. He cracked his knuckles. Stretched his neck until he heard *Pop!*

He really was losing it. How was she supposed to get to his house if she got four flat tires backing out of her driveway? Steven removed all the nails, parked down the street from her house, sat in his car, and waited.

"There's a proper way to end a marriage, bitch. You don't just walk out on the man who loves you, provides for you. You don't do that shit, Mona, and open your legs for another man." Tears burned his eyes as he cried, "You leave me no choice."

Maybe it was his fault she'd left him. Seeing Mona with Davis reminded him how happy they used to be. He should've cared more about her happiness than the half million he was paid per hit. Forget that. "This shit was her fault. All her fault."

In his line of work, his word was bond. The easy money came in bundles of ten to thirty grand. It was never his intent to kill, but he had to. Not much different from crooked cops nowadays, except the law wasn't on his side to protect him. No administrative leave if he got caught.

In situations where he thought it was okay to have Mona with him, she'd witnessed him take life. Again. And again. In Macon and Kansas City, she'd helped him cover up evidence that could send him to prison. Their marriage, once priceless, wasn't worth a damn.

"Her ass has that same evidence. After all

I've done for her!" he yelled, punching the vinyl dashboard. "Ow!" He spread, then curled his fingers thinking, "She probably has it hidden at the lab under some alias." His wife could probably make one call and he'd be arrested.

Never should've taken her out of her mother's house into his. Her mother, he thought, then shook his head as he calculated a clever plan that would nicely involve Mrs. Ellington. Mona's mom started all of this. "Provide for her daughter's every need shit." If she hadn't spoiled her daughter, maybe Mona wouldn't be so damn self-centered.

Eight o'clock, no Mona. Nine o'clock, she wasn't there. Ten o'clock, same. He was used to sitting in his car for much longer hours surveilling their homes. He knew Mona wouldn't go straight to his house without coming to hers first, but he'd waited long enough.

Starting his engine, he drove to the other side of town, near the Bakersfield Arch, stopped at Buck Owens Crystal Palace. Four beers later he made his way down a dark road to a nearby strip club. Handing the cashier thirty dollars, he said, "Cover plus twenty singles."

Soon as he sat in one of about seventy

empty, plush red velvet chairs, a woman dressed in a tight black and white striped shirt with her cleavage bulging and her ass barely covered in a black pleated skirt asked, "Would you like something to drink?"

"I'm good," he said, feeling the buzz from the brews he had earlier. Besides, he knew all she had to offer was soda, with or without ice.

None of the all-nude strip clubs in town served alcohol. Didn't make any sense to be sober with pussies shining in your face. But it didn't matter. He wouldn't be there long enough to see the first girl slide her Brazilian-waxed pussy down the pole.

He sat passing time contemplating another plan just in case Plan A didn't work out to his satisfaction.

MONA
CHAPTER 31

November 2010

"Why do you love me so much?" she asked, not feeling worthy of his affection.

For a moment, Mona missed her mother. Now that she was older, she understood that her mother had done great things, had good intentions. Instilling confidence, self-respect, and self-worthiness in her was something Mona couldn't put a price tag on.

"Forget about how Steven acted a fool earlier," she thought while relaxing on Davis's couch. Steven should be grateful she'd given him over five consecutive years of her life. Perhaps the best years, but she was in her prime and fertile enough to have a baby by Lincoln. Was that a smart way to show she loved him? Not really.

She smiled at Davis, thankful he couldn't read her mind. Davis was so enamored with her he overlooked her lies, or outright missed her sudden interest in another man.

The six months she'd dated Davis, he'd showered her with flowers and gifts every week. He loved surprising her and she enjoyed letting him. She smiled at Davis. He probably had a Thanksgiving present that he'd give her tomorrow, that was if she was around to get it.

Three artificial orchids, pink, brown, with a hint of white, dangled from his mantel above the wood-burning fireplace. He said he'd put them there because those orchids reminded him of her pussy. Framed in silver, their picture was neatly placed beside the plant.

She sat at the opposite end of the sofa. His foot was nestled between her thighs, cradled in her crotch. She pressed the tip of her clit deep into the arch of his foot.

He wiggled his toes, then said, "You've been awfully quiet since that incident with Steven."

Mona knew she shouldn't have told Davis Steven's name. She hadn't done so until today. Davis and Steven seeing one another was not her decision. But she had decided there was no way she was going to Steven's house tonight. And her relationship with Davis had to end tomorrow.

"You wanna talk about —" He paused,

then said, "You let me know if you want to discuss him or what was in that note, wherever that is."

She shook her head. She was pissed that Steven's shenanigans overshadowed her excitement about Lincoln's text. Maybe relocating to Seattle was perfect timing. She'd reply to Lincoln in the morning when Davis dropped her off at her house.

"You're special. You're good to me. No, make that great. I love the way you spoil me. How you massaged my feet the first day we met, wow. And you pamper me all the time. Your spirit is wholesome, so pure. Like the essence of an angel."

Mona hadn't given Davis any special treatment; she was just being herself. But since most women didn't do the extras, she understood how he felt.

"I can't say no to you, Mona. Your smile makes me smile. Your dreams encourage me to dream. Your zest for life energizes me. Your Southern drawl, your hospitality, and those delicious dishes you cook make me happy, especially that filé gumbo. Not to mention how you do those naughty things to me that no woman has ever done." He paused, then continued, "You're the only woman I've dated whom I can't find one thing about that I don't like. Not a one.

Does that answer why I love you?"

"I know you do, Davis," Mona said before squeezing his big toe.

"Mmmm. See. That's what I'm talking about. After six months, you still do that. Your touch feels so good, honey. I was going to wait until tomorrow for Thanksgiving dinner at my parents', but I can't."

Davis hurried to his bedroom, retuned to the living room, knelt beside the sofa. Holding her hand, he frantically opened the black box, then gazed into her eyes. "Mona, marry me?"

Was his proposal rhetorical? She wanted the Denzel Washington proposal in *American Gangster.* Life was all about the fairy tale. Death was always looming in the background. For all she knew, Steven could've killed another person since she last saw him. It'd be better if someone, anyone, killed Steven. Then she wouldn't say "Yes" to Davis's proposal, but she would say "Yes" if it were Lincoln asking again.

Mona stood, placed the ring inside the box, then snapped it shut. She interlocked her fingers with his, then led him to his bedroom. She placed the box on his dresser as she stared into his eyes.

Davis eased the spaghetti straps of her silk nightgown over her shoulders. The pink baby-doll gently fell to the floor and draped around her ankles.

"I wanted to surprise you. Ask in front of my family tomorrow. But I love you so much, Mona, I can't wait, I . . ." he said, turning to reach for the box. "I'll make the announcement to my family at dinner while I'm saying what I'm thankful for."

Mona pulled him toward her, kissed the rest of his words into her drooling mouth. She scooted onto his flannel sheet, then spread her thighs. "Show me how much you love me." She waited for Davis to join her. He removed his pajama pants, then lay his naked body atop hers.

Sadly he said, "You didn't answer me, Mona. I want you to be my wife." His eyes fixated on hers. The wide head of his manhood lightly touched the spot where the arch of his foot was moments ago, then slid into the opening of her vagina.

Mona held Davis close, put her chin on his shoulder, trembled as she climaxed all over his dick. Her ankles instantly locked around his waist. Staring at the ceiling, she said, "Let's not talk about marriage right now. Take me slowly. I need to feel every inch of you inside of me" *for the last time.*

Marriage for Mona wasn't an option. Not that she wouldn't have divorced Steven to marry Davis, that was, if Lincoln hadn't resurfaced. But even if Lincoln had never texted her, she still wasn't in love with Davis.

STEVEN
CHAPTER 32

November 2010

Dressed in all black, Steven sat in his recliner missing his family, who were miles away in Selma. Family holidays were sentimental for him. Every Thanksgiving he sat at the table with the ones or the one he loved. For the first time in his life, this year was different. He knew he'd have to drag Mona by her hair, tie her to their dining room chair, and force-feed her if she were going to dine with him tomorrow. Perhaps he should move back to Selma.

Maybe hearing his mother's voice would erase the thoughts of what he'd planned to do in a half hour. He checked the time on his cell phone — eleven-thirty p.m. in Bakersfield, one-thirty a.m. in Alabama. "What the hell," he said, deciding to phone home.

On the third ring, his mom sleepily answered, "Buttercup, you okay?"

"Yeah, Ma. I'm good. Just needed to hear your voice."

"You haven't been laid off because of that oil spill over in the Gulf, have you? I heard y'all got a new governor. Thank the Lord that rich lady didn't win. Buttercup, did you know that Meg lady spent over one hundred and seventy-eight million dollars and a hundred and forty-four million was of her own money and she still lost that race. People with all that money shouldn't have all that power to control people's lives, especially if they ain't living right. You sure you doing good, Buttercup? You don't sound like yourself."

He laughed out loud. Only his mom was allowed to call him by the nickname she'd given him. He'd fallen in love with both peanut butter cups and Mona Lisa before his tenth birthday.

"Yeah, Ma. I still got my job at the oil company," he lied. He'd have to lie about having his job or explain how he earned his money. If his mom knew he'd killed several people she wouldn't kill him, but the shock would cause her to nearly beat him to death.

"How's Mona? It's been six months. That's why you calling me. To tell me she's home."

He wished. "Nah, Ma. She ain't back."

"I saw her mother the other day at the grocery store. We were both getting the trimmings for our turkeys. She said that William Lincoln boy was discharged from the Marines two years ago. Told me he had PTS or PST, you know that disorder when you ain't quite right in the head. Said she wished she'd known that before she gave him Mona Lisa's number. Anyways, you tell Mona hi for me when you see her. I love you, Buttercup."

That bitch. Now he hated Mona even more. His flesh crawled like he was burning in hell. Sweat drenched his face, soaked his shirt. He didn't care.

"I love you too, Ma," he said, ending the call. Steven picked up the bottle beside his recliner, guzzled the remaining whiskey, then hurled the bottle at Mona's picture hanging on the wall.

The bottle and the frame shattered into small pieces. His heart weighed heavy like a flock of birds in the Gulf drenched in petroleum. "That bitch ain't slick. Davis is her decoy. The whole time she's been claiming to be unhappy with me, she's been plotting to leave me for Lincoln." Mona had made his decision easy.

Polishing his gun, he stared at her dented picture. Mona Lisa was still the most beautiful woman he'd ever held. She was a Southern belle with hypnotic charm. Her flesh was smoother than butter.

He rewound in his mind to the first time he'd had sex with her. It was his first unforgettable blow job. The second he released himself inside of Mona's mouth, and she swallowed every seed, he'd instantly fallen in love with her. No girl had done that.

"Now what do I have!" he shouted, then slammed her picture to the floor. "A wife that sucks every man's dick except mine. I hate you!"

He sat in his chair, checked the bullets in his gun. Never could be too sure. Worst thing he'd imagined was shooting to kill but getting shot because of a missing bullet. He screwed on the silencer. Opening a fresh bottle of bourbon, he gulped half of the contents, then placed the bottle on his coffee table. He'd save the other half for a nightcap with Mona. Whether he had to pour the whiskey down her throat or douse her dead body with it, either way her ass had a toast coming.

Mona's eight hours were up. He knew exactly where to find her. He stepped outside. What he was about to do might silence the gossip about the Harper family tragedy in Bakersfield. Whoever killed that wife, her mom, and children was a heartless murderer.

Maybe if he were heartless, he could forget Mona.

Steven concealed his gun in a fresh bubble envelope. He had a heart and a loving mother. And although he didn't have any kids, there was no way he could kill a defenseless living being. Five people lost their lives that day in Bakersfield. He'd watch the entire episode on *Dateline NBC: The Mystery of the Lost Weekend*.

"Fucking coward." The person who did that shit was a punk. The jury on the case wasn't much better. Whether the dude did it or not, how the hell do you convict anybody based on association of evidence but have no proof? Perhaps the same way he'd done with Sarah. Sarah not being able to prove where the money came from didn't make her guilty of murdering Calvin. But the police were so eager to pin the case on someone to make themselves look good, it didn't matter. Lots of innocent people went to jail because law enforcers were gunning to outdo one another.

Mona claimed she could prove him guilty. Tonight he'd give her another opportunity.

"That's it! Her ass was going to have me

locked up so she could leave Davis and be with Lincoln and I'd be behind bars out of her way. Hell, no, bitch!" He was meant to call Katherine and his mother.

He stepped onto his porch, locked his door, then trotted across his lawn toward his SUV.

"Hey, Steven. Happy Thanksgiving," Ms. Velma called out from her front yard.

No one in this town knew what he really did for a living except Mona. In a few minutes, no one alive would know his truth.

He smiled. Waved. "Happy Thanksgiving Eve to you, Ms. Velma."

Mona had five minutes to make the right decision.

Ms. Velma was always happy. Anyone who needed food, clothing, or shelter could depend on her. If she had it to give, they didn't have to ask twice.

Well, Steven had something else to give, so he got in his truck, put the yellow envelope on the passenger seat, and headed to Davis's house.

Mona
Chapter 33

November 2010
Midnight.

Hot water showered their naked bodies. Mona lathered the cotton washcloth. In small circular motions she gently washed Davis's shoulders, kissed the center of his spine, then massaged his back.

His palms flattened against the tiles. "The hot water and your hands feels so good, baby," he moaned, hanging his head forward. "Be honest. Do you love me, Mona?"

Thankful his back was to her, she kissed his spine again. It was more of a good-bye kiss for her. Davis was her transition man. He was there to help her escape from Steven. He was fun. He was great in bed. Davis was a good man. And if it weren't unladylike, she'd compliment him for a job well done. The alternative for her was to crush his heart or settle for being in bed with another man she wasn't in love with.

"Stay right here," she said. "Close your eyes. I have a big surprise for you."

He turned, looked down at her. "What now?"

"You know you love my surprises. Just do it, baby. I still have eleven hours. Remember, you started this twenty-four hours thing, not me."

Melancholy dilated his pupils. His irises were hazed with desperation. "Put my ring on. That's what I want more than anything right now," he said, then closed his eyes.

She faced Davis toward the white ceramic tiles. "And no peeking."

As she got out of the shower, the memory of Steven's voice momentarily influenced her mood, shifting her thoughts. She wondered if she should tell Davis to take her home. She'd feel better if Steven had completed what came across as a threat earlier. "If you're not back in our house by midnight, Mona." Then what? Forget Steven. He was not going to make her miserable in her own mind.

Hesitant, she slipped on her engagement ring, happily picked up her cell phone, then skipped to the kitchen to contact Lincoln.

STEVEN
CHAPTER 34

November 2010

Airport Road was almost a straight drive from his house to Davis's home. His speedometer registered twenty-five mph. He stopped at the 7-Eleven, bought a beer to chase his whiskey. Continuing to his destination, a few blocks down he passed the gas station. He was now closer to the airport.

To his left was open field; to his right were single-family dwellings. He drove another mile, then turned right into a fairly new subdivision. The neighborhood was quiet. He parked his truck on the opposite side of the street, about fifty feet from Davis's front door.

He surveyed Davis's house. A room, once dark, suddenly became illuminated. The silhouette dancing on the curtains matched the one he'd seen countless times at Mona's house when he'd spied on her. Her shadow swayed.

He tiptoed across the street and through the alleyway alongside Davis's property. The front room lights were off. Steven ducked, crept below Davis's kitchen window, and headed toward the backyard. A light in a back room was on. Steam covered a small rectangular sliding window.

"Hurry up, Mona! The water is getting cold!" a man shouted, giving Steven his exact whereabouts.

Steven tugged on the ceiling-to-floor sliding glass door. The door was locked. No problem for an expert like him. He dug into his pocket, retrieved a flat metal hook, jimmied the lock, lifted the latch, then slid the door open. Once he was inside Davis's house, Steven didn't care if Davis or Mona saw him. He held his gun at his side, tiptoed into the bedroom, then scanned his surroundings.

Quietly he entered the bathroom. A tall male's shadow was inside the shower. Hands above his head, he leaned against the wall. *That's interesting.* Steven removed the white bath towel from the rack.

"It took you long enough," he said. "Hurry up before I open my eyes."

Whoever said "Timing is everything" was right. Unbeknownst to Davis, he'd never open his eyes again.

Steven opened the shower door. In one sweeping motion, he placed the towel over the back of Davis's head, slammed his face against the tiles, held it there, then pulled the trigger.

Davis's body slumped into Steven's arms. Careful not to fire his gun again, he pointed the barrel away from his body. He dragged the body into the living room, lay Davis across the large area rug, sat on the sofa, sat his gun underneath the coffee table beside his foot. Mona's voice resonated from the kitchen happily singing, "Hey boy, I really wanna see if you can go downtown with a girl like me. . . ." Her singing faded into humming.

Steven removed a cigarette from his shirt pocket. It was too wet to light. He sat there wishing he had the bottle of whiskey in his car to wash down his beer.

How fucking long is her ass going to be in the kitchen? He'd give her a few more minutes. If she didn't come out, he was going in to get her.

MONA
CHAPTER 35

November 2010

Although she was craving to hear his voice, this wasn't the best time to call Lincoln, so she replied to his last text message of When are you coming? with I'll book my flight in the morning. OMG, I will be in your arms by eleven a.m.

After retrieving an icy cold bottle of champagne from Davis's refrigerator, Mona got two glasses from his cabinet. This was cause for a celebration of new beginnings. Surely Davis would understand. She'd do her best to let him down easy.

Death and the end of relationships should be celebrated. That way there wouldn't be so many depressed people mourning over the inevitable. Death was the only thing that was unavoidable and final.

The ending of their good relations would be a joyous occasion to acknowledge their fond memories. It was best to disappoint him now.

She spread her fingers. "This sure is the most spectacular ring I've received." Four, maybe five carats. "Must've cost him six months' salary. I think I'll keep it to show my appreciation." She smiled. "He did give it to me."

After slowly peeling the foil from the champagne bottle, she untwisted the metal cap. She wrapped her hand around the cork, cautiously maneuvering it back and forth. The cork began to rise with each motion. The anticipation of the loud noise excited her. She swayed side to side. "Here we go. One, two . . . get ready, Mona Lisa . . . three."

Pop! The cork ejected, but the sound she'd heard wasn't that of a cork popping. Or was it? Her mouth caught the overflowing bubbles. Mona swallowed, frowned, then leaned her ear toward the kitchen door. Was that the sound of the shower door slamming?

"You'd better not be getting out!" she shouted.

The constant shushing of the water probably drowned out her demand. She doubted that Davis had heard her. Mona searched the kitchen, found honey. She reached into the refrigerator, got the whipped cream, set the items on a silver platter. She pressed an empty glass against the lever outside the refrigerator door until crushed ice was filled to the rim.

A mouthful of ice while sucking his dick and massaging his shaft with honey and whipped cream would drive Davis insane. She'd make sure to use the whole can and swallow every sticky drop.

She powered off her cell phone, placed it on the tray. Didn't want Davis to accidentally discover her messages from Lincoln.

She filled both flutes halfway. Maybe she'd give him a bubbly blow job. "Here I come," she called out. "You'd better still be in —"

The tray slipped from her hands. Bubbles poured from the green bottle creating what resembled bubbling red candy apple mix. "What in God's name have you done? Jesus, Steven . . . Noooo!"

Calmly he said, "You're going to wake up his neighbors. I know you don't want that."

He flipped his forearm upward, glanced at his wrist. The watch she'd bought him for their first anniversary was covered in blood. He wiped the face, looked at her. "It's past midnight."

Mona heaved until her insides were out. Davis's lifeless body was faceup on the living room area rug. Vomit spilled into her hands, seeped between her fingers, then splattered onto the floor.

"Why did you have to kill him?" she asked, staring at her cell phone drowning in blood and vomit.

"I don't think he's dead . . . yet. And you didn't see me shoot him, nor do you see me with a weapon. But as I recall, there *was* a gun in your purse with your fingerprints on it." He picked up his gun, pointed it at her.

"You low-down son of a bitch. Shoot me. I don't care." She stared at the barrel, wishing it were her lying on the floor. Mona's head drooped; she looked at Davis's chest. There didn't appear to be any up or down movements. Did Mona care enough to check for a pulse? What if Steven was going to shoot her too? "Steven, please. Please don't. You bastard! This is why I hate you so much!"

"Can you keep it down?" he said, placing the gun on the coffee table.

He shoved it toward her. Her gun wasn't the murder weapon, his was. She thought about trying to beat him to his weapon, but it was closer to him. He knew she didn't have the courage to shoot him.

Steven grunted with anger. "I warned you! Make up your mind, Mona. A few hours ago you were shouting to all of Bakersfield,

'Davis, please fuck me harder,' now you're telling me, 'Steven, please. Please don't.' What, Mona? What's wrong with you? I'll tell you what your problem is. You're too eager to open your damn mouth and legs at the same time without engaging your fucking brain. You screw every man in this town except your husband? What kind of wife are you?"

That wasn't true. Mona was a wholesome kind of woman with morals and values before she married him. Sure she was a wild child, but her adventures were fun. Her problem was she loved new experiences and she made decisions too fast. Her heart, not her head, opened her legs for Davis just as it had for Steven.

Davis was the only man she'd sexed since leaving Steven. Mona prayed she could catch the first flight to Seattle. Hopefully she could convince Lincoln to be her alibi and that her one-way ticket was okay with him, because there was no way she was going back to Steven or staying in Bakersfield.

"You selfish bitch. You just gon' stand there and let your so-called man die without . . . Aw, hell, no! Is that an engagement ring where my wedding ring should be?"

Mona didn't respond. She headed to the bedroom for her clothes.

Steven rushed toward her, forced her from the hallway to the living room, then flung her to the carpet. "Sit your ass down and don't move. And take that damn ring off. You are my wife!"

"You don't love me, Steven. Admit it. You're scared that I'm going to turn you in. If I were, I would've done so months ago. What woman in her right mind would've done for you the things that I've done? What sane woman would want you?"

A thousand capillaries zigzagged, turning his jaundice-colored eyes beet red. "Bitch, take that damn ring off!"

This was not the time to argue. She had to get out of the house. Sitting in a puddle of blood, Mona remained calm. She removed the ring, sat it on the rug. The ring was one more piece of evidence that could link her to Davis's murder.

"You know what, Mona . . . go. Just leave. Go and get yourself together. We'll work things out later. I'll clean up this mess I've created."

Killing had become second nature to Steven. That was the reason she'd left him. He could take life as though there were no God. Mona didn't want to see death anymore. Not this way.

For years, Mona had lived under Steven's

roof determined to keep him happy. Leaving her mother and father in Selma, she regretted she'd become estranged with her family. Sitting next to a dead body, she realized she hadn't chosen Steven. He'd chosen her. If she'd known Steven was going to kill Calvin McKenny that night, she never would've asked to accompany him.

Keeping her eyes on Steven, Mona stood. Davis's blood streamed down her ass and legs and dripped from her fingers. How was she going to get to her house? The airport was closer. If Davis weren't dead, Steven would definitely finish the job.

Mona went into Davis's bedroom, saw the sliding glass door open. She closed it. At this point evidence didn't matter. There were many of her prints throughout his house.

Mona filled the tub with hot water, added lots of milk and honey bubble bath. "Who am I fooling?" she thought, scrubbing her body in the oversized tub. Mona cried uncontrollably. *If I don't go back to Steven, I'm going to end up in prison.*

"Mona, I'm leaving," Steven said, standing in the doorway. "But I'll be back to get you and you can help me clean up that mess. Everything will be all right," he said, closing the door.

240

He spoke as if the carpet were stained with merlot. "Son of a bitch, bastard, mother-fucker, I wish you were the one dead," she whispered.

She was not helping him clean up. This time instead of covering up for Steven, Mona would have to worry about protecting her own ass.

The bathroom door opened again. He stuck his head in, then said, "Don't think about leaving me. I'll kill the next one too if I have to."

STEVEN
CHAPTER 36

November 2010

The bloody mess wasn't what he anticipated having to clean up. His adult life wasn't what he'd envisioned at all. Perhaps the problem was he had no vision for his future. He was simply existing as opposed to living. So deep into the mayhem, he couldn't quit killing unless they fired him. The job he'd just done was out of jealousy, rage, and of his own free will. No check was on the way.

Steven sat in the living room waiting for Mona to finish bathing. Davis's body was lifeless. Should he leave the body where it was and burn down the house? No. Arson created more evidence than it destroyed, especially if what he intended to go up in flames survived the fire. Should he wrap the body in the rug, then dump it deep in the grass field across the street? He had a better idea.

Mona would definitely be questioned

about the murder. She might have to serve time, but that was okay. He'd divorce her, put money on her books. She should take the wrap for him. That was the least she could do for cheating on him. Better for him to get another wife than for him to become somebody's bitch behind bars.

Steven relaxed, believing he wouldn't be linked unless Mona exposed him. Obviously Davis thought Mona was a single woman. He hoped Mona hadn't told Davis, his friends, or his family that she had a husband. One less connection to him. But he couldn't believe that his wife accepted another man's engagement ring.

What was she thinking?

Mona entered the living room. Her wet and stringy hair clung to her neck, soaking her T-shirt. "My decision is the same. I'm not going to your house, Steven," she boldly said, holding a half-full garbage bag in one hand, her purse in the other.

"What's that? All the shit you had over here?"

Picking up her blood-drenched cell phone and the engagement ring, she placed them in a large Ziploc plastic bag, then put the bag in her purse. "What difference does that make? All you need to know I just told you. But in case your comprehension is still all fucked up, I'll say it again. I'm not going to your house, Steven. Good-bye."

He picked up his gun, stood, snatched her biceps, then pushed her onto the front porch. He locked the front door from the inside, then closed it. Steven opened the passenger door of his SUV.

"Get in," he said, shoving Mona onto the seat. He threw her bag and purse on the floor, slammed her door, got in the car. He put his gun in a black plastic bag, placed the bag in the compartment on the driver's side, then drove off.

Cruising along Airport, he stared at Mona. "What's your damn problem?"

Silence surrounded them. He focused on the road until he got to his house. "Get out," he demanded, picking up his black bag.

"There is no pleasing you, Steven!" she yelled. "That's why I left you. Now take me to my house before I call the police and tell them everything!"

Slap! His backhand landed across Mona's cheek. She'd screamed loud enough for the neighbors to hear, and he smacked her hard enough to shut her ass up. Her face slammed into the leather headrest. That was the first time she'd made him hit her.

"Now say something else." He stared at

her. "Get the fuck out!"

Mona held her face, got her bag and purse.

If he had to kill Mona, so be it. He was tired of her ass too.

She got out of his SUV. He followed so close behind her, if she stopped, he'd step on her heel. She looked over at Ms. Velma's house. The living room light came on. Quickly he pushed Mona in their house, then locked the door.

He shoved his keys into his pocket, put the black plastic bag on the coffee table, pushed her into the recliner. The bottle of whiskey fell over. "Nah, I don't trust you." He snatched her from the seat, pulled her with him into the garage, got a roll of duct tape. He dragged both Mona and a dining room chair into the center of the living room, then shoved her in the seat. "Hold out your wrists."

"You don't have to do this. Steven, please. I'm not going to leave."

"I'm not going to ask you to stay and I'm not going to ask you again. We've done things your way for the last six months. Your time is up. Now we can do this my way or we can do this my way . . . got it?"

Extending her arms, Mona Lisa cried.

"Something's wrong with you. Shut up,"

he said, wrapping the duct tape around her wrists three times. Then he did the same to her ankles and ended with one wide strip around her body.

He frowned. Taping her up was too easy. Mona didn't say a word. She didn't fight back. Her smart ass was plotting something brilliant, no doubt. He'd have to hurry back.

"Don't leave me like this!" she yelled to his back. "Take me with you. You know you need my help."

Nah, taking her with him was what she wanted. Mona brought this shit on herself. Steven slapped a strip of tape over Mona's mouth, slammed his front door, got back in his truck.

"Hey, Steven!" Ms. Velma shouted from her porch. "I thought I heard you come in. You going back out already? Everything okay?"

The sun would rise soon. He had to finish the job. "Hi, Ms. Velma," he said, concealing his disgust with Mona.

"You can have Thanksgiving dinner at my house tonight. Steven, you left . . ." Her words trailed off.

Steven didn't have time to listen to Ms. Velma. He had to bury Davis's body in a place where no one would find the remains unless he wanted them to. With countless boarded-up abandoned buildings on Mona's side of town, a vacant house on Dr. Martin Luther King Jr. Boulevard might be the perfect hiding place for Davis's body.

Getting Mona Lisa to do as he said, that was his greatest challenge.

MONA
CHAPTER 37

November 2010
Lord, please get me out of here before this man kills me.

Soon as Mona heard Steven's SUV pull out of the driveway, she rocked back and forth in the chair. Each time she leaned forward, she pushed harder. "Aw, shit," she said, almost tilting over on her face. Quickly she leaned back, steadied herself, then started over.

Balancing on her two feet that were taped at the ankles, Mona hopped toward the door as though she were on a pogo stick. Three hops and she noticed Steven had left the black bag on the coffee table. If he needed what was in that bag, he'd be back real soon. That meant she had to hurry.

She jumped twelve inches at a time. If she could make it to the porch, she prayed Mama V would be standing on hers.

Mona heard footsteps coming up their

front stairs. Her heart pounded, praying Steven wouldn't catch her trying to escape. God only knew what he'd do. She glanced around, started hopping backward fast as she could trying not to fall over. Trying to get back to the indentions in the carpet where her chair was.

A familiar voice said, "I'd better close Steven's door for him."

Frantically, Mona rocked until she was on her feet. Hopped three times. She wanted to scream, "Wait! Help! Mama V!" but she couldn't.

As the door was closing, Mona hurled her body and the chair onto the coffee table. Risking hurting herself was her only hope of being rescued.

The door slowly opened. Mama V peeped inside. "Chile, what is going on in here?" She hurried to Mona, tugged at the tape on Mona's mouth. "Wait here," she said. "This doesn't make any sense." After sitting Mona up, Mama V headed out the door.

Mona screamed, "Don't leave me!" But she couldn't separate her lips. Her words were muffled desperation drowning in her throat. Mama V was already out the door.

"Mama V, please don't call the police." Tears streamed down Mona's face. If the police showed up, she and Steven were going to jail. Deservingly so. But was it really her fault she'd married a murderer?

Mona's biggest fear was Steven returning before she got out of his hellhole. Nothing in the house had changed over the last six months, except her photo on the wall was mutilated.

Mama V rushed in carrying a bottle of cooking oil and scissors. She doused Mona's mouth with oil. She massaged the oil under the edges, then cut the thick gray tape binding Mona's ankles, wrists, and body. She saturated the tape stuck to Mona's mouth with more oil. Mona worked one side of the tape, loosening the edges. Mama V gradually lifted the other side.

The adhesive lifting from her delicate skin was painful. She didn't care. All Mona wanted to do was get out.

Finally, her mouth was free. Mama V reached for her wrists.

"I've gotta go. Thank you so much, Mama V. I love you."

"Mama V has done a lot of things to help people, chile. But I ain't never seen no foolishness like this. A man tying up his wife. Steven needs his ass whupped, but I know how to deal with his kind. Wait until —"

Mona frantically shook her head. "Don't

get involved. Can you please give me a ride to my house?" Mona picked up her purse. That was all she needed. She stopped, picked up the black bag. She smiled. She had another piece of evidence he needed more than her.

"Give me a minute," Mona said, rushing into the garage. She grabbed a black plastic bag, shoved the stapler gun inside, placed the bag on the coffee table, then rushed out of the house.

KATHERINE
CHAPTER 38

November 2010

Katherine sat in her mother's living room. She felt good watching Jeremiah suited up in his football uniform. He was so handsome. But if her son earned one scholarship to college, he was going to college. The way he ran that ball down the field constantly reminded her of Lincoln. Whenever Lincoln did get a chance to see Jeremiah play, she knew he'd be proud of his son.

Did she make the right decision to help Lincoln? She hadn't heard from him since she'd wired him the money two days ago. No "Thank you, Katherine." Or "I got it." And although she hadn't seen him yet, at least she knew he was alive.

Eventually he'd meet his son. She'd placed a framed eight-by-ten photo of Lincoln in Jeremiah's room when her son turned two. The next day, her mother removed the picture, saying, "Our baby doesn't need to know his father until Lincoln is ready to be a father." She'd disagreed with her mother and put the picture back by her son's bedside.

Another photo of Lincoln hung outside her son's bedroom door. Each time Jeremiah pointed at a picture of Lincoln, he'd say, "That's *my* dad." Hopefully Lincoln would come home soon so Jeremiah could meet the man behind the uniform and hear all about how his daddy served his country.

Covering the national news continuously increased her compassion not just for Lincoln but for all vets, especially those who had seen the worst war had to offer, then came home and literally slept on American soil.

Desperately she wanted to hug Lincoln. Thank him for whatever he'd done while serving their country. Maybe she'd take a trip to Seattle, try to find him. Not tell her mom where she was going but ask her mom to keep Jeremiah for a few days. Makeda could help out if she wasn't busy studying for college finals.

"Come on, Mom, I want to get to the game early," Jeremiah said, tugging her hand.

Katherine sat on the sofa. She didn't feel like moving. Her mind said get up but her body protested. She was tired. Tired of going, and going, and going. Tired of pretending to always be happy so her child wouldn't see her sad. Tired of acting like they had lots of money when month to month she didn't know how she'd pay his tuition.

"Give Mama a minute, sweetheart. Go get your grandmother."

"She's already in the car waiting for us. This is our big Thanksgiving Day game. If I'm late, I won't start. Coach will bench me, and Makeda won't see me score the touchdown I promised her." His brown eyes pleaded more than his words.

Makeda had proven to be heaven sent. She chaperoned Jeremiah and his friends on Friday nights. The ten thousand–dollar check Steven told Mrs. Cunningham to give her was also a blessing.

Katherine wanted to tell her mom, "Lincoln sent a partial child support payment," so her mother wouldn't hate him so much. After all her mother had done to support Jeremiah, Katherine couldn't tell that lie.

Being a lead anchorwoman was great, but the salary increases were barely enough to cover her expenses. The money Steven had given her would help pay down her student loans. Another one hundred twenty thousand dollars to go and she'd almost be debt free.

The private school she'd selected for Jeremiah was more than she could comfortably afford. If she didn't get approved for a grant before Christmas, she'd have to find a sponsor for the next school year or her son would miss out on great educational and athletic opportunities.

"Mommy, please, come on."

Lost in her thoughts she'd forgotten he was standing by the doorway watching her. He tugged her hand again. She pulled away.

"Mommy promises. You're not going to be late, baby. Go get in the car. I'll be out in ten minutes tops."

Katherine waited until Jeremiah was outside. He slammed the screen door in protest. Normally she'd discipline him for that, but he had feelings too. She picked up the cordless. Dialed his number. Immediately she got his voice mail. That was a sign she shouldn't have called him. She placed the phone on the charger. Tears blurred her vision.

Lord, what am I doing? I can't take on a second job. I know You'll make a way. The extra money in her account felt good, but with so many unpaid bills it was already spent.

Putting on her happy face, she opened the screen, then closed the front door. The home phone rang. Quickly she shoved open the door, ran inside, and answered, "Hello." Without looking at the caller ID, she hoped it was him calling her back.

"Hey, Katherine. It's me, Lincoln."

Though she was happy to hear his voice, that wasn't whom she'd called. "Hi" was all she got out. Tears streamed down her cheeks. She was overjoyed to hear his voice again.

Why was she so damn happy to hear his voice? The last time they'd spoken, her mother told her to demand he pay the back child support. When Lincoln tried to explain, her mother hung up the phone, saying, "And you'd better not call him back."

Southern parents believed if their children lived under their roof, no matter what their age, they had to live by their rules. The princess-cut diamond earrings Steven had given her were in her jewelry box. "A man that gives a woman an expensive gift like that is after one thing and one thing only. And I'm not raising any more babies," her mom had said. Katherine had to make more money so she could move out as soon as possible.

"I'm sorry I didn't call sooner. I called to

say thanks for helping me out. I promise I'll pay you back every penny. I called because I'm ready to see my son."

As much as she loved Lincoln, Katherine shook her head. "We're struggling to come up with enough money to take care of Jeremiah. I mean, I have student loans I've got to pay. I'm still living at home with my mom. It's hard." She cried, staring at the gold band on her ring finger.

"I know your mom doesn't like me, but you can't be doing that bad. You just sent me two grand."

She understood how he could conclude that. "But you have no idea where it came from."

"You're right. Look, I'm trying real hard to get myself together. I'm on a good track now, and seeing my son will give me a reason to fight harder for something good. I might have a sponsor to help me."

A sponsor? To help him with what?

"Lincoln, we need a sponsor. We need you to help us. You owe us almost fifty thousand dollars."

Katherine hated that she sounded like her mom, but if she had what he owed her she wouldn't have to struggle. Money wasn't what she wanted from Lincoln most. She wanted his love, tenderness, and compassion. She wanted Jeremiah to have a real father, not a photo dad. She wanted them to become a family. She wanted to be Mrs. Katherine Lincoln. And damnit she wanted to feel him inside of her again. She was a young woman with unfulfilled womanly needs. Casual dating and casual sex was fun, but that wasn't her preference.

"Is that all I'm good for? Money?"

Katherine frowned. Her voice escalated. "Don't go there with me! I just sent you" — she paused, looked over her shoulder to make sure her mom wasn't standing in the doorway — "two thousand dollars that I could've used for our son's tuition. I didn't ask you any questions. I didn't tell you to join the military, and I sure as hell didn't expect you to walk away and never send me a letter or call me or nothing. You didn't even call to find out if I was pregnant!"

She could've gone on and on with a long list of what was truly Lincoln's fault, but what would that prove. He knew he was an absentee dad.

"You're right. I'm sorry, Katherine. I made a big mistake. I've made a lot of mistakes. Forgive me. I promise I'll pay you back and I'll start sending you money for Jeremiah soon. Thanks to you, I didn't have to sleep on the street last night. I got me a room at the Warwick until my apartment is available on the first. Once I'm situated, then can I see my —"

"Momma, come on! You promised. I'm going to be late!" Jeremiah yelled from the doorway.

"Katherine, is that him? Put my son on the phone. Let me say —"

She whispered, "I can't just spring this on Jeremiah. I've got the weekend off. I'll try to come to Seattle to see you tomorrow. We can discuss it then. We've got to go. Bye."

Katherine typed the name of Lincoln's hotel and the phone number registered to her cordless in her cell. She dried her tears, then smiled wide at her son. "I love you, baby." She kissed Jeremiah, then hugged him tight. "Come on here, boy! Let's go get this W!"

She'd find a way to continue providing for her son without Lincoln's help. And he could see his son. But first she had to look Lincoln in his eyes and ask a long list of "Why's."

STEVEN
CHAPTER 39

November 2010

No corpse.

No crime.

No charge.

No conviction.

How long would it take for Davis's body to decompose? How long would it take for any possible DNA matches to vanish?

Steven wondered how many missing persons were never found. His plan was more clever than Mona would imagine. He'd pried loose a boarded window at the back of an abandoned gray house that had been on the market for over a year. The FOR SALE sign was weather-beaten and leaning to the side. He'd dumped Davis's body and the rug inside, then resealed the wooden frame.

Maybe he'd make an offer the Realtor was sure to accept, record the deed in Mona's maiden name, have the property gated off, then have NO TRESPASSING signs nailed to the fence.

Dragging his feet, he bypassed Ms. Velma as she waved. "Hi, Steven!"

He was too tired to respond. Entering his house, Steven shook his head. He kicked the chair to the floor. "Fuck! I knew I shouldn't have left her ass here."

Oil and shit was all over his coffee table. The duct tape that should've kept Mona's mouth shut was on the floor.

Running through his house he shouted, "Mona!" knowing she was gone. What he didn't know was how long. "Mona! Where the hell are you?"

Steven went outside. Stared at Ms. Velma. "Where'd she go?"

"Where'd who go?"

"So you didn't see Mona leave my house?" Steven stomped down his stairs, stood in his front yard, kept staring at his next-door neighbor.

"Nope. Didn't see her come back home."

"You sure?"

"Yep. Ain't seen her in six months," Ms. Velma said, leaning on her column. "The turkey'll be done by four. Come on over and watch me carve it while you tell Mama what you're thankful for," Ms. Velma said, going in her house.

Liar. Ms. Velma knew something. And she

261

wasn't his damn mama!

Steven went inside, slammed his door. He picked up the black bag on his coffee table. Ripping open the plastic he yelled, "What the fuck is this?"

The staple gun from his toolshed was inside and his gun was missing.

"All right, have it your way," he said.

Steven went into the kitchen, got a bottle of whiskey, opened it where he stood. He gulped half the contents, then picked up his cell phone. This time when he dialed, he wasn't thinking about calling Mona, and he wasn't phoning his mom.

"Hello, I'd like to terminate one of my numbers," he told the customer service assistant. "Yes, the number is 334 . . ." He continued giving Mona's number. Now she'd have to get a new number.

"You do understand once we deactivate the number you can reactivate that same number later. You don't have to get a new one unless your time expires. May I suggest that if you're not sure, you temporarily suspend the number? That way it's easier to reactivate it. Or you can call back and terminate it later."

He didn't want to hear all that. "Terminate it now!"

Ending that call, he stood in the same spot

in his kitchen, downed the other half bottle of whiskey, then made another call.

A woman answered, "Bakersfield Police Department."

"Yes, I'd like to report a stolen vehicle."

MONA
CHAPTER 40

November 2010

Thank God, Mama V had taken her home.

The wisdom of that woman should never be underestimated. Mama V had told her, "Divorce him immediately. If you need me, all you've gotta do is call me. Mona, you go and you stay gone. Don't come back to this town for nothing. Don't contact Steven and tells your people not to give him any information on your whereabouts. Any man that'll tie you up like that will sho 'nuff kill ya. And don't worry about me. He don't want none of this."

Mona wasted no time getting in and out of her house. While she was home, she stuffed her backpack with her last book of blank checks, her laptop, charger, and a few pair of underwear. She secured both her guns inside the vented hood over her stove. Where she was headed, she'd only need protection of her heart.

Her 4Runner was a catalyst to permanently get her away from Steven and to the airport. Not BFL in Bakersfield. Mona was almost at LAX. Her decision to depart from Los Angeles to Seattle was based on the greater availability of flights.

Without a functioning phone, Mona felt naked and disconnected from the world. She wasn't able to contact Lincoln nor had she memorized his number. But he'd invited her to visit him, and she was determined to get her man back.

She parked the car in long-term parking at LAX. Mona shoved the black plastic bag with Steven's gun in it underneath the passenger seat, then locked the door.

Chasing the airport shuttle, she yelled, "Wait for me!"

Eventually someone would report Steven's car abandoned, but neither his gun nor his 4Runner was registered in her name. She didn't care what happened to Steven. If she could've blown up his SUV with him in it and had no witnesses, she would have.

"Thanks for waiting," she said, settling in a seat closest to the driver. "Do you know of a wireless store close to the airport where I can purchase a cell phone?"

"Yes, but it wouldn't do you any good. It's Thanksgiving Day, lady."

Damn. How soon could she get a phone? How was she going to get Lincoln's number?

Handing the driver a ten-dollar tip, Mona slung her backpack on her shoulder, hung her purse on the other, then exited at departures. Holiday travelers formed long curbside check-in lines that blocked the automatic sliding glass door entrance. Kids were in strollers, luggage was mounted on carts. Everybody was in the way.

You don't own the airport! Move, people. Move!

All I need is to buy a ticket, she thought, eyeing longer lines inside at check-in and ticket purchase. So much for getting to Seattle by eleven. It was already noon.

Thirty minutes later she stood in front of a ticket agent. "I'd like to purchase a one-way ticket to Seattle."

"What date would you like to leave?"

"The next available," Mona said.

"The next flight is tomorrow at three p.m."

"Tomorrow! I need to leave today! I know you have something. Please, lady, check again! It's a family emergency."

No way was Mona staying in Los Angeles overnight when she could spend the night in Lincoln's arms. She'd . . . "Never mind."

266

She walked away, then hurried back to the agent. "On second thought, I'd better get the ticket for backup. One-way, please."

Stuffing her ticket in her backpack, Mona headed downstairs and got on the first rental car shuttle. She picked out an SUV, handed her ID and contract to the clerk at the gate. "How far is it to Seattle?" she asked.

The guy slid his window wider, stared at her, then asked, "As in Washington?"

Mona rolled her eyes, nodded. Her lips tightened. "No, as in California."

"Oh, you got jokes? I'm not the one who needs directions. Just know that according to your contract you cannot take that car," he said, pointing at her SUV, "out of this state," then pointed toward the ground. "If you're going to Seattle for real, for real you need to change your contract." He tapped on a few keys, then enunciated, "Seattle, Washington, is one thousand one hundred and forty miles, airport door-to-door."

Mona sat for a moment. She'd thought it was closer. Based on the distance, she wouldn't get to Seattle until Sunday. Getting out of the car, she handed him the keys. "This doesn't make any goddamn sense."

"Neither do you," he said. "They don't pay me enough, lady. Don't make me stoop to scoop your poop. It ain't happening."

Mona walked ten feet toward the rental car shuttle, then froze. She went back to the clerk. "Get out of the car. I've changed my mind."

"Why does that not surprise me?" he said, turning off the engine.

If she was going to be in Los Angeles overnight, she had to be mobile.

STEVEN
CHAPTER 41

November 2010

"That was stupid, Steven," he told himself. Maybe he wasn't close to clever after all.

"Why did you terminate Mona's cell phone number?" That was the easiest way to track her ass. No telling where his car was, but even if the police found the car, that wouldn't lead him to Mona. She hadn't used his credit cards in over six months. He didn't know where she banked.

"Fuck!" He could only blame himself for being that dumb.

Sitting in his recliner, he guzzled a half bottle of whiskey. His cell phone interrupted his intent to polish off the other half.

He answered, "Hi, Mom. Happy Thanksgiving."

"Hey, Buttercup. Happy Thanksgiving. Your dad says the same. How you doing? You having dinner with Mona, I hope."

He loved his mother. Never wanted to

disappoint her or his dad.

"Ma, we talked about this two days ago. Six months didn't cut it. Mona is gone and she's not coming back. What am I gonna do now?"

He felt like a child asking his mother for marital advice, again. He could transfer title of the car to Mona's name. Nah, stupid idea.

"A lot can happen in forty-eight hours. No use in crying over spilled milk. It's time for you to move on. File for a divorce. That way if she starts charging up your cards, you won't be responsible. You've got to protect your credit and the Cunningham family name. Once your divorce is final, get yourself another woman. I don't understand these men sleeping around with a whole lotta women 'cause their woman done left them. You ever thought about dating that news reporter girl, Katherine Clinton? I know she's spoiled already, but she's raised that kid the same way I raised you, and that says a lot about her integrity. She's the marrying kind."

Divorcing Mona wasn't happening. He had too much invested to let his marriage go. Plus, Mona had his gun. Oh, shit! What if she left it in the car and the police found his bloody gun and his car?

Steven dropped the cell in his lap, covered his ears, then screamed, "Fuck!"

"Buttercup! Buttercup! You okay?" his mom shouted. "Don't let that devil grab ahold of ya. You not going crazy, are you? Answer me! Richard! Come here. I think Buttercup is falling apart! We might have to go back to California."

Picking up the phone, he quickly composed himself. "No, don't do that. I'm okay, Mom. I just jammed my finger," he lied.

"Go rinse it off and put some Neosporin on it. You still got that job at the oil —"

"Yes, Ma, yes," he lied again. And what good would ointment do? "Let me call you back, Ma. I love you. Bye."

Steven ended the call and drove to Mona's house. Quickly he picked the lock on the back door, entered her kitchen, then locked the door behind him.

He'd try to remember some of the forensic tips Mona had taught him. There was no use in him dismantling the stove's hood; he'd find nothing inside the vent. She was smarter than taking her own advice. He rolled the refrigerator six inches from the wall, inspected the back, nothing unusual. There were no secret compartments on the cabinets, inside the light fixtures, or under the grooves of the travertine floor.

Hurrying to the bedroom, he checked the mattress, frame, headboard, and nightstand. He didn't discover any important information. He opened Mona's closet. There was a chest on the top shelf. As he scooted forward what he hoped to be a plethora of treasures, the wooden box slipped. A dozen or more dildos banged on his head, then fell to the carpet.

"Fuck this." Steven kicked the vibrators out of his way, then left the way he'd come, out the back door.

MONA
CHAPTER 42

November 2010

Thank God for credit cards.

This time she had more credit than cash in her purse. She would've had a few grand in her pocket had she known Steven was going to act a fool. Didn't expect to be in transit overnight. Holding on to the three hundred dollars she had, Mona's hotel incidentals were charged. She had access to the room, phone, Internet, minibar, dining service, and whatever else she needed for the night.

Sitting on the bed, she prayed for Davis's family. They probably knew by now that something terrible had happened to Davis. Knowing Steven, the police may never find Davis's body.

In a moment of silence, Mona recalled the first night they'd met. Wondered if he'd spoken his destiny into existence. If they'd decided to do one thing differently — go to

Disneyland, not stop at the arena, or not eat at the café — he might still be alive. If she hadn't left him alone in the shower with his eyes closed and his back turned, he could've defended himself. Or if she hadn't gone to the kitchen, she could've protected Davis by shooting Steven before he entered the bedroom.

One decision made Davis's death final. But which one?

The holiday gave her an excuse to call her parents. Dialing their number, she wondered if her old room was the same or if her mom had given her things away and made it available for guests.

"Hello." The baritone voice was familiar.

"Hi, Daddy. You're home. Happy Thanksgiving." She was happy to talk to her dad.

"Hey, Mona Lisa. Why haven't you called? Your mother has been worrying about you. Where are you? How are you?" he asked.

Wow, she hadn't seen or spoken with her parents in over five years. The sound of her dad's voice brought back fond memories of the few times he was at home. "Guess I'm a chip off the ole block." They laughed, then she said, "I'm good. I'm in Los Angeles." She didn't want them to know she was headed to Seattle.

She made small talk until she felt comfortable telling them the real reason she'd called. "So, what did Mom cook?"

"Actually, I cooked for your mom today. We've been spending a lot of time together since my other friend passed away last year," he said, sounding sad.

Wow, her dad had more than one lover, more than one family, and her mom took him back just like that? "I need to speak to Mom. Is she there?"

"Honey, Mona Lisa is on the phone."

Honey? Since when?

"Hi, Mona. You all right?" her mother asked.

"Happy Thanksgiving, Mama. I'm good. I'm in LA."

"Where's Steven?"

Mona should've been prepared for that question. Didn't want to hear her mother say, "I told you so." They sounded happier than ever, like newlyweds on their honeymoon.

"He's in the back," Mona said.

"Took you too long to answer. You never were a good liar, Mona Lisa. I heard the hesitation in your voice. What do you need?" her mom asked.

"I know, Mama. It's complicated. I'll explain later. I'm calling because Lincoln called me. Told me you gave him my number. My cell phone is damaged and I need his number so I can call him back. Do you have it?"

"No, I don't."

"Mama, please. I have to get in touch with him."

"Mona Lisa, I told you I don't have that boy's number. His grandmother called, asked for your number, and I gave it to her."

Now who was lying?

"Can you call his grandmother on three-way and ask her for Lincoln's number? Please, Mama."

"No, I'm not calling her and that's final. Changing the subject, you hear that Sarah McKenny got the death penalty for first-degree murder. Now, before you say anything, I know something ain't right. I can feel it. Sarah didn't kill Calvin. Is that why you and Steven had to leave town all of a sudden after Calvin's murder? Y'all seen something? Is that why you married him, Mona Lisa? You covering up for him? You out there in the world making foolish mistakes? Don't you ever come back here with blood on your hands, little girl, you hear me?"

The marriage hadn't happened in that order, but her mom's intuition was eerie. If Mona had known what Steven was going to do before she'd said, "I do," she never would've married him. Mona knew if she confessed everything to her mom, her mother would go straight to the police.

"Sorry I called, Ma. Tell Daddy I love him," she said, then hung up the phone before her mother figured out too much.

There had to be another way to get in touch with Lincoln. Maybe Katherine had his number.

LINCOLN
CHAPTER 43

November 2010

Katherine wasn't serious about visiting him, was she?

Lincoln sat in his room watching anything except football. Just in case she was, he texted Mona, Plans changed. Don't come now. Wait until I contact you with the okay. His text wasn't a request. It was a demand. To make sure he didn't receive her calls or texts, Lincoln blocked Mona's number.

Next week would be better to talk to her. He'd be in his apartment. She could help him pick out furniture for his place. And he could kiss Mona Lisa one last time. If he honestly had a chance to get his family back, they were his priority. He'd have to find a job to support them. Hopefully one he could keep without getting fired. But would getting a job mean he'd have to give up his housing voucher? He'd better check with his Prime Care doctor first. The government had too many hidden rules in their manuals.

Lincoln turned on his radio, danced in front of the television. His combat boots were strapped to his feet. His dick slapped thigh to thigh. He only removed his shoes to shower and sleep. The room wasn't that big but, "Sleeping on fresh sheets every day beats the hell out of sleeping on the street," he said, moonwalking on the carpet. More than being happy, he was grateful his life was looking up. Plus. . . .

Downing two sleeping pills with a cola, he prayed he'd fall asleep before sunrise. He stared at himself in the mirror. Despite his trials and obstacles, his abs and ass were tighter than ever. His chocolate thighs and muscular biceps were well defined. Neither his hair nor skin looked or felt as good as it used to, but it was getting there. He had housekeeping leave him extra lotion, shampoo, and conditioner. A trip to the barbershop and one of them spa treatments wouldn't hurt either.

Opening the newspaper, he pulled out the classifieds. Maybe he could get on with that seafood company over on Shilshole Ave. They had over six thousand employees. Surely they could benefit from his strength and skills. Or he could get a desk job at the

Veteran's Administration. They owed him that much.

His cell phone rang. He checked the ID. "Hey, this is a surprise," he said.

"Katherine gave me your number," she said.

"Wow, Katherine did that? That was nice of her. Grandma, how are you?"

"If I wasn't in this hospital bed, I'd come to wherever you are and beat your behind, young man. Why haven't you called us? Were we that bad of grandparents that you left here and never called, or wrote, or sent us a picture? Your mama said you never called her, either. Nobody's heard from you. Not even Katherine and your son. Oh, Lincoln, he looks just like you. Don't be like your daddy was. Your son needs you. What's wrong, baby? Don't you know we love you?"

Shaking his head, he was not forgiving his father for taking the easy way out. For the first time in years, he cried. He wept so loud and hard, it was hard for him to swallow. "I love you too, Grandma."

The things he'd gone through weren't her fault. What he'd experienced overseas he wouldn't wish on the enemy. And he would tell. No one would believe any human beings could be that cruel.

"Baby, you hush. Ain't no reason for you

to be crying. Now, I'm calling you 'cause I want you to come see me. This ole bag of bones might not see the New Year roll in, and your grandfather and I want pictures with our grand and great-grand together before the Lord calls me home. They're sending me home tomorrow. Said there's not much else they can do for me here. Promise me you'll come see me."

Lincoln wiped his eyes, his nose, his jaw, his eyes again. He sniffled. "I promise, Grandma. I promise."

When he thought no one loved him, he learned that was a decision he'd made. Not them.

STEVEN
CHAPTER 44

November 2010

Maybe his mom was right about Katherine being a good woman. Familiarity made him comfortable with the idea. He could lure Katherine in like he'd done with Mona. Get her so intertwined in his past that she'd be the ball connected to his chain. He might go down. She'd go down faster. He didn't want it that way, but he had to give the woman with him a reason not to turn him in if she discovered his truth.

Steven sat in his recliner. It was ten o'clock in Selma. He'd take a chance. He needed an adult to talk to other than his mother. He dialed Katherine's number.

The phone rang four times before she answered, "Hey, Steven. Happy Thanksgiving."

This was the first time Katherine's voice sounded sweet and sultry. "Hey, I was calling to say I'm thankful for your help on the

Sarah case."

Somberly she said, "You haven't heard?"

"Heard what?"

"Sarah got the death penalty. I reported it yesterday. You think she really did it?"

Damn. What he'd detected in Katherine's voice wasn't sultriness, it was sadness. "Nah, I hadn't heard the news. That's horrible. Guess I've been too busy dealing with my own problems."

"I've been trying to figure out where Sarah got the money from. That's the main thing Davenport is holding on to. Why Calvin? Why Sarah? Why —"

Steven interrupted. "Compared to what's happening with Sarah and your long list of questions, my situation is starting to look up. My best advice is, don't get involved at all."

Now he had to keep in touch with Katherine. She was too curious. If she started probing for answers, she might find out that his name was indirectly attached to all those cashier's checks.

She laughed a little melodically. "Listen at me. You're the one who called me."

Could a woman of Katherine's caliber genuinely fall for him? He'd have to develop a strategy to reel her in. He'd start with trying to make her sympathetic. Women were natural nurturers, especially mothers.

Sadly, he said, "Mona left me. I thought she was coming back, but I don't know where she is."

"So that's why she called me."

His voice escalated. "Mona called you? For what?"

"She said she had some urgent information for Lincoln. She wouldn't tell me what it was. I'm not a high school teenager anymore, Steven. I'm a woman. I don't have time to play games."

Urgent information. That Mona is a great liar. "So did you give her his number?"

"I had no reason not to. I mean, I hope Lincoln does right by his son even though we haven't gotten married yet. But if Lincoln isn't going to take care of Jeremiah, or make me an honorable woman, I'll have to keep doing the best I can with what I have. My hundred thousand dollar student loan will have to take a backseat to my son's tuition."

Steven gulped his whiskey. He didn't want to seem too anxious to financially help Katherine. Now that he knew her hook, he'd reel her in slowly. Katherine could be his bait to catch Mona's ass.

"I've got to go. Let's talk soon," he said, ending their conversation.

For now he was done asking questions of and answering questions for Katherine. Steven went into his bedroom, packed his suitcase. The next time he questioned Katherine would be face-to-face in Selma.

Mona
Chapter 45

November 2010
The number Katherine had given her was scribbled on a notepad in front of her. Anxiously, Mona dialed nine, one, the area code, and the number from the cordless in her hotel room. She paced from the door to the window repeatedly.

"Answer the phone. Come on. Come on," she said, clenching her fist.

"Thank you for calling the Warwick Hotel," a woman said.

"What the hell?" Mona said, then hung up.

She was supposed to get Lincoln or his voice mail. She checked the number again, dialed the number again. "If Katherine didn't want to give me the number, all she had to do was say no."

"Thank you for calling the Warwick Hotel," a woman said.

Mona hung up. She dialed the number a

third time, got the same message, and hung up again. She decided to do what she should've done first. Mona powered on her laptop and logged on to her cell phone account.

Invalid user name or password popped up three times. She called the company and discovered, "At the subscriber's request, we can no longer provide you access or information regarding this account. I'd be happy to start a new account in your name."

Mona ended the call. She didn't need help with setting up an account over the phone when she didn't have a phone. First thing in the morning, she'd go to the wireless store, open her own account, buy a new phone, and get a new number with a 212 prefix or something so her parents and others wouldn't know where she was unless she wanted them to know.

The more she thought about Steven terminating her number, she thought, "That's a good thing." Now he couldn't track her whereabouts from her calls.

Mona dialed Katherine's number. "Answer the damn phone!"

Katherine answered. "Mona Lisa, I'm going to ask you to stop calling me. I don't know what you're up to, but whatever it is, I hope what Steven told me isn't true."

Frowning, Mona hesitated, then said, "If you didn't want to give me Lincoln's number, you shouldn't have."

"I did give you his number. Don't call me again. If you do, I'm going to the police. Bye," Katherine said, ending the call.

Going to the what? "Bitch, you don't know me." What the hell did Steven tell Katherine? And why was he talking to her anyway?

Mona slammed the cordless on the base. The battery popped out. She didn't care. She wondered how much Katherine knew. And whatever happened to the clothes that Steven said had to be destroyed the night he killed Calvin? There wasn't time to get rid of that evidence. So where'd he put them?

Seattle first. Then Selma. That wasn't the smartest thing to do. Mona should go home first and search Steven's house in Selma.

She sat on the bed. *Her car?* She prayed it wasn't so, but knowing him, that's exactly where he stashed everything.

Damn!

KATHERINE
CHAPTER 46

November 2010

Her decision was finalized.

The suitcase by the door had everything she'd need for her weekend trip to Seattle. Jeremiah's photos and video footage of a few of his games were in her carry-on. She wished she could stay longer than two days, but she had to get back by Sunday to anchor the Monday morning national news on *Morning to You, America.*

"Bye, Mama," she said, giving her mother a hug.

"I wanna go with you," Jeremiah whined.

"What did I tell you about shortcuts? It's 'I want to go with you.' "

He stared at her with those eyes just like his daddy's, eyes that pleaded more than words. "Mama, I want to go with you to Atlanta."

She hated lying to her mother and son, but there was no way she could tell either the truth. "I'll bring you something back." Hopefully, his dad. "Now, go back to bed. Four o'clock is too early for you to be up."

Kissing her son, and hugging her mom again, Katherine put her suitcase on the passenger seat, then headed to Montgomery for her connecting flight to Dallas/Fort Worth.

The drive from Selma to Montgomery's Dannelly Field airport was a welcomed hour of solitude. She made sure she drove the speed limit along U.S. 80 for two reasons. One, she feared getting stopped by the police in the dark. Two, she didn't want to collide with any animals.

Parking, checking in, and getting through security consumed more time than her road trip. It was too early to eat; a breakfast sandwich would be cold by the time she was hungry. A club sandwich and a cup of fruit would have to do.

Waiting to board, she dialed the number to the hotel. When the operator answered, Katherine said, "Lincoln, I mean William Lincoln's room, please."

"Certainly, I'll put you through."

Confirming he was still a guest, Katherine ended the call before he answered. In eight hours she'd be face-to-face with the man she hadn't seen since high school. Was he the same? Did he look better than when she last saw him? Would he find her equally or more attractive? Would her heart forgive him for abandoning them?

Settling into her seat, Katherine prayed Lincoln had more answers than she had questions.

LINCOLN
CHAPTER 47

November 2010

"Huh. What?"

He sprang from his bed. Squatted. Slapped his face. The inside of his left, then right hand pressed hard from his forehead to his chin. Felt like bugs were crawling on him. Standing tall, he stared at the clock, at the ringing phone, then into the space in front of his face.

Rattling his head, he looked at the clock; it was 2:14 in the afternoon. He picked up the open bottle of sleeping pills that was on the nightstand. He peeped inside. The prescription he'd filled two days ago was all gone. He couldn't have taken the remaining ten pills at once.

"Shut the hell up!" he yelled at the phone. Unable to sleep all night, he'd just dozed off an hour ago. "Damn!" He scratched his stomach.

He went to the bathroom, stood over the

toilet, let his dick hang as he emptied his bladder. A red thong was on his vanity with a note. *Thanks, soldier. It was my pleasure serving you.*

Shaking himself, the phone rang again. He snatched the phone from the wall. "What!"

The voice on the other end asked, "What room are you in?"

"One, two, one, two, two," he said, then slammed the phone against the receiver.

Good. Whoever owned that piece of butt floss was coming back to get it.

His phone rang again. "Stop fucking calling me!"

"What room are you in?"

"I just fucking told you, bitch! One, two, one, two, two!" He slammed the phone on the hook.

Wiping his dick with a white towel, he noticed red lipstick smeared on his shaft. "Fuck, Lincoln. Why did you bring that 'ho to your room last night?"

Last night he watched television. Went for a walk to the liquor/grocery store across the street, bought a six-pack of beer and two bottles of tequila. And . . .

"Damnit, Lincoln, you did let that trick convince you to let her suck your dick."

That probably explained his pills being

gone. "Oh, shit!"

He ran into the room, picked up his pants, shoved his hand in one pocket. Empty. Checked the other. Nothing. "Fuck!"

Knock, knock, knock.

I'm kicking that bitch's ass. He put on his pants. His underwear and T-shirt were still on the chair. He hurried to the door, jerked it open.

Heaving, he froze. His heart softened. All that angered him dissipated as he stared into her eyes.

"Can I come in?"

He shook his head in disbelief, opened the door wide. Scratching his temple, he said, "I thought you were kidding." He took her suitcase. "Yes, come in."

He wanted to say, "You won't believe what just happened to the money you sent me," but that wasn't appropriate.

"Mind if I use your bathroom?" she asked, pushing open the door.

He dropped the suitcase, jumped in front of her. "I forgot to flush the toilet." That was the truth, but he really needed to hide that note and that nasty thong.

Lincoln closed the door. Looked around for a safe hiding place. The black bag that the blow dryer was in seemed safest at the moment. After stuffing the prostitute's belongings inside, he tied the drawstring in a military knot, flushed the toilet, then opened the door.

"Why did you call me twice?" he asked, not knowing what else to say to her.

She was still the most gorgeous woman he'd seen. Slightly thicker in the breasts and hips, but he liked it.

"I only called you once," she said, entering the bathroom.

He called the front desk. "Hold all my calls until I notify you otherwise."

That trick wasn't slick. But he didn't want her creeping up on him. Nah, she wouldn't come back after stealing his money. Doubted she was that stupid, but he'd find her. And when he did, she'd swear he was her pimp. She had an ass whupping coming from him if she didn't have his cash.

It was a good thing he'd paid for his room in advance. But what about the incidentals he'd incurred. How would he pay for those? There wasn't enough money to cover his extra charges. He could leave without checking out. Or persuade Katherine to take care of his bill.

"Certainly, Mr. Lincoln," the operator replied.

Who the fuck called the second time?

Lincoln couldn't believe she was standing

in front of him. He wanted to hug her, kiss her. He picked her up, twirled her around. "I must be dreaming," he said, feeling the happiest since the last time he'd seen her. "You hungry? You want to go downstairs to the restaurant and eat? You tired? You want to rest? You want to take a shower? Anything you want to do, anything. Let's do it."

Katherine sat in the green oversized chair facing the bed. She placed her purse on the magazines scattered on the small round table next to the chair. He wondered how much cash she had on her. Maybe if he made up a story about what happened to the money she'd given him, she'd give him some more.

"Lincoln, why? I need to understand why you never contacted us?" Tears trickled down her cheeks. Katherine wiped her eyes.

He noticed she wasn't wearing the ring he'd given her. Assuming his comfort position in opposition, he sat on the edge of the bed facing her, clamped his hands together, spread his feet six inches apart, then stared at the floor.

"Please don't cry. I didn't mean to hurt you."

"Doesn't matter what you meant, it's what you did. To me. To our son. Why, Lincoln? I really need to know. And look at me. I have to see your eyes," she said.

He watched her dry her tears again. He cried like he'd done when his grandmother told him she loved him. Any attempt to gain sympathy was worth the effort.

"Do you love me, Katherine?"

"William Lincoln, please don't make this about you. Please. If you don't want to tell me, say so, and I'll get a separate room, go back to Selma in the morning, and never contact you again. I'm here to get answers, not answer your questions." She didn't blink. Her eyes were wet, but there were no more tears.

Lincoln wiped his face. "I . . . I . . . I . . . I love you, Katherine. I never meant to . . . I don't know what happened to me."

More like "I'll never tell you what happened to me," but based on her tight lips, he doubted she'd care about that either. Vigorously, he shook his head trying to erase the horrible thoughts creeping into his mind. He prayed he didn't have a flashback that triggered a panic attack. She'd just gotten to his room. Didn't want to scare her away.

"If you're done talking, I'm leaving."

"Fine, you want the whole truth?"

She nodded. Her lips got tighter. Katherine remained silent.

"When you told me you might be pregnant, I thought you were setting me up. Trying to trap me with a child to make sure you got a piece of whatever you thought I was going to get paid." He stared at the empty space between his feet.

"I'm listening. And I'd appreciate it if you look at me and stop staring at the floor."

He stood. Paced in front of her. The small space between the chair and the bed forced his leg to slide along the side of the mattress. "My first year wasn't so bad. I traveled to Okinawa for six months. Didn't contact anyone. Not even my grandparents. I was trying to find out who I was. What I wanted. What my purpose in life was. I told you I made the decision to join because of my grandfather, but day one in the service I resented him because it was more his decision than mine. I should've gone to college."

"How could I trap you with a baby when there was no guarantee you were going to go pro, Lincoln? Players get injured all the time. And I loved you with every part of my fifteen-, sixteen-, and seventeen-year-old body." Katherine opened her purse. "I've worn this ring almost every day except for the time I was in the hospital giving birth to our son and now. I held on to the hope that one day you'd come back to me. But you didn't. I've come to you. So if this ring doesn't mean anything to you, I can have closure, and," she said, placing the ring in his hand, "and you can have this back."

His Adam's apple lodged in his throat. He clenched the ring in his palm. Wow, she'd worn his gold ring for over ten years. Had she sexed another man while wearing his ring? He shook his head again. Didn't want those thoughts creeping in either.

"Katherine, I don't have any excuses for not contacting you. I love you. I still love you. Seemed like the longer I took to call, the easier it became not to call anyone. And I —"

"Did you call Mona Lisa?"

He shook his head. Technically he hadn't called her. He'd texted her.

"You're sure?"

Did she know something he didn't about Mona? Best to stick with his first response, since that was the truth. "No, I haven't called her. Haven't seen her since graduation day."

"Um, huh. Continue," she said, crossing her legs.

"Nine eleven changed my life for the worse. Honestly, I didn't think I was going to survive Afghanistan or Iraq. Being an expert shooter saved my life many times, but I couldn't save —" He stopped speaking. Choked up again thinking about Randy. "The military taught me my main purpose was to kill. But I couldn't save my best friend. Katherine, I'd love to tell you I'm the same man you last saw, but I'm not."

"What do you —"

The chopping sound hovered over the hotel. He grabbed her. Threw her to the floor. Covered her body with his. "Stay down! Don't move." He crawled to the nightstand, got his gun, peeped out the window.

Katherine sprang to her feet. He knocked her back down, kneeled beside her. "Stay down! It's not safe."

Lincoln stayed by her side, protecting her like he'd done other soldiers. "I should've never walked away from Randy," he cried, then wiped her face.

Katherine moved his hand. "Stop it." She peeped out the window. "It's a helicopter. Lincoln, my God, what happened to you over there?"

KATHERINE
CHAPTER 48

November 2010

Would she regret having made the trip to see him?

She already had one dependent. Didn't need another. Katherine had a choice. She could get out of his hotel bed, get dressed, and leave a day early. Or she could stay by his side until tomorrow and pray he gave direct answers to her questions.

They lay pillow-to-pillow facing one another. His arm hugged her hip. Her hand caressed his shoulder. A craving to feel him on top of her, inside of her, made her twitch.

"That was nice. Good morning, beautiful," he said. "You have no idea how many times I've dreamt of this moment. I want to make love to you too, Katherine."

If he had protection, perhaps they'd make love before her departure. The urge to orgasm lingered between her thighs, tingled on the tip of her nipples. She kissed him.

Twitched. Kissed him again. Yes, she definitely was still in love with Lincoln, but she had to address the more important matters with a clear mind. "We have a lot to discuss."

"Yeah, I know." The disappointment in his voice lingered.

The stiffness in his dick pressing against her thigh lessened. Sex was not the solution to their plethora of problems.

Yesterday, once the helicopters and planes stopped flying over the hotel causing him to push her to the floor several times, draw his gun, then peep out the window, she lay in bed beside him exhausted. Their time together had progressed with Lincoln describing one gruesome war story after another. The worst, he'd said, "I can't tell you." She couldn't imagine it being worse than what he'd graphically described — decapitation, amputation, rape, murder. She wondered if he'd done any or all of those things and more. He'd described death so vividly, the stench of decomposing flesh was stuck in her nostrils.

"Have you smelled a dead rat?" he asked.

She had and it was horrible.

"Close your eyes and recall the odor. Now imagine it's not one rat but a thousand. They've been dead for a month. Someone takes a handful of the rotted flesh, stuffs all of it into your nostrils," he said.

When he had said that last night, she almost threw up.

He concluded his description with, "Now inhale deeply and you're almost there. Imagine this malodorous stench is trapped inside of you for years."

At that point she'd gotten up, ran to the bathroom, vomited until her insides ached. She'd rinsed her mouth and nose, trying to erase the picture he'd painted in her mind.

There had to be a way she could help him. A loan from Steven, or she could do another favor for him, earn a few more thousands of dollars that she wouldn't have to pay back. She was so indebted to her creditors, earning the money would be best. The sun had set and was now rising, shining through the curtains, beaming on Lincoln's chest. She envisioned kissing his nipples, then trailing her tongue down his abs to his navel and below his pubic hairs.

She'd dozed off several times, but each time she'd awoken, Lincoln's eyes were wide open. Sympathy sex wasn't what she wanted to give him. She felt bad for him. His parents didn't care about him? Why? He thought his grandparents didn't care either. Why had he felt that way? Without his giving a definitive response, she was closer to understanding why he hadn't contacted her.

"Maybe you're afraid to love anyone," she said, gazing into his eyes. His pupils seemed hollow, like a dark tunnel she could journey down and never reach the end.

"More like afraid to be abandoned by someone I thought loved me. Especially my mom and dad. Katherine, if you'll have me back, please don't ever leave me. I survived the war. Kind of," he said, then chuckled. "But my heart can't survive the ticking of a time bomb not knowing when or if it'll explode."

He started weeping like an infant, buried his face in the pillow. "I'm sorry. I hate for you to see me like this." He swallowed his pain and sorrow.

A man, strong, muscular, handsome, and possibly more vulnerable than her, lay beside her naked in countless ways. She was closer than ever to becoming Mrs. Lincoln. Her next dream could come true by Jeremiah's tenth birthday. But was she dreaming? Would a marriage to Lincoln survive his mental disorder? Would he be a good father or freak Jeremiah out?

"Don't you ever sleep?" she asked, touching his face. "You were up all night and kept me up too."

"Only when I'm medicated. Otherwise, I'm afraid to sleep. My mind never sleeps. Soon as I close my eyes, the war is like a movie constantly replaying in my head. I don't want you to see that side of me. The way I wake up sweating, shouting, paranoid. It's like constantly living in the war zone. My body is here. But my mind is still in Iraq. No one can catch or save me."

She had one more day to be with him before heading back to Selma. "I don't think anything can freak me out more than what happened yesterday."

"Don't be so sure. You haven't witnessed my worst panic attack. I'm not sure I have either. Having PTSD scares me. I'm afraid of myself. That's why, even though I really want to be with you, I have to wait until I can afford better treatment."

"Better treatment? What are you talking about?"

"The cost for a private doctor to properly diagnose and treat me could cost six figures. The VA has a long list of patients like me. No real help. Just meds and more meds to numb the pain. They're treating the symptoms, but until they address the cause, I'm a walking time bomb. I'm so afraid that one day I may not be able to pull back. One day,

I may draw my gun, think I'm in Afghanistan, and pull the trigger. I fear who might be on the receiving end of the bullet."

That comment helped Katherine decide what to do next. "Lincoln, come back home with me. I know enough people to get you professional help. My therapist can help you."

He frowned. "I can't afford to take care of you and Jeremiah, let alone pay for a shrink. I refuse to let you help me. Soldiers are strong. We make a way out of no way."

"But you don't have to be this strong. You can lean on me."

"And what? Become another mouth to feed. I can't do that. I won't do that. When I'm better, I'll let you know. Besides, I'll be home for Christmas. I promised my grandmother. Can I see my son then?" he asked, looking sad.

"I almost forgot," Katherine said, easing out of bed. She opened her suitcase, retrieved her DVD player and photo album. "I brought videos and pictures of Jeremiah to show you."

Lincoln sat up. "Wow! Really? Okay, let me throw on something, run across the street, grab us something to eat and drink, and we can spend the rest of the day with you showing and telling me all about my son."

"Can't we just order room service?"

"I'm out of my meds. Gotta self-medicate to minimize the anxiety. I need a little more than food, if you know what I mean. Oh, can you spare a few dollars?"

A puff of air shot from her nostrils. Her eyebrows grew closer. "What happened to all the money I sent you?"

"I used it for this room and a deposit on my apartment. I'll pay you back. I promise."

"Please, don't make me any more promises." She was glad she had helped him, so a few more dollars didn't matter. She opened her purse, gave him fifty dollars.

"Since you're already naked, take a shower. Get her ready for me. When I get back, we're celebrating. And I'm putting my ring back on your finger." Opening the door, he looked back at her and said, "We are going to finally get married."

Katherine had enough problems. She wasn't sexing or marrying him. "Hurry back. I'll set up the DVD player."

MONA
CHAPTER 49

November 2010

Mona exited the elevator at the twelfth floor. "One, two, one, two, two," she mumbled, checking the room numbers. Her heart thumped with anticipation. What did he look like? Had he gained weight? Was he still handsome? Taking a deep breath, she could hardly contain herself.

When she got to the corresponding room, she inhaled again, covered the peephole. She had her new 4G camera phone positioned to take his picture. Had to capture the surprised look on Lincoln's face when he saw hers. Sort of surprised look, because he knew she was coming but had no idea she'd arrived.

Tap. Tap. Tap.

Smiling wide, soon as the door opened she released her finger from the camera image. "Surprise!" Mona stepped back.

"What did you for . . . get?" Katherine

asked, opening the door.

"Aw, hell, no!" Mona said, staring.

For a few seconds, Katherine froze in the doorway. Her forearm covered both her breasts; her hand cupped her pubic hairs as she crisscrossed her knees.

The door started slowly moving closer to Mona, closer to shutting in her face.

The moment was worth capturing twice. Mona stuck her foot in the doorway, took another picture of Katherine from behind. Her ass was wider than Mona had remembered when they were in high school but tight and firm as it had appeared years ago underneath Katherine's form-fitting dresses.

Mona hadn't gained much weight, but seeing how perfect Katherine's body was, Mona wished she would've exercised instead of following Steven on his jobs. If she was going to stay in Seattle with Lincoln, Mona had to get in better shape and find a job. Maybe she could do forensic work for the police department or she could contract as a bounty hunter.

"What in the hell are *you* doing here?" Mona asked. "Where's Lincoln?" Not awaiting an invitation, she pushed open the door, entered the room, and slammed the door. She started to secure the latch but changed her mind. Didn't want to trap herself in a small room with Katherine.

"This is why you called me for his number? Get over him, trick-a-Mona-i-ous." Entertaining herself, Katherine laughed softly, then sternly said, "He doesn't want you. He hasn't wanted you since tenth grade. You like drama. You enjoy ruining people's lives, don't you?"

Oh, this bitch got insults? We'll see who's laughing when I'm done with her ass.

"If he didn't want me," Mona said, digging in the purse, "he wouldn't have given me this engagement ring." She held the ring in front of Katherine's face.

Katherine walked away, opened her purse, held up the same-style plain band except hers was gold. "That's probably the ring your husband gave you. Lincoln gave me this engagement ring."

Mona tried to one up Katherine when she said, "He gave me my ring on —"

Katherine interjected, and proudly said at the same time as Mona, "Graduation day."

What in the world is going on here? After all these years Lincoln was trying to play both of them? If he was messing with Mona's intelligence, the play Mona would run on him would rank at the top of every player's playbook.

Tired of staring at Katherine's erect

310

nipples, Mona said, "This is too much. You need to put some clothes on. Where's Lincoln? How long have you been here? Don't answer that. I don't care. Get out. Lincoln invited me to come see him and you're trying to trump me. Get your ass out. Now!" Mona wondered but wouldn't dare ask, Did you fuck him?

She discretely sniffed the air. It didn't smell like sex.

"I don't know what he's ever seen in you. You're wild and out of control."

"You'll never see what any man sees in me, because I don't do females. You don't need to know," Mona said, wishing she had one of her guns. She'd never killed anyone and she wouldn't shoot Katherine, but she'd scare her ass for sure.

Katherine countered, "And you don't need to know what he sees in me. You're one sinful woman. You need Jesus. You want them both? You've got a husband. Why don't you go back to Bakersfield and be with Steven," Katherine said, stepping into her underwear.

Mona walked to Katherine's suitcase, rummaged through her belongings. "You've got to go before Lincoln gets back," she said, tossing Katherine a black dress and a pair of slip-on, two-inch heels. "Put that shit on and get out while you can."

Picking up the photo album that was spread across the bed, Mona flipped through it. "Cute illegitimate kid. Can't wait for the paternity test." She tossed the album in Katherine's suitcase along with the DVD player and the laptop.

"That's . . ." Katherine began, then shook her head.

"That's what? Shut up and keep it moving," Mona said, then went into the bathroom, gathered Katherine's toiletries, packed those too.

"Hurry up, bitch. You've got to get out of here."

"I'm not going any —"

Mona gripped Katherine's neck with one hand, stared her in the face. Katherine couldn't breathe. Her face turned beet red.

"Woman to woman, Lincoln is mine. I'm asking you politely. I'm not going to ask you again." After shoving Katherine onto the bed, she threw Katherine's clothes on top of her. "Put that on." She zipped, then dragged Katherine's bag to the door. Tossed it into the hallway.

"You've got two minutes to get dressed in here or you can get dressed out there."

"You'll get yours," Katherine said, quickly pulling her dress over her head. "You can take care of his broke butt. And while you're at it, give him the two thousand and fifty dollars I loaned him so he can pay me back."

"Not a problem." Mona opened her purse, wrote Katherine a check for the full amount. She shoved Katherine into the hallway and flung the check in Katherine's face. It floated to the floor. "Here, bitch. If this is all it takes to buy your uppity ass, bank on the fact that you won't get Lincoln back. And if he tells me you're lying about the money you claim he owes you, I'll stop payment on this check before you can cash it."

Katherine looked at the check, hesitated, then picked it up, put it in her purse. "I don't want him anymore. I hate him and I hate you! This drama is so unladylike. He's all yours," she said, throwing her hands in the air, repeated, "All yours."

"Um-hum. Thought so. You ain't gave me shit. I took him from you," Mona said.

"Just like I'm going to take Steven away from you," Katherine said, rolling her suitcase down the same carpet Mona had traveled fifteen minutes ago.

"Why don't you tell our story on national news," Mona yelled, slamming the door.

Hopefully this was the last she'd see of or hear from Katherine. She needed to go home and take care of her kid instead of chasing a man across country.

Now that Katherine knew where Mona and Lincoln were, Mona was more concerned with Katherine telling Steven. How much did she know? Steven was definitely jealous enough to show up in Seattle. Katherine might not be bluffing. And he was crazy to make good on his threat, "I'll kill the next one too, if I have to."

Mona would kill Steven before she'd let him harm Lincoln.

Lincoln
Chapter 50

November 2010

As Lincoln roamed the streets of Seattle, it started to rain. That prostitute's worst nightmare would confront her if he caught her with his money. Determined to find the chick that had stolen all his cash, Lincoln stormed down Lenora Street toward P.F. Chang's.

At every corner he stopped. His head snapped to the left. He closed one eye, focusing on distance. Trying to spot the lady in five-inch heels and a short pink dress who left her thong in his room, the eagle-eyed precision he'd used while in Afghanistan beamed with magnified intensity. He turned the opposite direction, scanned both sides of the street.

There were too many people — mostly interracial couples, white females clinging to black men — for him to see past all of them. Some of the men and a couple of women he recognized from the VA clinic. Maybe the prostitute's stroll was over, but his hunt was just getting started.

Clenching his fist, he shouted to the sky, "I declare war!"

People around him scattered. Lincoln realized that taking that female to his hotel room had complicated his situation. It was Saturday evening. He needed the kind of help Katherine couldn't give him. The Prime Care doctor could help by refilling his prescription, but the clinic was closed. Monday was too far away. Drugs. He needed drugs to take the edge off of his anxiety so Katherine wouldn't witness his other side. He had no choice but to self-medicate with an off-the-shelf substance.

The things he'd done to that prostitute earlier he wouldn't dare do to Katherine. Not intentionally. The sex was rough the way he liked it now. He didn't care about the hooker's feelings. She was paid twenty dollars to service him. He knew he shouldn't have fucked her raw, but he did. Compared to being shot at for years, having unprotected sex meant nothing. Lincoln shouldn't have rammed his dick up the prostitute's ass, but he did. He shouldn't have taken his dick out of her ass, stuck it in her pussy, then made her perform oral sex on him, but he'd done that too.

All the rough sex he'd had with her did not include him coming. That had made him frustrated, angry to the point of wanting to beat her. But he didn't. What else had he done to her? The last thing he recalled was her telling him to relax, her making him a warm cup of tea, then watching him gulp it down. Next thing he remembered, Katherine was at his door.

Stopping in front of a small café with two tables and a few chairs outside, he placed his hand over his heart. His breaths grew shorter and closer together.

"Are you okay, mister?" a little boy asked.

Lincoln stared at the kid. His eyes narrowed. "Get away from me!" he yelled, then ran fast as he could for as long as he could in his combat boots. He screamed, "My God, please take the demons away."

Staring at the flashing red hand, he stopped in the middle of the crosswalk, dropped to his knees in the middle of the street. He prayed for a car, a truck, a bus, or a miracle to end it all. A driver slammed on his brakes. Lincoln motioned for him to keep coming.

Covering his ears, Lincoln pleaded, "No. Don't stop! Please don't stop," to the driver slamming on his brakes. The bass from the car thumped hard enough for him to feel the beat moving the ground beneath him.

That little boy he'd seen moments ago didn't look much different from the kid that had the suicide bomb strapped to his body when Randy was killed. Not much different from some of the kids he'd killed in order to save his own life. Tears poured into his gritty hands as he bowed his head to the asphalt. He cried, "Why me? What did I do to deserve this?"

I know I'm going crazy, but I can't stop it. Can't stop them. Can't stop the demons from creeping into my head.

Someone tapped his shoulder. "Get up, man. Are you okay? Are you all right, dude?" the stranger asked, trying to lift him to his feet.

Lincoln pushed the guy away, sprinted. Three blocks back in the direction of the hotel, there she was. "You!" he shouted.

The woman in the red heels and short pink dress ran. He chased her. "You gon' give me back my money!"

Money. All he'd worked for was gone. Money. A piece of paper dictated the quality of his life. She ran fast. He ran faster. Closing the gap, he was steps away from tackling her.

Stretching his arms, he yelled, "That's

right. I'm on your ass."

He grabbed her hair. "I got you!"

She stumbled. Her left, then right shoe flew high in the air. Her body fell to the ground. A long, jet-black wig was clenched in his fist. She tucked her arms, rolled her body toward him like a bowling ball, sprang to her feet, then ran in the opposite direction.

Lincoln stared at the wig, slammed it to the ground as he stood watching the barefoot woman run down Lenora Street. Maybe they were more alike than they were different. Perhaps she was one of him, a war vet trying to survive.

Katherine was probably wondering what was taking him so long. Lincoln wasn't sure he was ready to go back to the room to see Katherine, to see pictures of Jeremiah. What if the pictures freaked him out? What if seeing his son triggered a panic attack?

The worse feeling was that Lincoln never knew what would cause him to explode or how he'd respond. He made his way back to the hotel, crossed the street, then entered the liquor store.

"Give me as much whiskey as I can get for this fifty," he said, slapping the bill on the counter.

STEVEN
CHAPTER 51

November 2010

The conversations in his head had gotten old. He was tired of bitching to himself about how his wife had betrayed him. How revenge was inevitable. Yeah, yeah, yeah. He scolded himself, "Do something about it or shut the hell up."

Steven exited the plane at Montgomery International. He sat at the gate for a few minutes flooding his mind with evil thoughts of all the things he'd do to get back at Mona.

People watching, he wondered, How many holiday travelers were in transit to unite with partners they couldn't stand? He mouthed, "Mona Lisa, your days are numbered. For real this time."

A woman could seriously fuck up a man's mind. His wife was probably somewhere all bubbly sexing another man while he was sitting in an airport sexually deprived. No more masturbating for him. The next time he came, he'd come inside of a woman.

Smoking, downing a bottle of whiskey, and being with another woman might help ease his tension if he didn't get blue-balls. Steven stood, shook his legs to adjust his erection, made his way to baggage claim. Maybe he'd lie, say he'd tried to locate Mona, post his divorce in the newspaper, and get him another wife without Mona knowing.

What type of woman would love him? He never thought of himself as attractive and doubted Katherine ever noticed him in an intimate way.

With the exception of giving her those earrings and few thousand dollars, he hadn't done anything for or with the woman. He wasn't a complete stranger to Katherine. He might have a chance if he treated her and her son well.

Women generally liked men that were good to their kids. Christmas was coming up in a few weeks. He could buy her son more presents than he'd imagine getting for the holidays. Buy her a new car she couldn't afford, and if he were lucky she'd show her gratitude. Sex him real good. Maybe even fall in love with him.

Most women appreciated a good man but

didn't want one. Mona wasn't . . . after all he'd done for her. *Forget her.*

"Steven."

Now he was hearing voices. He imagined someone called his name.

"Steven."

This time he was certain. He looked over his shoulder. The one person he wanted to see was the person he saw dragging her luggage, strolling toward him.

"Katherine?" he said, smiling wide. *Damn, she looks better in person.* Not wanting his manhood to greet her first, he said, "Odd meeting you here. Where're you coming from, or going to, I should ask?"

She had on a black dress and heels. Her makeup was fresh, lipstick inviting. He longed to kiss her lips, but that would be inappropriate. Didn't keep him from lusting. His dick expanded an inch or two down his leg.

"Good to see you," she said, giving him a hug.

Her perky breasts pressed against his chest. He hugged her. *Damn.* She wasn't wearing a bra. *Were those her nipples he felt?* He didn't want to let go, but he had to. If no one was watching, and if she'd let him, he'd bend her over the carousel, take her for a ride on his horse.

"You were in Bakersfield two days ago. You didn't tell me you were coming home."

"A lot can happen in two days," he said, thinking about where he'd left Davis's body.

Katherine exhaled. "Isn't that the truth."

"I needed to come home and check on my parents and my house. I should rent my place, but then what would I do with all my things?"

"You mean yours and Mona's things. Sorry, I shouldn't have said that. Your parents, they're okay?"

He was hoping Katherine would've taken the bait and inquired about renting his house. What grown woman wanted to live with her mother? "They're fine. Just being a good son," he said, hoping to gain cool points.

"Are they picking you up?" she asked, standing tall. Her breasts thrust forward.

Trying not to focus on wanting to feel those nipples against his chest again, he answered, "No, I'ma hop on the bus."

"No, you will not. You don't have to do that. I'm parked in long-term, so you're riding with me. That is, if you don't mind my little sedan." She headed toward the parking exit.

Taking her bag, he followed her. Her ass was amazing. The way her dress separated her cheeks made him want to separate them more.

"Jeremiah and I both could use more leg room, but my car is almost paid for," she said, laughing. "I'm going to use the check Mona wrote me to pay it off. That is, if it's any good."

Steven froze behind her in the shuttle doorway. "What did you just say?"

Katherine sat and placed her purse on her lap. "My car is almost paid for. I'm going to pay it off."

"With?"

"The check Mona wrote me."

"That's what I thought I heard." Not wanting the other riders ear hustling, he sat quickly and was quiet until they arrived at her car at long-term parking.

When she unlocked her car, he opened the driver's door. "Get in. I've got our bags." Steven tossed both bags in the trunk, hurried to the passenger side. Getting in Katherine's car, he said, "Mona Lisa Cunningham wrote you a check. What for?"

"I loaned —" she said, then stopped. "It doesn't matter. Long story. The check is in her maiden name. I just better not see her crossing the street while I'm driving."

The bitterness in her words mirrored his sentiments about Mona. He wanted to ask

Katherine about Lincoln, but he wasn't prepared to hear her say, "I love him." If Steven got involved with Katherine, he'd have to help raise Lincoln's son. He could handle that, but would Lincoln be cool with it?

"Like that? You'd run over her?" he said. "What you're saying doesn't make sense. Why would you do that?"

"Yes, exactly like that," Katherine said, untying the scarf around her neck.

"Damn! What happened to you?"

"Mona Lisa happened, that's what. That crazy woman strangled me."

He shook his head. One of the things he loved about Mona was she had backbone. Steven doubted Katherine fought back while Mona choked her. But when were they close enough for all that to happen?

"You might have to keep a scarf on for a few days until that heals. Otherwise, a lot of people are going to call into the station asking more questions than me."

"I know. She did this on purpose. She's the most evil woman I know."

"That makes two of us. But you can always sue her or have her arrested," he said.

"No, my reputation is more important than Mona. She'll get hers."

He still wanted to know where she saw

Mona but would ask her later. Instead he asked, "Can I see the check she wrote you?"

Frowning, Katherine questioned, "Why?"

"Just curious."

"About?"

"Never mind," he said, not wanting to force the issue. He'd find another way to see the check. He was determined.

Katherine stopped at a red light, dug into her purse, handed him the check, then drove slowly when the light changed to green.

They'd be on the U.S. 80 for at least a half hour. Long enough for him to get to know her better. Best if she didn't learn too much about him, so he'd ask most of the questions.

Damn, so that's where she banks. Why didn't I figure that out? It is the only major bank in both Selma and Bakersfield. "Can I keep this?"

"What?" Katherine slowed down, glanced at him for a second. "No, you cannot. I told you I'm paying off my car with that money."

"Okay. Calm down, Miss Independent Woman. I'll double the amount. But I need to keep this check."

"Double?"

"Double. And a date. Let me take you out," he said, admiring the way her dress dipped between her thighs. When she glanced at him, his eyes darted toward hers.

"Double and a date. It's a deal. But business before pleasure. When can I get my check?"

"Tonight," he said with a smile.

He wasn't sure how long it had been for her, but it had been way too long for him. If he were luckier, he'd get a date and get laid.

MONA
CHAPTER 52

November 2010

Ten hours had passed since she'd kicked Katherine out of Lincoln's hotel room. Where in the world was he? Had Mona escaped being unhappy with one man only to face being disappointed by another? He had to come back; his gun was in the drawer, his backpack on the floor.

Were Katherine and Steven setting her up? Why was Katherine in Lincoln's room naked? He'd better not have fucked her. Mona felt trapped in the unknown. So many questions, but there was no one to question.

If she left the room, she couldn't get back in unless Lincoln was there. In case she had to leave abruptly, she refused to get too comfortable. She'd showered earlier, put on a fresh pair of underwear and her old clothes.

She could check into a separate room.

Maybe the room next door was unoccupied. Wasn't like Lincoln knew she was there. If she were in 12124, she'd hear him come in. She could knock on his door. If he asked about Katherine, she could go off on him and say, "Why the hell you asking me about her? You invited her to see you too?"

Kicking Katherine out and staying in his room was her right. He'd invited her. Mona picked up the cordless, pressed the dining button. "Yes, I'd like to order two steak dinners medium, a bottle of merlot. Make that two bottles of merlot. Two large bottles of water. And a pint of strawberry ice cream."

The ice cream with chilled strawberries could drizzle between her vaginal lips and give her orgasmic chills. If Lincoln arrived in time for dessert, he could taste her stickiness. If not, she'd entertain herself, then shower again. At the moment, Mona was what she hadn't been in years — bored.

"That'll be one hundred forty-seven dollars cash."

Cash meant Lincoln didn't have a credit card, or like she'd done in Bakersfield, he didn't give them his credit card to cover incidentals. "No problem," Mona said, ending the call.

She stood in the window. If Lincoln never showed up, at least she had enough money to leave, but where would she go? Definitely not back to Selma anytime soon. Didn't want to deal with her mother's suspicions. Maybe Katherine called Lincoln. They could be cozy and she could be lying naked next to Lincoln at a different hotel or in a different room.

Mona dialed the front desk. "Katherine Clinton's room."

The receptionist said, "Hold, please."

"Aw, hell, no. This can't be happening."

"We don't have a guest by that name," the receptionist said.

Mona exhaled with relief. But where was Lincoln? He had to come back for his things. "Ughhh!" She'd give him until tomorrow. If he wasn't back by then, she'd leave.

The keycard lock clicked.

Mona hopped with joy. She wasn't sure if she wanted to get in the bed, bury herself under the sheet, and surprise him or hide behind the door. Or in the bathroom. She grabbed the white down-feather comforter, wrapped herself up to her neck, then stood facing the window with her back to the door.

The door opened, then closed.

"I'm sorry, baby," he said. "I should've been back earlier."

Mona sniffed the air. The familiar stench

of whiskey invaded her nostrils. She heard a loud plop, turned around. He was facedown on the mattress fully dressed.

Standing at the edge of the bed, she turned his head sideways to get a clear view. "What happened to you?"

There was no response. Lincoln didn't move. His face was covered with dirt. She removed the combat boots from his feet. Undressed him. She checked his pockets — room key, ID, and thirty-six cents. After placing his items on the nightstand, she got the plastic laundry bags from the closet, put his clothes in one. She tossed his filthy shoes into the other bag. Surely they could clean a pair of combat boots. Sitting at the desk, she filled out the dry cleaning slips, then hung the bags outside the door.

Knock, knock, knock. "Room service."

Mona tossed the comforter on top of Lincoln. Opening the door, she'd forgotten about the steak dinners but was glad food had arrived. "Please be as quiet as possible," she whispered. "You can roll the table over there." She pointed at the space between the wall and the bed.

She glanced at the check. An eighteen percent gratuity was included. She gave the delivery person one hundred and fifty dollars, then closed the door, secured the latch.

Sitting on the edge of the bed, she poured a glass of wine, then carved tiny pieces of steak. As she sipped the merlot, she stared at Lincoln.

Freshman year at Selma High, he was the sexiest boy she'd ever seen. All the girls were flirting with him, including her. Mona noticed how he walked tall and proud like he was a superstar. Later they'd all find out that William Lincoln was more than a star; he was a savior of sorts. He saved the football program from being terminated. Led their school to championships four years in a row for the first time in the school's history. He stood up to bullies who picked on smaller kids. He'd always done what was right for others.

On their first date, he didn't try to go all the way with her. Although her hormones were racing to feel his naked flesh next to her innocent body, he took his time, waited until she convinced him she was ready.

Finally, tenth grade, they went all the way. Afterward, she'd worried if he'd treat her the same the next day. Would he respect her? Would he still love her? Would he tell everyone?

The next day he'd brought her a signed football to school. Said, "Hey, Mona Lisa. Catch."

She'd caught the ball with one hand, tucked it to her side like he'd taught her. When she looked down, the ball was signed, "Lincoln loves Mona Lisa forever . . . my gurl . . . 09/01/1998. At fifteen she thought love was forever. Now that she was twenty-eight, sitting less than two feet from him, she knew she was right.

Tossing footballs, rolling around on the field, kissing him in the hallway between classes were some of her best memories. When he'd wrapped his arms around her she felt safe, like nothing or no one could hurt her, except him. She still felt that way.

Mona exhaled. Deep in her heart she realized he was still the love of her life. She knew there was a purpose for her being there with Lincoln. She prayed the purpose was positive. Why wouldn't it be?

STEVEN
CHAPTER 53

November 2010

What a difference one woman made in his overall attitude toward women. His wife made him hate women. He'd invested too much in her. Trying to make her life his life, he realized work, Mona, and conversations with his parents were his only constants.

The woman who gave him a ride home yesterday made him want to fall in love with her. He thought he loved his wife, couldn't live without her. His wife made him laugh, but she didn't make him happy.

Steven clapped his hands, stomped his foot, nodded his head while singing aloud, "I'm gonna have a little talk with Jesus . . . Tell Him all about my troubles . . ." He sat in church between Katherine and Jeremiah. Ms. Clinton was seated three pews in front of them.

Although his visit to the house of the Lord was an unanticipated first date, it brought him back to his childhood roots. He knew a lot of lyrics to quite a few of the spiritual hymns he'd learned growing up. Would God really forgive him for *all* he'd done? There was only one way to find out, but Steven wasn't ready to fully repent for his sins and he did not get up when the pastor said, "The doors to the church are open." He had a few more premeditated sins to commit before giving his life to the Lord.

Katherine whispered in his ear, "Thanks for coming with us."

He smiled, nodded. The pleasure was truly his. Funny how one person could have a positive impact in his life. Katherine made him want to be a better man. Though he'd admit he led Mona down a crooked path, Mona never made him want to detour.

"Do we have any visitors with us today?" the pastor asked.

Three people stood. Katherine tapped his knee. He shook his head.

No way. The way he saw it, they were all visitors, transients. He wasn't different from the so-called members that showed up every now and then or on holidays. Maybe he'd be back next Sunday. It was too soon to make that commitment.

"Will the church stand for the benediction," the pastor said, lifting his hands to the congregation. "May the Lord watch between you and me, when we are absent one from another . . . Amen."

When church ended, Steven said, "Jeremiah, why don't you come with me while your mother talks with her church members. We'll be outside," Steven told Katherine.

Katherine smiled. "Make sure you keep an eye on my baby."

A way to a mother's heart was through her kids. For Steven, that was common sense. He heard what she said, but his thoughts heard, "Baby, keep an eye on my baby." Twenty-four hours in and they were off to a decent start. At least he hadn't done anything she hadn't approved of.

Deciding to let Katherine take the lead on establishing their relationship, he chose to do things that he hoped would make him irresistible. Unlocking his car, Steven told Jeremiah, "Look at what I have," holding up a football. "Let me see how good you can catch."

Jeremiah threw his suit jacket on the seat. "Let me see how good you can throw. And don't be afraid to go long," he said, running into the open field next to the church.

Steven motioned for Jeremiah to go farther back. "Keep going. A little more." He threw the football about twenty feet.

Jeremiah snagged the ball with one arm. The same way his dad used to do in high school. "Told ya! I'm good! Let's go for thirty!" he yelled, firing the ball back.

Steven threw the ball about thirty feet, and Jeremiah jumped in the air, caught the ball with two hands this time. Steven was impressed.

They got about two dozen throws in before Katherine came to the field. "Okay, that's enough. Let's go."

"Mom, Mr. Cunningham is great! Can he come to my game Saturday?"

"Have you asked him?"

"Mr. Cunningham, can you come to my game on Saturday? Please," Jeremiah asked, tossing the ball in the air and making it spin.

"If it's okay with your mom, I'd love to come."

The part about "I'd love to come" applied more to Katherine than it did to Jeremiah.

Katherine smiled. "We'd love for you to come."

Hopefully he wouldn't have to wait until Saturday to find out if Katherine tasted better than Mona Lisa. "Let's go get something to eat," Steven said, leading the way to his car.

MONA
CHAPTER 54

November 2010

"Wake up! Wake up!"

Mona Lisa sprang forward, sat up straight. Her heartbeat felt like a snake's tail rattling in her chest. Her neck stiffened, eyes stretched wide. "What are you doing? Are you crazy?" She closed her eyes, fell backward onto the pillow. "Please don't point that gun at my face." Heaving, she held her chest.

The memory of Davis lying in his own blood flooded her mind. What had Steven done with Davis's body? What would Lincoln do with her body if he killed her? "Mama, I've got to make my own mistakes" echoed in her head. If she died right here, would her mother care enough to have her body flown back to Selma? Would she have a respectable funeral? Would Steven find out about all her money and get it?

"Sit the fuck up!" he demanded.

She sat in a slumped position, praying he wouldn't pull the trigger that his finger touched. His naked flesh stood before her. His manhood hung low. Maybe she should've left his boxer briefs on him.

"Where the fuck are my shoes? My clothes? My laptop? My drawers? And where the fuck is Katherine?" he asked, pointing the gun at her head. "Don't fucking lie to me or I swear I'll shoot you."

Mona Lisa scooted back on the bed, leaned against the headboard. She pulled the covers over her naked body. "I . . . oh, damn." That was his laptop she'd tossed in Katherine's luggage. "Katherine took your laptop when she left."

Lincoln shook his head. "She wouldn't do that. You're lying!" He moved closer to her, shoved the tip of the gun deep into her temple. "Where the fuck are my shoes? My shoes, bitch. Where the fuck are they?"

Bitch? If he didn't have that gun to her head, she'd have his bitch, all right.

"Those boots stunk up the place. I put them outside the door last night so they could be dry cleaned."

He ran to the door, snatched it opened. "There ain't shit out here! Why you fucking messing with me? Why are you here?"

Okay, trying to explain things to him

wasn't working. "I'll go get your shoes and your clothes," she said, getting out of bed.

Slam! He closed the door with brute force. The framed picture above the bed fell flat onto the mattress.

"Damn! What's wrong with you?" She escalated her voice, hoping someone would hear them arguing and report their disturbance. "Obviously you invited me and Katherine here. You're trying to play the both of us and maybe you're the one who got played. I told you, she took your laptop. And she left you that ring that she claimed you gave her the same day you gave me mine." Mona pointed to the night-stand next to the bed. "And you know what? You can have this one back too!" Mona said, throwing her ring to the floor.

She wanted to pitch the cheap silver band at his stupid head, but that might make him hurt her. "I'll go get your clothes," Mona Lisa said, quickly putting on her pants and shirt, no underwear. Getting out of Lincoln's room alive was her priority.

He started crying like a baby, then abruptly stopped. He shook his head, picked up the cordless. "Yeah, do you have a dry-cleaning order for me?"

Regretting she'd ever touched his clothes, Mona eased toward the door. If she couldn't escape, at least she could lock herself in the bathroom and call for help.

He hung up the phone, then ran to her. "Where do you think you're going, soldier? You don't leave until I say so." He snatched her biceps, pulled her an inch from his face. "You're not going anywhere until somebody brings me my clothes, and that's an order."

Whoa. His mental instability was frightening. Did he know who she was? Did he know who he was?

"I can buy you more clo—"

His massive hand choked the remaining words down her throat. She couldn't breathe. Clawing at her own neck, she struggled to wedge her fingers beneath his. Suddenly her feet were no longer touching the floor. She tried kicking, but her legs barely moved.

"You'd better pray my boots come back, or I'll have your head on a platter," he said, releasing her to the floor. "You won't be so lucky next time, Mona Lisa Ellington."

Her body slid to the carpet. Afraid if she got up he'd flash again, she decided to lie there until his clothes were delivered. What in the world happened to him? She wished it was all a game of flag football, but this was real. Now she understood this might be the reason why he hadn't contacted her sooner. She almost wished he hadn't called her at all. She thought about sitting up slowly.

Poop, poop, poop, poop, poop, poop, poop. The familiar nonstop puttering of a helicopter hovered over the hotel.

He ran to the window. Peeped between the curtains. Looking over his shoulder, he yelled at her, "Stay down, soldier!"

Tears clouded her vision. She blinked them away. The man who always wanted to do what was right for others no longer knew the difference between right and wrong.

His naked body dove onto the carpet, then crawled toward her. He whispered, "We have to stay quiet until it's safe to fire back. The one thing we never do, soldier, is retreat."

There were so many things she wanted to say but didn't dare mention. His upper body covered hers. His palm pressed against the nape of her neck, forcing her to kiss the carpet.

Knock, knock, knock. "Laundry service."

Lincoln's eyes widened. He sat up, braced his back to the wall, pointed his gun at the door.

Mona lifted her head, then whispered, "It's okay. It's your shoes."

"My shoes?" he said, sounding like a two-year-old.

First she wanted to escape from him. Now she realized she had to protect him. "Yes, baby. Your shoes. I'll get them for you. You sit right here on the floor."

Slowly, Mona got up, cracked the door just enough to take his belongings, then shut the door. She opened the heaviest bag first, held up his clean combat boots, sat them beside him.

He snatched them, peeped inside. Shoving on his left boot, then his right, he cried, "Randy, I thought I'd lost you, man. I promise I won't ever let this happen again."

Randy? Who was that?

Lincoln got up, sat on the bed with nothing but his shoes on, stared at the black flat screen. He spread his feet six inches apart, interlocked his fingers, then stared at the floor. He whispered, "I need help, Mona Lisa. The things I've seen and the things I've done . . ." His words trailed off. Tears fell, staining his newly cleaned boots.

Mona sat beside him. "I'm not here to hurt you. I'm going to help you. You want me to call Randy?" she asked, holding his hand.

Again in a childlike voice, still staring down, he answered, "I can't. Randy is dead."

She knew a part of William Lincoln was dead too. His sadness made her sad. Quietly she sat beside him, held his hand. Mona had no idea what it was like to lose a best friend because she'd never had one.

KATHERINE
CHAPTER 55

December 2010

"Five, four, three, two." The producer pointed at her.

"Good morning to you, America, I'm Katherine Clinton. A house fire erupted an hour ago near the six hundred block of King Street. The oldest child, a seven-year-old, is being considered a hero. The boy and his two siblings were trapped in the blaze. From the second story of their burning home, the little boy tossed his one-year-old baby brother and two-year-old sister into the arms of firefighters standing on the ground before jumping from the window himself. The blaze is almost fully contained. The whereabouts of the mother and father are unknown. The cause of that fire is under investigation. We'll keep you updated. . . ."

Reporting had become second nature to her. The good and the bad, she left it all at the station. Katherine wished Lincoln could've left what happened overseas, overseas. Lincoln hadn't called her since the day she'd left Mona Lisa in his room.

The pain in her heart for Lincoln gradually became an illusion, while the love in her heart for Steven became an evolving reality. Was it smarter to love the one who loved you? Or did love mean waiting for her son's father to make them a family?

Katherine went to her makeup room, sat in front of the mirror surrounded by bright bubble lights. Every day she sat here, she felt like a star. She retrieved her purse from the locked drawer beneath the table, pulled out her cell phone. Dialed his number.

The phone rang three times before he answered. "I've been meaning to call you. I've been through a lot late—"

There comes a time when a woman has to take charge of her heart.

Interrupting him, she said, "Save it, Lincoln. I'm not calling for an explanation or an apology. I'm calling to let you know you owe me fifty-six thousand dollars and I want every penny. If you don't want to see Jeremiah, that's going to be your decision, but I'm going to petition the courts to order you to pay child support. I hope Mona Lisa gave you back your ring, because I'm done with you." She wished being done meant being over him. But it didn't. But in time, she would be.

"No, Katherine, don't say that. I do want to see my son, you know that. I never said I didn't want to see him. I'll be home for Christmas, and I'll get you some money before Christmas, I promise. And I still want to marry you. It's just that I have to get professional help for my condition first."

Was there a limit to how many times a person should be a fool for the same person? The tone of his voice was starting to irritate her.

"Blah, blah, blah. Save it. Is that what you told Mona? Everything isn't about you, Lincoln. I'm sorry for you and for whatever happened to you while you were in the military, but there are no excuses as to why you've treated me like shit for the past ten years. And like a fool I waited for you. Nothing I do anymore is about you. It's about me. If I don't have my money by Christmas, I don't care if the court takes all of your money. You'll get exactly what you deserve. Goodbye. Oh, and tell Mona Lisa I'm not done with her yet. Bye, Lincoln."

Ending the call, Katherine felt relieved. Whether she filed with the court before Christmas or not was not the point. Lincoln needed to know she was done with him.

Her phone rang. "What, Lincoln?"

"My laptop. Mona said you took it."

"Correction, she gave it to me when she packed my things and kicked me out of your room. I'm giving the laptop to Jeremiah as one of his Christmas presents. He needs a computer for school. And that doesn't count toward your child support. Bye."

Ending the call, she exhaled heavily, refreshed her makeup, made her way to the green room. This time instead of her mother waiting, Steven was there.

He greeted her. "For you. For appreciation of your friendship." The dozen long-stem white roses were the first bouquet any man had given her. Katherine's smile was wide and tight as she blinked away her tears. "Why are so nice to me?"

"Because you deserve it," he said. "You ready?"

"Depends. Ready for what?" She was ready for a real man in her life. And Steven deserved to have a real woman. Not some immature, unfaithful trifling wife like Mona Lisa. Mona and Lincoln deserved one another.

Steven interrupted her thoughts. "I have one more surprise for you," he said, leading her out the front door.

When she saw the beautiful red bow sitting atop a brand-new white Mercedes ML350 SUV, she said, "No way. I can't accept that. This is too much."

He handed her the keys. "You can leave it there if you'd like. It'll be there tomorrow when you come back to work. But since I drove it over here, I was hoping you'd give me a ride home."

As she tiptoed to the passenger side, her knees trembled with every step. She peeked inside.

"Just touch the handle," Steven said, standing behind her so close she felt his breath on the back of her neck.

When she touched the inside of the door handle, the doors unlocked. He opened the door. "Get in. I'll drive us to my house. You're too nervous."

En route to his house, she asked, "Why do some men act like parenting is optional or part-time? I don't regret having Lincoln's baby, but as much as I spend on Jeremiah I should've been able to buy this car if I wanted to. But I can't afford this. Am I wrong if I keep Lincoln's laptop and give it to my son?"

Steven stopped the car. "You have his laptop? How? Why?"

"Mona packed it in my suitcase before she put my bag in the hallway. Obviously she thought it was mine."

"What if there's something on his hard drive that you wouldn't want your son to see? Give me the laptop and I'll buy Jeremiah a new one. But take me home first."

Katherine was tired of talking about Lincoln and thinking about Mona. "So is this your way of getting me to your house?"

"I'm not gonna lie. Yes, it is. You don't have to come in if you don't want to. But I hope you come in for a little while."

The SUV was a dream come true and she was most grateful. But Katherine didn't want to go in his house. Not because she didn't want to give herself to him. She'd decided that a week ago, before he'd given her a Mercedes.

"Can I be honest?" she asked, touching his hand.

"I'm not taking this car back."

"I'm not giving it back." She wasn't that proud that she'd give back a man's gift. Her mother taught her that a woman had to learn how to accept a man's gifts without attaching her own strings or allowing him to tie strings to her.

"Be honest about what?" he asked.

Clearing her throat, she said, "I haven't come inside your house, one, because you're married. And two, because you're married to Mona Lisa. She's not wrapped too tight, and I just don't feel right having feelings for you while you're married to her."

If he asked for his SUV back, that would be understandable. If he didn't, that would be okay too. She wasn't attached to material things and his circumstances made her feel detached from him.

He drove up his long driveway, parked her car in front of his garage. "How about we enter through the front door and you can stay in the living room? I'll make us lunch. Then I can tell you about my plans for Mona Lisa. That check you gave me came in handy."

"The living room. How far away is the bathroom? In case I have to go."

"Not far enough," he said.

They laughed for a moment. She'd seen the way he looked at her in a man's eyes before. In Lincoln's eyes. The lingering, lustful look that said, "I want you so bad."

"There's a bathroom off the hallway. It's by the bedroom, but this one isn't inside the bedroom. You'll be okay. If you start to feel uncomfortable, you can leave. I'll pick up the laptop tonight."

His words about her leaving comforted her. His going to church with her allowed her to trust him a little more. His closeness to her son and the fact that her mom liked him made her want to like him a lot. But she couldn't. That wasn't the smart thing to do. But was love smart?

No, love wasn't. They say if it's too good to be true, it usually is.

CHAPTER 56

December 2010

The fact that Katherine wanted nothing to do with him bothered him more than Mona doing everything for him. He'd never asked for a handout. Wasn't used to a woman providing for all his needs, including sex.

Mona called from his living room, "Come on, Lincoln, darling. We're gonna be late for your appointment with your Prime Care doctor. And we have to go to Bed Bath and Beyond and get a blanket. Then we can eat at the Hard Rock Cafe. And our last stop will be to pick up the Christmas tree."

Practically overnight, Mona had furnished his entire one-bedroom apartment down to the silverware in the kitchen drawer. The living room had a cerulean suede sofa on one side and two big, black high-back suede chairs with wing sides on the other side. A crystal coffee table divided the sofa and chairs. A twenty-inch round table draped with a blue cloth was positioned between the two chairs. A sixty-inch flat screen on an entertainment stand faced the sofa. A surround sound system was wired throughout the apartment. He had state-of-the-art technology, but nothing beat the king-sized bed in his bedroom.

How was he ever going to ask her to leave without her being pissed off? Especially with her paying all his bills and giving him money.

"Give me a few minutes," he said, locking his bedroom door.

It was two weeks before Christmas. He had to call Katherine and his grandmother. He turned on the iPod player Mona had bought. Turned on the woman who turned him on while he was sexing Mona, Nicki Minaj. Nicki's breasts and ass were amazing. Watching her videos excited him. Mona used to excite him, ten years ago. Not now. Her motherly ways were appreciated, but no man wanted to bed his mother.

When Katherine answered, he asked, "Can you ever forgive me? I know I messed up."

"Nothing has changed on our end, Lincoln. Nothing."

Her "nothing" seemed cold. Final.

"I'm coming home in a few days. I'd like

to see my son. Please, Katherine. Can you keep him out of what I owe you?"

"You get the child support papers I sent?" she asked.

"Yeah. I got 'em." She made him regret giving her his address. Said she wanted to send pictures of Jeremiah.

Sternly she asked, "You got my money?"

"I'll get it. I promise. I just need some time."

"Call me back when you've got it."

"Kat—" His phone went silent. "Hello." He glanced at the screen. Her name and number were no longer displayed.

He glanced at the nightstand, picked up Mona's checkbook. This wasn't the first time he'd contemplated doing this. Mona had paid for so much, a few thousand more shouldn't hurt.

Flipping close to the end, he peeled a blank check, put her book back in its place. Better to ask for forgiveness. He had to see his son. Surely she'd understand. He folded the check, opened the Bible his grand-parents sent him to the twenty-third Psalm, placed the check inside, then closed the Bible. He unlocked the bedroom door.

He clapped his hands so hard that he jumped. Scared himself a little. "Whoa." He took a deep breath, shook his head. "Let's get rollin', Mona, baby." He kissed her, followed her out the door. They entered the garage, got into Mona's new black-on-black Lexus GX. If she'd just marry him he wouldn't have to ask her for anything. Her money would become his money. How much money did she have?

"Mona, baby," he said.

"Yes."

"I know you said not to ask again about how you can afford all of this, so I won't, but why haven't you responded to my proposal? Are you ever going to say yes to that?"

She became silent for a moment, looked at him for a few seconds, then said, "I'll give you the right answer at the right time. Let's just focus on getting you to your appointment."

He didn't want to forge her signature to that check, then place it in the bank account she'd opened for him, but he would if he had to. She'd taken him to the bank with the check the government had given him. Said if she needed to transfer money to his account, their banking at the same institution would make it easier. Was she telling the whole truth or did she have an ulterior motive? They'd sat with her banker, and in less than an hour he was also a customer.

"I was wondering. I've never asked anyone for a financial favor. But I was wondering if you could loan me sixty thousand. I told you my grandmother is sick. I want to go home next week before Christmas to see her. And —" He paused, wanting to say, "Forget I asked," but said, "I was hoping to help make her comfortable in her last days. You don't have to answer now. Think about it." His ulterior motive was to see if Mona would hesitate about the dollar amount.

If she wrote the check, he'd get a cashier's check and send fifty-five thousand to Katherine. He'd use the other five to go to Selma and maybe Chicago. And he'd keep his word to Mona and pay her back soon as he could.

She parked in the lot at the clinic. "We'll discuss it later. But if it's for your child support for your son, the answer is hell, no. I don't mind taking care of you, but I'm not supporting him."

That sounded like a no, but he'd wait for a definitive response. If he stuck with his original story, maybe she'd help him out. He should've kept his child support issues from Mona, but she'd asked so many questions that it was easier not to lie to her. If he'd gone to college, then gone pro, he wouldn't be anyone's dependent.

"If you want to go home, I'll get our tickets for Christmas and I'll make our hotel and rental car arrangements," she said.

"And I have a surprise for you tomorrow," he said.

"A surprise? Well, alrighty then, I can't wait. I hope you didn't spend more than the weekly allowance I've put you on. You have to learn how to save money."

He got out of the car, opened her door. She followed him into the clinic. Their wait in the lobby was a half hour before he heard, "William Lincoln." They followed the nurse, waited for her to take his vitals, then the nurse led them to his Prime Care doctor's office.

"Well, hello, William. Hi, Mona," the doctor said. "Now that you're in your new place, things should be better for you, William. I see you brought your friend again. Y'all have a seat."

Better was relative. Yes, he had a roof over his head. Yes, his place was nicely furnished. Yes, he was having sex on a regular basis. No, he wasn't cured from his PTSD. He struggled not to think about anything that would trigger his anxiety.

"I'm trying, doc," he said. Assuming his comfort position, Lincoln stared at the floor between his combat boots.

Tapping him on the knee, Mona whispered, "Look at the doctor when he's talking to you."

The doctor looked at Mona. "Thanks, young lady." He shifted his eyes to Lincoln. "You make sure you keep her around. This here woman cares about you." He tapped on his keyboard, then mumbled, "Now, let me see . . . ah, yeah. Do you need any med refills, William?"

Lincoln hated that herding cattle feel. In and out in ten minutes, then the doctor was on to the next patient.

Mona answered, "Yes, he needs a stronger prescription for sleeping because we're going to be on a plane before his next visit. I can't have him freaking out in midflight. And a refill of the antidepressant. And just in case, I think you should give him a prescription for pain. All name brand only. I don't want Lincoln taking generics."

That was sobering. Lincoln wanted to push Mona out of her seat onto the floor for handling him like a kid.

"Well, that's not a problem," the doctor said. "I have that list of therapists you requested. Have you given more thought to sponsoring William's additional health care? More drugs, stronger meds, that's not the solution. William could benefit greatly from having a therapist. Here," he said, handing Mona a list of names. "And he could use a good HMO. My recommendations are on the list too. William will never be cured from PTSD. It's like having HIV —"

Lincoln interrupted, "Excuse me, doc, that's a bad analogy."

"You're right, William. But you get my point. No matter how much meds you take, a panic attack can happen when you least expect it. Maybe hypnosis can help. I don't know. But what I do know is that woman is your guardian angel. Mona, if you have any questions about my referrals, don't call me. Call them."

Mona stood, reached for the prescriptions. "I've got it from here."

Lincoln was done watching the doctor and Mona tag one another as though they were the only two on his team and his opinion didn't matter. He stood, shook the doctor's hand for the first time.

"Oh, I almost forgot. Here's two tickets to the Seattle–Atlanta game on Sunday. Don't bother thanking me. My wife said I can't go."

Mona reached for the tickets. Lincoln beat her to them. Outside the doctor's office, he stopped. He looked down at Mona.

"I'm a grown-ass man. You don't have to

control every damn thing."

She replied, "I do. And I will."

"Then marry me."

"Let's go," Mona said, leading the way.

Steven
Chapter 57

December 2010

Holding on to her morals to not disrespect another woman's home, Katherine refused to sex him in any room of his house. He didn't know if he should believe she was telling the truth about setting standards or if she was using her principles as a way of getting out of having sex with him. Today he was eradicating all obstacles.

"Hey, you were great as usual," he said, handing her a dozen pink roses. He kissed her cheek. "I have a huge surprise for you."

"Thanks, let me put these in water. I'll be right back," she said as she walked away.

From the back, her body was beautiful. Toned calves, smooth silky legs that would feel amazing wrapped around his waist, and shiny dark hair that he longed to run his fingers through.

He could've picked up a few bounty-hunting contracts while in Selma to help keep his mind off of her, but his pursuit of passion took precedence. Luring her in with his lethal tongue was necessary before the inevitable. Eventually she'd have to fuck him or make a choice to either cover up his wrongdoings or report his scandals on the news.

Katherine returned to the green room smiling. "You are unbelievable. Please don't stop spoiling me, but I don't know how many more surprises I can handle."

This surprise might be his if she didn't accept his gift and later follow through with having sex with him. "Let's go." They walked out to the parking lot.

No, she didn't have to sex him because he'd given her an SUV she couldn't afford, paid her son's tuition in full for the remainder of the school year, and gave her enough cash to keep her comfortable. But he was determined to discover why she accepted all he had to offer but wouldn't suck his dick. That was the least she should've done.

"I'll bring you back to your car," he said, opening his passenger door. He got in on the driver's side, leaned over. "I have to blindfold you."

Katherine held up her hands, blocking his. "Oh, no. I'm not letting you do that. Knowing you, your surprise might be a house."

He wasn't ready to be that generous. "Trust me. It's not," he said. After placing the blindfold over her eyes, he drove in the direction of their destination.

The money he'd spent on Katherine, thanks to Katherine giving him that check Mona had given her, was siphoned from Mona Lisa Ellington's bank account, not his. There was more than enough left in Mona's account to buy Katherine a half-million-dollar home on the Alabama River, but if he'd done that, what would there be left to do? She wouldn't need him.

Mona's check had all the information he needed — routing and account numbers as well as her P.O. box — to wire funds to his account. He'd ordered checks from Mona's account, had them mailed to his house, then slowly started depleting her financial resources. Even if Mona discovered the debits, he had a backup plan to achieve his ultimate goal of making his wife penniless.

"We're almost there," he said, driving twenty miles per hour.

"I can't stand it! I want to take this off so bad, Steven. Please, can I?"

Sex him until the last seed spilled out of his balls? Yes.

He liked the way she begged. "I'll let you know when."

The upside of knowing the banker was that the guy had graduated from Selma High the same year as Steven. Initiating casual conversation, he talked about Mona Lisa as though they were the happiest couple. Steven had asked the banker questions about his family, complimented him on his success, then slipped in the request to reorder checks on Mona's account. "Oh, and update the mailing address too," he said, giving the banker his address. If the banker lost his job for being too trusting and casual, that was his problem.

They arrived at Capitol Hill in nearby Prattville. He valet parked, gave the attendant the keys, then hurried to Katherine's side. "Okay, I'm going to take off your mask."

She checked out her surroundings. Frowned at him. "A hotel, Steven? For real? What kind of Christian woman do you think I am?"

"Chill out. We're having lunch. Then I'll take you to your car."

Steven escorted Katherine to the Presidential Cottage, opened the door.

She stood in the hallway staring at him. "Lunch? In a hotel room? Really?"

Exhaling, he said, "I ordered room service. I'll call and let them know we're here. I thought you'd appreciate the privacy since you're a celebrity of sorts."

"I must say this is impressive and a slick move on your part. So I guess this is the part where my panties are supposed to be on the floor and over there?" she said, then laughed.

"Take your time, but that would be nice," he said. She was kidding. He was not.

The spacious suite had a king-sized bed suitable for a queen like Katherine. The comforter, decorative pillows, and old-fashioned wooden headboard faced the fire-place.

Knock, knock. "Room service."

Katherine headed toward the door, opened it. "That was fast."

"You can place the tray in the living area," Steven said.

Everything had been prearranged, including payment for the bill. Two hours tops was all he had before he'd have to take Katherine back to Selma to pick up Jeremiah from school. One solid hour of sex was all he needed.

"We don't have much time. What would you like to do first?" he asked. "Eat or relax in the tub?"

MONA
CHAPTER 58

December 2010

Her heart was filled with secrets. Some she'd cherish. Others she'd buried.

They'd made their way to the football game. Lincoln was so excited one would've thought he'd bought the tickets.

"You're sure you're okay with this crowd?" she asked, worrying about him embarrassing her. They should've watched the game at home on television.

"Baby, I feel great!" he said, sitting in his seat. "I've never been to a professional football game."

Perhaps she should relax. Some of the things she'd taken for granted were big deals for Lincoln.

The announcer said, "Please rise for the national anthem."

Lincoln stood tall, proudly faced the flag, placed his right hand over his heart. She clamped her hands behind her back, faced the field. She hadn't given much thought to the words she'd listened to innumerable times.

The crowd belted, "O'er the land of the free and the home of the brave."

"Land of the free," she thought. *Really?* "And the home of the brave." *Seriously?* Yeah, Lincoln was brave to serve his country, but what had his country done for him? The military was one step above free labor. That was what "the free" meant to her. What would happen if all servicemen protested, demanding higher wages?

She was glad to pay for his treatments. Accompanying Lincoln to his first therapy session two days ago made her consider getting help for the murders she'd witnessed. Her mind wasn't right either. Her coping mechanism was to escape her reality by suppressing images of what happened. It was almost like she'd never met Davis. Like her time with him was all a dream. If she stayed far from Steven, maybe no one would associate her with his killings. If she could push the horrible memories all the way to the back of her mind, maybe they'd stay there.

"Mona Lisa, will you marry me?"

The shocking words he spoke lingered beneath the cheering crowd. It was two minutes until the end of the second quarter. The fans created a wave — one section at a time. They stood, tossed their arms in the air, then sat in their seats. Her could-be-fiancé pointed to the heavens. The banner flying behind the airplane above the field was printed with the same proposal.

The chill bumps on her body traveled from her head to her toes as the crowd gave them another rolling wave. The stadium was packed, the Seahawks were down, and at that very moment the sky grew darker. Rain would be welcomed right now.

Her answer should've been obvious. But it wasn't. He didn't know.

Mona's head hung. Facing her lap, she whispered, "I'm not the marrying kind," as she stared at the pink polish on her finger-nails. The troll genie was in her purse. Was the crowd waving again? The roaring sounds of excitement, the standing ovation in her peripheral vision, gave her relief. Sounded like the home team had tied the game. She prayed the cheers weren't for her.

Genie, please make his proposal go away.

Make the extra point good, she thought, hoping to keep the attention off of her. Why was love so damn unpredictable? How long had he planned his proposal? How much did he spend on the ring he was holding in front of her face? When did he have time to buy a ring? The plane flying the banner must have cost more than he could afford. Where did the money come from? How could she say no?

Rain was always expected from the Seattle clouds, and misery was what she'd grown to expect from marriage. From childhood to adulthood, the unknown lurked in her shadow. One step forward, two steps back. That was the waltz she'd danced all her life until she'd reunited with the man sitting next to her.

If she said yes, would this be the one time she could take a step forward and not get pushed back or knocked down? Mona picked a popcorn crumb from her thigh, then twirled it between her fingers.

Lincoln tilted her chin upward, then kissed her lips. Gazing into her eyes, he said, "I know I've had it hard, baby. Thank you for being here for me. Say you'll be my wife and I promise to love and protect you, always."

She knew he could keep her safe, but she wasn't the person he'd have to protect if he slid his ring over her knuckle and left it there. Her life was more than complicated, it was cursed.

Mona glanced at the banner waving in the

air and prayed the bounty hunter she'd left in Bakersfield wasn't watching the game. Then she prayed Steven wasn't in the stadium. No matter how far she traveled to get away from Steven, she always felt he'd eventually find her.

Looking over her left, then right shoulder, Mona said, "Baby, we need to go. I promise I'll give you an answer when we get home."

The man she loved sat beside her holding a diamond ring in front of her awaiting a response. The plane circled the stadium again with the banner whipping the wind.

Why hadn't he taken her up in a hot air balloon, decorated it with her favorite colors — pink and purple? He could've had a chilled bottle of champagne, got on one knee, and no one would've known except the two of them and God. That's the only witnesses she wanted.

The ring. Surely she couldn't miss the sparkling solitaire in his hand or the fading gleam in his eyes.

He asked again. "Mona Lisa Ellington, will you marry me?"

Mona's silence lingered until halftime was over. Most of the fans resumed watching the game. The ones closest to them mumbled, "If it don't fit, don't force it, dude." "What's wrong with her?" "See, that's why I'm proposing before spending my money on all that other shit like buying a ring."

Softly she said, "I heard you the first time, Lincoln. Give me a moment."

To do what? Let him down easy. Maybe she should tell him about Steven and let Lincoln decide if marrying her was a chance he wanted to take. Things between them weren't perfect, but they were good. She enjoyed using her money to help him recover from his trauma.

Mona Lisa married the wrong man. Her only way out of their marriage was death. That's why she hadn't bothered filing for a divorce. If she said yes to the man she wanted to share the rest of her life with, she knew her husband would kill him too.

KATHERINE
CHAPTER 59

December 2010

"Where'd you get the money?"

"What difference does that make? I gave you what you wanted, now I want to see my son. I'll be in Selma tomorrow."

"Did you get it from Mona?"

She knew Lincoln didn't have that kind of money. Sending her a cashier's check for fifty-five thousand dollars in his name eliminated their court date. What if he filed for custody? Or visitation?

"Who's that on the phone?" Steven asked, kissing her lips.

"It's Lincoln. He's coming to Selma tomorrow."

Steven smiled. It wasn't his normal happy-to-have-pleased-me-first smile. This smile grew like the Grinch's and didn't stop until his lips could spread no wider.

"Ask him if Mona is coming with him."

Katherine asked, "Will you be by

yourself?"

"Tell that nigga in the background I said none of his fucking business. You'd better not have another man raising my son."

Stepping a few feet from Steven, she said, "Are you serious? You've never seen your son."

"Exactly."

"Well, you'd better not bring Mona around my son," Katherine lamented.

"So what's this conversation really about?" Lincoln questioned. "Money or control? I gave you what you asked for. Now give me what I deserve."

Steven moved closer to her, then whispered, "Ask him again about Mona."

"Is Mona coming with you?"

"Put that nigga on the phone! Why is he worried about Mona?"

The conversation grew more complicated by the second. Katherine muted the phone. "Steven, please. This is my situation. Please let me handle this." She unmuted her cell, walked away from Steven, then whispered to Lincoln, "Are you going to marry her?"

"Katherine, where is all this coming from?"

"Answer the question, Lincoln."

"Let's just say she's coming. Whether she's with me or not is irrelevant."

"Call me when you get in. Oh, and just in case you didn't know, if you do plan on marrying Mona Lisa Cunningham, you might be engaged to her for an eternity. She's already got a husband," Katherine said, ending the call.

"Whew! I don't know what to do about this one. Mona is coming too, and I don't want her anywhere near my son."

Katherine collapsed on the king-sized bed in the Presidential Cottage in Prattville. The suite had become their getaway.

Steven pulled her up. "Why did you tell him that Mona was married?"

"Because I don't think he knows. She's stringing him along."

"Don't lie to me, Katherine. Are you still in love with him?"

She nodded. "A part of me will always love William Lincoln. I can't change my past, but I can have a change of heart. Besides, he is Jeremiah's father. I don't want to have this conversation," she said, standing.

"It's okay, baby. So Mona is coming?" Steven asked, guiding her back to the bed.

"You're questioning me about Lincoln, but why are you so obsessed with whether or not she'll be here? Do you still love her?"

Steven leaned his head back, laughed

loud, then seriously said, "No."

He wasn't avoiding answering her question. Katherine crossed her legs, folded her arms across her breasts, sat on the edge of the bed, and became silent.

"I said no. I asked because I can call a lawyer and have the divorce papers prepared and have Mona served while she's here. That way I can do right by you and ask you to marry me."

Was marriage sweeter than the icing on the wedding cake?

From what Katherine Clinton had witnessed of her mother never having been married, her mother's life didn't seem too bad. Sure she struggled as a single mother, but she was at peace with her decision. The incidents Katherine had experienced between couples around her made her question whether married people were happier than those who chose to be single. Married people going through a divorce were some of the most vindictive people she knew.

Would marrying Steven complement or complicate her life?

Steven kneeled beside the bed, opened her legs, slid her hips to the edge, then buried his lips in hers. His tongue fluttered on her pearl. He smothered her pussy with passionate kisses. No man had made her feel so good.

She still hadn't broken her morals. They never had sex in his house. But were her standards correct since she was technically still sexing a married man? She had womanly needs that deserved to be fulfilled. Having her needs met by a man she might like half as much or not at all would still be fornication. Was one sin greater than the other? She'd pray for answers the next time she knelt at the altar.

Her mother loved Steven. Her son was crazy about him. Did they like Steven because of his elaborate gifts or because he was a man who spent lots of money on them?

Katherine's body trembled with womanly pleasure. After she'd finished cuming in his mouth, she returned the favor.

Easing his dick in her mouth, she enjoyed the way his erection felt inside of her. She sucked hard, stroked slow. She sandwiched his manhood between her breasts while sucking his head.

Steven rolled her over, spread her legs, then penetrated. "Baby, I have to feel you raw. Please don't say no. I promise I'll pull out before I cum."

She knew she should've denied him access. Made him put on a condom like they'd done each time before. Her mind said no. Her body rolled him over, straddled his dick, then mounted him. Her body, her hips, her pussy devoured his dick with each stroke.

A lustful, greedy sensation she'd never felt before deep inside her womb had a mind of its own. Grinding. Winding. Thrusting. She found herself moving more than him. She rolled her hips harder.

"That's right, baby. Get it. Get your dick. Ride it, Katherine. That's my girl," Steven said, pushing his dick deep inside her.

"Oh, my God!" she screamed, clawing, his chest.

She felt his throbbing penis releasing sperm so deep inside of her. She doubted the semen had far to travel before breaking through one of her eggs.

In a matter of ten minutes, Katherine prayed she hadn't made another bad decision.

LINCOLN
CHAPTER 60

December 2010

"Where are you spending Christmas?"

"Stop trippin'. I keep telling you, I'm not sure."

"Oh, so you have no problem with me spending my money on you, but you have a problem with me asking you questions? Are you staying at the hotel with me as planned?"

Lincoln sighed heavily. "No. I told you I changed my mind. I'm staying at my grandparents'."

"And I can't stay at your grandparents' so I have to sleep alone at the hotel?"

He really wanted to snap and push her out of the car she'd rented. The drive from Montgomery Regional Airport to his grandparents' house was almost over. His break from Mona was near. Being in the military was unbearable, but Mona was impossible to please.

Looking out his driver's side window, Lincoln suggested, "Why don't you stay at your mother's house until we go back to Seattle after the New Year?"

Bam! Bam! Bam! Mona stumped on the dashboard.

"Pull over to the side of the road," Mona said, grabbing the steering wheel.

"Let go!" he yelled, breaking her grip. "You're crazy!"

"No, you're crazy! What the hell is wrong with you! Are you saying we're not keeping the New Year's Eve plans I made to take you to New York? I just spent a thousand dollars on airline reservations."

The argument wasn't worth it. He'd survived more serious situations. Breathing deeply, he fought to hold back the anxiety attack brewing inside him.

"Like it or not, you are going," she yelled.

Nobody told her to buy those tickets to New York. She was the one who raved about how much fun she had there one summer and how they'd have fun watching the ball drop in Times Square. Maybe if she'd asked him, he would've gone. But the plan was all hers.

"Answer me!" *Slap!* Her hand landed against the side of his face.

His foot pressed the pedal to the floor.

The car accelerated from sixty, to seventy, to eighty, to ninety, to a hundred, to a hundred and twenty. He swerved between cars on U.S. 80. Gaining on a eighteen-wheeler, he cut to the left at the last moment.

"Ahh! Stop it, Lincoln, you're going to kill us!" Mona's eyeballs protruded from the sockets as she gripped the sides of the seat. "I'm sorry! I'm sorry!" She constantly apologized.

Determined to get away from her, he slowed down enough to safely exit and drove straight to his grandparents' house. He held on to the car keys and confronted Mona. "You want to control everything about me. I'm not a child. I have a child I need to see. And when the fuck were you going to tell me," he shouted, "that your ass is already fucking married?"

Mona's jaw dropped. "I, I, I —"

"Save it, Mona! Katherine told me and I didn't want to believe her, but I can see she's the one who told me the truth. Not you!"

He released the trunk, got out of the car, slammed the car door. Mona got out of the car too.

"Let's talk about this," she pleaded.

Lincoln removed his duffel bag from the

trunk, slammed the trunk, then threw the car keys at Mona. The keys hit where he'd aimed, in her chest. He wanted to throw them in her face but didn't want to be responsible for taking her to the hospital if he put her eye out.

"Oh, my God," his grandfather cried out. "Honey, you're not going to believe this."

His grandfather ran to him. Lincoln was prepared to apologize for his treatment of Mona until his grandfather wrapped his arms around him and started crying. "Grandson, it's so good to see you. Your grandmother is really going to think she's died and gone to heaven. Let me take your bag."

"I got it, Grandfather."

"What you think, an old man like me can't carry a heavy load? Boy, give me that bag," he insisted.

Lincoln glanced over his shoulder at Mona. If that was his last time seeing her, it would be all right with him. She sped across the driveway, across the lawn, and onto the street.

His grandfather stopped. Turned around. "Who in the world is that?"

"Nobody important. Just someone who gave me a ride."

Entering the house, Lincoln's grandfather

dropped his bag by the door.

Lincoln had one more of Mona's checks in his bag, and this time he'd write it for enough to cover his expenses for six months. Since she wanted to make him financially dependent, she'd support him his way, not hers.

MONA
CHAPTER 61

December 2010

"Excuse me. Run that by me again?"

"Miss, your debit card transaction wasn't approved," the cashier said.

On her way from Lincoln's grandparents' house yesterday, she'd stopped at the gas station/convenience store across the street from her hotel in Prattville. She was pissed that she'd had to spend the night alone, so she'd downgraded from the Presidential Cottage to a standard room with a king-sized bed. The two bottles of merlot she'd bought last night were empty.

She placed the bottles outside her room, near the door, then made her way back to the convenience store for the cashier to tell her what? She wasn't up for his foolishness. She needed two more this morning and she needed them now!

Had to numb the pain in her heart. After all she'd done for him? Now she understood

how desperately wanting someone who
didn't want you caused people like her
husband to drown their sorrows with alcohol.

Lincoln's fast driving made her accept
responsibility for pushing him too far.
Christmas was five days away. She had to
get back with Lincoln before he got with
Katherine and his son.

"Run it again," Mona insisted, watching
him scan both bottles of wine. She swiped
her card, entered her PIN number.

He shook his head. "It's not approved,
miss."

Mona handed him a fifty to show she
could afford her purchase. She grabbed her
bag, got in her car, and drove straight to
her main bank branch in Selma.

Not signing in or waiting for an invite, she
approached the banker, sat at his desk. She
plopped down her Bakersfield driver's
license and her debit card. "What the fuck
is happening with my account? Why
couldn't I" — she placed the two bottles of
wine and the receipt on his desk — "pay for
this with my card? Why! When I have over
two million dollars at this bank."

He stared at her. "Calm down. We'll get
to the bottom of this."

"Calm down! Don't tell me to calm the

fuck down! It ain't your money, but if you don't figure this out it sure as hell is going to be your problem."

He glanced at her ID. "Hey, your husband was in here about a week and a half ago."

"And?"

"Steven Cunningham, right?"

"And? What does that have to do with my —" Mona froze. *Damn!*

She quieted herself. "Now I really need to know what's happening with my money." After scribbling her account number on a piece of paper, she watched him tap on his computer keys.

He frowned. Tapped on a few more keys. "Damn," he mouthed. "This can't be right."

"What can't be right?" she asked, sitting on the edge of her seat.

He went to the printer, handed her five sheets of paper. "Did you approve these?"

The first check was payable and paid to William Lincoln, sixty grand. The second, to Steven, sixty thousand. The third, to Steven for a hundred grand. The fourth to Steven for two hundred fifty thousand. And the fifth, yesterday for a hundred thousand payable and paid today to William Lincoln, had overdrawn her checking account.

"Is this correct?" the banker asked. "Your

husband reordered checks on your account."

Mona countered, "He's not on my account. Did you approve that?"

"He's not? Are you sure?" The banker's eyes stretched wide. "Um, I can explain. Because he was only reordering checks, I thought it was okay."

She pounded her fist on his desk. "You'd best start looking for another job, mister. Close that account and give me ten thousand dollars cash from one of my CDs. I'll decide by tomorrow where I'm transferring my other investments, but I will not be a customer here and this bank will give me back my money and I don't care if they have to take it out of your check or your ass, you hear me!" Shoving the copies of the checks and the cash in her purse, Mona left the bottles of wine and exited the bank without saying another word.

Sitting in her rental car, Mona dialed Lincoln's cell. No answer. She called again, again, again, and again, but he didn't answer. "That's okay. You can't hide from me forever," she said, driving off.

Mona drove in front of the *Morning to You, America* television studio. "What is this? Fuck with Mona Lisa Day?" Her mouth hung open. She made a U-turn, parked across the street. She could've made a scene that would've prompted any witness to dial 9-1-1. Instead, she sat in her rental outside the studio and watched them.

Steven's car was parked in front of the building. Mona slumped in her seat, watched him. Katherine danced out the door, got into Steven's car. "Aw, hell, no." Mona made another U-turn, followed them. Careful to stay several cars behind, she trailed them all the way to . . . the hotel where she was staying?

She wanted to jump out of her car and commence whipping Steven's ass like she was a guest on an episode of *Cheaters*. Her legs began to shake uncontrollably. She rubbed her thighs. She didn't follow them. If they were checking in, she could find out by calling and asking for Steven's or Katherine's room, but that wouldn't confirm what room they were in. Maybe she could pretend she was Katherine's assistant, say Katherine left her laptop and she had to deliver it to her. *That's stupid, Mona. They'll know you're lying.*

She thought for a moment, then said, "Yeah, that'll work." A smile crept across her face. Mona had the hotel's number stored in her phone from when she'd made her and Lincoln's reservation. Mona retrieved the number, called the front desk.

The receptionist said, "Thank you for —"

Mona cut her off and began speaking really fast. "Yes, this is Detective" — she made up a name — "Casey from the Selma Police Department. We've been advised a Katherine Clinton, news reporter, just entered your establishment with a Steven Cunningham. We have a warrant for Mr. Cunningham's arrest, and we want to make sure Ms. Clinton is not harmed. It's urgent for Ms. Clinton's safety that we know what room they are in." Mona tried to sound official like when she worked for the police department.

"We've never had anything like this happen before. I —"

"Now, miss, now! While you're trying to make a decision, a woman could be murdered in your hotel and you could be charged with obstruction. What room are they in?"

The receptionist blurted, "He's in room ten twenty-nine. That's the Presidential Cottage on the top floor. What else should I do?"

"Nothing. Don't tell anyone. You may have just saved a woman's life. Let us handle this. Don't make any calls or everything could backfire and your guests could be endangered."

"But —"

Mona cut her off again by ending the call. She went directly to the top floor. Used the guest phone in the hallway. Disguising her voice, Mona called their room. "Yes, Mr. Cunningham. Sorry to disturb you, but there seems to be a problem with your SUV."

"A problem? What kind of problem?"

"We're not sure. Please come down to valet immediately."

"Sure," he said. "Baby, something's up with my car. Get her ready for me. I'll be right back."

Baby? Mona hid near the elevators, behind the ice machine. She saw Steven pass by. She heard the elevator ding. Soon as she heard the elevator doors close, she hurried to his room, knocked on the door.

When Katherine opened the door, it was like déjà vu. Her ass was naked. This time Mona Lisa didn't outstay her unexpected visit.

"Go tell this, bitch!" She punched Katherine in the face, dragged her naked ass along the carpet, into the hallway, then closed the door. "And while you're at it, tell Lincoln you're fucking my *husband*." Mona was so angry she kicked Katherine in the ass.

"If you think that hurts, just know that I'm not done with your trifling behind yet," Mona said, walking away. She got on the elevator, went straight to the lobby, got in her car, and drove to Steven's car.

She lowered her window. "You wanna play bitch swap or dick swap? I've got something for your ass too. Keep that bitch. But you're giving me back my money. All of it! By the time I'm done with you, you'll need a new set of balls."

Shit was about to get real ugly really fast.

Mona had to make her way to the gun shop, but first she had to confront Lincoln about her money.

STEVEN
CHAPTER 62

December 2010

Mona Lisa was no match for him. She should know that.

Their brief confrontation was his first time seeing her in almost a month. Seeing her convinced him he'd done the right thing by moving on. He'd upgraded from an immature girl. Now he had himself a real sexy, fun, career woman who made him happy in and out of bed.

Mona acted like she was bad, as though she could make him pay for her pain and suffering. She didn't know what it felt like to take a person's life. He doubted she could aim a gun at him, then pull the trigger, even if her life depended on it. In order to shoot someone in the head and then watch them die meant Mona would have to be fearless. She was undoubtedly afraid of being on the receiving end of a bullet. He wasn't.

Mona was the reason he'd killed Davis. Depending on Lincoln's intentions with Katherine, Katherine would become more of a motivation to kill Lincoln than Mona. Once Katherine let him into the sacred space between her legs and that special spot in her heart, she had become more significant to him than Mona Lisa.

Steven hurried to his floor. Walking toward his room, he saw Katherine was crying and curled in the fetal position in front of the door. He ran to her, opened the door, scooped her into his arms, then carried her inside.

"What the hell is wrong with her?" Katherine cried, holding her face. "Crazy bitch."

The only time he'd heard Katherine curse was when she referred to Mona. Moving her hand, he said, "Damn! Aw, damn. Baby, I'm so sorry," then kissed her cheek. Her left eye was purple and slightly closed.

"She's going to pay for this," Katherine vowed.

"I got this. Baby, you stay here. I know what I have to do."

"I will not. What if she comes back? What if this gets to the media? Take me home right now, Steven," Katherine said, getting dressed. She grabbed her purse, then stomped out the door.

Katherine stared out her passenger window. She was quiet on the thirty-minute drive to her house. There was no point in explaining anything to her until she said, "Steven, I've really enjoyed our time together."

Interrupting, he turned off his engine. "But."

Softly she sighed. "I can't do this anymore. I mean, I have a son to raise. A public image to uphold. Look at my face," she said, crying. "I have to doctor on this all night and cover the bruise with makeup tomorrow. If my eye doesn't open all the way, I'll have to take tomorrow off. All because of you and her. It's just a matter of time before Mona shows up at my job. I can't afford to get fired. This has gotten out of control. You can't even stop her. I like you, Steven. But I love myself, my son, and my mother more. My family is all I've got."

What kind of female liberation bullshit was that? She wasn't so liberated and in love with herself when she accepted his gifts.

"I know what you're thinking."

Actually he had no idea what he'd do to her if she abandoned him. He'd give her a day or two to make the right decision. If she chose wrong, he'd bury her six feet deep in the same grave with Mona.

"You can have back the car. I'll give you back the money I have left in my account, and I promise to repay you for Jeremiah's tuition."

He shook his head. "I suggest you keep it. Keep your mouth shut. And keep doing what we're doing." He yelled, "You take me for a fool!"

Katherine jumped in her seat, unfastened her seat belt.

He grabbed her arm, tightened his grip. "You think I'm stupid! You want him! You want Lincoln! You want to marry him and be one happy family, don't you?"

Frantically, Katherine shook her head, opened the door. "That's not true. You can't sit there and tell me you don't understand why I don't want to be involved with you."

Refusing to let go of her arm until he'd made his point, he said, "No, what you don't understand is I didn't buy you that car or give you that money."

She frowned. "But you gave all that to me."

He shook his head. "No, I didn't. Mona did. Mona's money paid for all of that, including Jeremiah's tuition."

"You're lying. She'd never do that."

"She doesn't know. But I have a feeling that her attack on you says she knows something. So see, you need me to protect you from her." A cynical smile spread ear to ear. He released his grip.

Katherine got out of his SUV, slammed the door so hard his windows rattled. That was okay. He had her right where he wanted her. She was an emotional train about to wreck, and he was the only person that could put on the brakes. If he did nothing, Mona would hurt Katherine again and again.

Driving off, he realized Katherine, Mona, and Lincoln were within his grasp. He could destroy each of them in one day. But he'd wait. He headed to his parents' house, let himself in. They were in the living room watching television.

"Hey, Buttercup. I've been worried about you," his mother said.

"I told you that boy was all right," his dad commented. "Hey, son."

He kissed his mom, hugged his dad, then sat on the sofa beside his mom. "What you over here worrying about?"

She patted his knee. "Remember the time when you were five years old? And you were outside playing in the front yard. And I told you to come inside."

"Yeah, Mom, I remember the story."

"Well, you didn't want to listen to me so I

had to come outside and get you."

He finished the story. "And if you hadn't come to get me I'd be dead because a drunk driver lost control of his car and ran into the yard where I was playing."

"Buttercup, that man drove over your bike. You could've been on that bike."

"What does that have to do with now, Ma?"

"I got that bad feeling again today. All I can say is, stay here with your dad and me."

"Dad, tell Mom I'll be fine. I'll be by tomorrow," he said, kissing her cheek. He hugged his mom. She held onto him longer than usual.

"Let the boy go," his dad said. "Bye, son. Regina, we'll see him tomorrow."

Steven got into his car, unlocked his glove compartment. He checked his gun, confirmed it was loaded. It wasn't him his mother had to worry about.

Driving off, Steven headed straight to Lincoln's grandparents' home. It was time to settle everything man to man.

MONA
CHAPTER 63

December 2010

"William Lincoln, get your ass out here right now!"

Mona Lisa stood on the porch, fists on her hips. The nearest neighbors were over fifty yards away. She doubted they'd heard her, but she didn't care.

"Lincoln!" she yelled loud as she could. "I said get your ass out —"

His grandparents' front door opened inward and the screen door swung outward, grazed her arm, hit the side of the house. "I told you not to come back here," he said, stepping onto the porch. "What's wrong with you? Are you crazy?"

Mona Lisa stepped closer to him. Her breasts touched his chest. She should've prayed for God's mercy and forgiveness for all she'd done, but that wasn't why she was there.

"How could you? After all I've done for

you." She stared up at him. "How could you steal from me? Steal my checks. Forge my signature. For real? You didn't think I'd find out? You think it's okay to steal from me? And you're bold. A hundred thousand and" — her voice escalated — "sixty thousand dollars." She grabbed his shirt.

He slapped her hands away. "Apparently you got it like that. You wanted to buy me, Mona. Consider me bought."

"Is that what you think? You've got it wrong. I was trying to help you because I care about you. I love you. You think I'd do all the things I did for you for any other man?" she said, feeling vulnerable.

If he held her right now, she'd melt in his arms like butter on hot bread. Why was she so weak for him? Her money didn't make her a woman. Wasn't as though she was broke. She had over two million dollars that she'd transfer into a new account at a different institution first thing tomorrow.

His strong arms wrapped around her. "You're right. I'm sorry. I shouldn't have done that. I promise I'll pay you back. But if things are going to work out between us, you've got to do things my way. And you've got to promise me you'll never lie to me again."

Her tears drenched his shirt. "I promise. I

promise."

"William, what's going on out here?" his grandfather asked, standing in the doorway. "I heard yelling."

"I got this, Granddad. She's okay," Lincoln answered. "Go back inside."

Lincoln squinted. Held his hand over his brows. His eyes shifted. Left. Right. Left. Right. He bypassed his grandfather. Entered the house, returned holding a handgun. He walked down five steps into the grass yard.

Dust filled the air. Mona coughed. She couldn't identify the car headed toward the house.

Lincoln's grandfather asked, "Why you went and got that gun? Who's that, Grandson?" Not waiting for an answer, his grandfather went inside.

The car sped up, headed directly for Lincoln. He ran back toward the yard. The driver slammed on his brakes, jumped out of the car, left the door open.

"You bad military boy," Steven said. "Pull the trigger."

"Steven, what the hell are you doing?" Mona ran toward Steven, begged, "Please don't shoot him. Shoot me if you have to shoot someone."

Looking over her shoulder, Mona stared at Lincoln. He dropped his gun in the grass.

His hands fell to his side. He closed his eyes as though he prayed Steven would pull the trigger.

Steven yelled, "Pick up your weapon, soldier boy!"

Lincoln didn't move. "If you came here to kill me, do me that favor."

Bracing one hand under the other, Steven aimed his gun at Lincoln. "I'd rather you fight back, but if you want to punk out, that's on you."

"Steven, don't do this. Not again," Mona cried. "You've got to stop this."

"I'll take it easy on you, soldier," Steven said.

Pow!

Lincoln fell facedown onto the lawn. Mona raced toward him.

Pow! Pow!

Her body collapsed next to Lincoln's. Her life flashed before her.

If only she had divorced Steven and said, "Yes, Lincoln, I will marry you," her entire life could've been different.

Her decision to marry Steven had changed her life forever.

KATHERINE
CHAPTER 64

December 2010

This was the hardest thing she'd ever have to do.

"Good morning to you, America, I'm Katherine Clinton, and at the top of the news is the update from yesterday's shooting. William Lincoln, a ten-year veteran, is hospitalized. We're glad to report his condition is stable. Also at the same hospital is Steven Cunningham. Steven is on life support. The man identified only as William Lincoln's grandfather was not taken into custody for shooting Steven Cunningham. Steven Cunningham trespassed onto the property with the intent to kill his grandson, and the grandfather shot back with a double-barrel shotgun. We'll continue to keep you updated on this story as we receive more information."

Katherine removed her lavalier, tossed it on the desk. She ran to the bathroom, leaned over the toilet. Her body was weak. How could she not have sensed that Steven was such a horrible man?

Maybe she was blinded by his kindness. Heaving, she regurgitated her breakfast — one cup of coffee. Her stomach contracted until it was empty.

After rinsing her mouth, she soaked a paper towel with cold water, patted her face. The nausea in her stomach frightened her. She'd felt this way once before.

She'd promised her mother she wouldn't do this again. How was she going to tell her mother that she may have broken that promise?

LINCOLN
CHAPTER 65

December 2010

"You have a visitor," the nurse said.

Lincoln didn't bother asking who it was, because he knew who it wasn't. Steven. He pressed a button on the remote to elevate his back, straighten his covers. Placed his gown over his bandaged shoulder where the doctor had removed the bullet.

"Okay, let 'em in," he said.

Seeing her face made him exhale, turn his back to her. "So now you want to see me?"

"I know. You have every right not to want to see me. I came to say, I apologize," she said, sitting on the side of his bed facing him. "I'm really sorry for all of this. Forgive me. When I heard about the shooting, all I thought about was how you could've died and never had the chance to see your son. And that would've been my fault." She cried.

"Get off of my bed." He had no empathy

for her. Didn't try to console or hold her. She had chance after chance to do the right thing. He sent her the money she'd demanded. She wouldn't let him talk to his son. He came to Selma. She still denied him his right to see his son. Now she stood by his bedside looking like a rag doll expecting him to forgive her?

"You're right. If I had died without seeing my son, that would've been all your fault. I could've died when Steven shot me. But I'm alive for a reason. I think getting shot for the first time in my life, as crazy as this may seem, has helped with my anxiety. When Steven pointed his gun at me, I wanted to die. I was ready."

Katherine cried. "Don't say that." She reached to touch his face.

Blocking her hand, he said, "Don't tell me what to say or how to feel. You don't care about me."

"That's not true."

"It is true and I'll tell you why. If you cared about me, you wouldn't have put a price tag on my sanity and my dignity. You have no idea what I went through in Afghanistan. No idea. I'm a proud Marine. I did what I had to to protect you and every damn body else in this country."

He became quiet. Leaned over, looked at

his combat boots beside his bed. Mona had made sure the nurse had them where he could see them when he opened his eyes. His throat ached with sorrow for all he'd done, wondering if God would ever forgive him for breaking several of His commandments.

"You're right, I don't know."

It was clear. Katherine was confused. He was done talking to her. "Is my son outside?" Lincoln asked, caring more about Jeremiah than Katherine.

"I wanted to see you first. I didn't want to tell him like this."

He yelled, "This isn't about you! Can't you get that? I need to see my son!"

She tried covering his mouth. He swatted her hand away.

"Don't get upset. I'm going to help you get better first. I'll do whatever it takes to help you get better. Then I can introduce Jeremiah to you the right way," she said, touching his hand.

"Get out! Get the hell out! And don't come back here or anywhere near me unless you have my son!" he shouted.

He felt the veins in his forehead and neck expand. What the fuck was wrong with her? Didn't she get it? All he wanted to do was meet his son. Hold him. Apologize to him, not her.

Mona may have had a hidden agenda for taking care of him, but Katherine proved one thing to him today: Mona Lisa had his best interest at heart. Mona could've left him in Seattle to seek medical help on his own. She didn't have to pay for his therapy sessions. Although he'd had only one session thus far, Mona had paid for twelve. She could've had him arrested for forgery. He understood her pain and how hurt she must've been to find out he'd stolen from her. He'd never do that to her again. But after all he'd done, Mona still made sure his boots were by his side.

And for that he could only repay Mona Lisa by giving her, and only her, his heart.

STEVEN
CHAPTER 66

December 2010

"Mr. Cunningham. Mr. Cunningham."

Steven heard an unfamiliar manly voice echoing in his ear. He opened his eyes to a needle in his arm. A tube flowing up to a plastic bag with clear fluids was connected to the needle. There was another tube, this one in his nose. The heart monitor connected to his finger was stable, but his heart wasn't. Would he die not knowing what true love was?

"Mr. Cunningham, I'm Detective Davenport from the Selma Police Department, and this is my partner. I'm going to ask your parents to go to the waiting room until we're done taking a report."

"Buttercup, I'll be right back when this here detective is done." His mother looked at the detective, then said, "My Buttercup wouldn't hurt a soul. I don't know what happened at that William Lincoln boy's grandparents' house, but I sure hope justice is served." She cried. "Look at my baby."

His mother cried louder. His father hugged her.

"We'll be back, son," his dad said, fighting to contain his own tears.

Leaving the room, his parents held on to one another. They'd done all the right things raising him. But every child's mind was independent of its parents. Steven wasn't sure what made him the opposite of his mom and dad.

Looking at the detective, Steven whispered, "Haven't I seen you before?" Steven could hardly move without his neck, chest, back, shoulders, legs, and feet hurting. "Can you get the nurse for me? I, I —" He exhaled.

The detective opened the door, then called out, "Can we get a nurse, please?"

A male nurse rushed into the room. "Are you okay, Mr. Cunningham?"

"I need something stronger for the pain. I'm hurting all over."

Did he deserve to die this way? He tried to imagine what his victims must've felt before dying. He was the lucky one. Maybe. Another few inches to the left and Lincoln's grandfather would've blown out his heart. Physically, that was. Emotionally, his heart was already gone.

"Here, take these," the nurse said, handing him four pills.

As long as the medication eased his pain, he didn't care what it was. Steven tossed them in his mouth, washed them down with the cup of water, then leaned back on the pillow.

"I'll be back to check on you in a few minutes," the nurse said.

The detective cleared his throat. "I'll get straight to the point. You're under arrest. You have the right to remain silent . . ."

Really, on his sickbed this dude was reading him his rights? Steven closed his eyes. Listened until the detective asked, "Why did you shoot William Lincoln?"

"Who said that?" Steven asked, not willing to admit his guilt.

"He did," the detective said.

"He's alive? Damn, I'm getting rusty." Steven didn't care about much at this point except his mom and dad. He didn't want them to know his truth.

"Why don't I think about that while you think about this. The woman that was with Lincoln, Mona Lisa Ellington-Cunningham, is my wife. They were having an affair. She's had an affair on me before. What —"

The detective interrupted, "What you

should do is answer my question, Mr. Cunningham."

"Please, call me Steven," he said, gasping for air. The tube in his nose irritated him. "I'll get to the point. There's a dead body in my wife's house in Bakersfield. You can have the Bakersfield PD verify this right now. She killed Davis Singletary. I was trying to avoid having this happen again. So you see, I'm really the hero here."

Steven adjusted his oxygen tube. Gasped. Then continued, "I was defending myself. William Lincoln drew his gun first. There was a gun by his feet. You had to have taken it as evidence. Right?

"You should know that my wife was also involved in the murder of Brian Norris in Macon, Georgia, and Terrence Vince, in Kansas City, Kansas. Now what was your question again?" he asked, glad he'd gotten that out.

Mona probably thought her name was clear, but he was determined to destroy her even if he had to do it from hell. "Oh, and the money she was paid to do it is in her bank account at . . ."

He'd decided to let Katherine be. There was no need to complicate her life any further. She deserved to keep all he'd given her, even if Mona's money did pay for it. If

Katherine was wise, she'd keep her mouth shut, keep the money and the car and the cash. Move on with life. Be comfortable.

"Oh, and the clothes Mona Lisa had on the night Calvin McKenny was killed are in her car, in the garage, at our house. I'm done covering up and lying for my wife. If I'm guilty of anything, it's trying to protect my wife."

Steven gave a description of the car, clothes. He was certain the detective already had his address, but he repeated it just in case.

"What were those names again?" Davenport asked. He watched the detective scribble notes on a pad. His partner did the same.

Katherine must've moved on already. He hadn't heard from her since he'd been in the hospital. His mom had mentioned she'd seen Katherine going into Lincoln's room. Steven knew he was right about her wanting to be with him. What made several good women want the same man? And he couldn't get one good woman without having to buy her love?

Mona Lisa wasn't a bad woman, but he'd corrupted her. Katherine was a good woman, but he'd tainted her. He wasn't a horrible guy, but he'd done horrible things.

"Oh, and while you're taking notes, Sarah McKenny is innocent." Steven pulled the oxygen tube from his nose.

Detective Davenport opened the door, called out for a nurse.

"Tell my parents I love them." Steven was feeling no pain. Closing his eyes, Steven asked, "Now what was your question again? Again."

It didn't matter what the detective asked or what the nurses or doctors would do. Steven decided this was the last time he'd close his eyes. He didn't want his mom and dad to see him being escorted from a hospital bed to prison. If they never took him into custody, his parents would always believe he was innocent. But he wasn't.

For the lives he'd taken, Steven felt he deserved to die, and he was ready.

MONA
CHAPTER 67

December 2010

"Are you sure?"

"Yes, I'm sure. Positive," Lincoln said.

She had to hear him say it again. Mona asked, "Are you absolutely sure beyond any doubt."

"Yes, my Mona Lisa. I'm sure."

"Okay, baby. I'll see you at the hospital in a few hours." Mona ended one phone call, then answered another. "Hello."

"Is this Mona Lisa Cunningham?"

"No, it's not." She never wanted to be associated with him again. She was determined to divorce Steven so she could move on with her life.

Firmly, he said, "I'm looking for a Mona Lisa Ellington-Cunningham."

Annoyed, she asked, "Who is this?"

"This is Detective Davenport."

Why didn't he identify himself first? Her heart thumped in her chest. *Damn!* She prayed Steven hadn't involved her in his shit. "Yes, this is Mona Lisa Ellington."

"I'm calling to let you know that your husband, Steven Cunningham, is dead."

Mona smiled. "Are you sure?" she asked. Steven's death would make her day perfect. She could surprise Lincoln and give him what he's been wanting for years.

"You sound happy," the detective said. "Why?"

"No, I'm not happy," she lied. "I let him make my life a living hell. I feel resurrected. Why are you calling me?"

"I'll get to the point. I need you to come to the police station for questioning."

"For?"

"You can come to us or we can come and get you, but you need to be here within the hour," he said. "You'll find out when you get here."

"Where is his body? I need to confirm what you're saying before we speak. And I need to consult with a lawyer."

"His body is at the morgue. You can bring your attorney with you. I'll give you two hours."

The only thing Mona needed to do was to tell Lincoln the good news in person. "I'll see what I can do," she said, ending the call.

Jumping in the air, Mona clicked her

heels. There was a God. She kissed her troll genie. Hopefully God would have mercy on her. Her only crime was associating herself with a murderer. She laughed out loud.

"Mona Lisa, what's going on in there? Are you all right?" her mother asked.

"I'm fine, Mama!" Mona was too excited to tell her mother the news. Didn't want her mother scolding her about rejoicing over Steven's death. Her mom would find out eventually. Mona was sure Katherine would report Steven's death on the morning news.

Unlocking her bedroom door, Mona kissed her mom. "Thanks for letting me spend the night."

"Don't thank me, thank your father," her mother said. "You hungry? I'm cooking breakfast."

"No, Ma. I've got some business to take care of. What's the pastor's number?"

Her mother turned to her. "Whose number?"

"The pastor. I need him to meet me at the hospital."

"I know that look, Mona Lisa. What are you up to?" Her mother walked away, entered the kitchen.

Mona was right behind her. Her mother picked up the house phone, dialed seven digits. "Yes, pastor. This is Sister Ellington.

416

My daughter needs to speak with you." Her mother handed her the phone.

Mona mouthed, "Thanks, Mom," then said, "Hi, pastor. Can you meet me at the hospital in an hour? I need you." She paused. "You can! Thanks! I'll see you there!"

This was the happiest day in her life. Mona hoped the coroner didn't call her to make arrangements for Steven's body. His parents could pay for his funeral and bury him any way they'd prefer.

"Whatever it is you're up to, Mona . . . don't," her mother said. "I know you."

"Everything is fine, Mama. I'll be back later. I've gotta go."

After the shooting, her mother didn't want her in the house. Her dad insisted she stay with them. Mona's mom was afraid Mona would make them a target. That Steven would show up at their house, and one if not all of them would be shot or, worse, killed.

Mona knew what her mother would soon find out. Their worries were over. Mona danced out of her parents' house and drove straight to the store on East Highland Avenue.

After hurrying inside, she tried on a few dresses, shoes, and veils. Making her way to the register, she said, "I'll take these."

"Don't you want me to bag those for you?" the cashier asked.

A bag contained the clothes she'd worn into the store. "Nope." Mona stood close enough for the cashier to scan the items on her body. She tilted her head toward the electronic gun. *Beep.* The price of the veil registered.

"That'll be five hundred forty-nine dollars."

Mona handed her five hundred fifty dollars, then headed to the morgue. She had to see for herself. The room was freezing. Hiking her white dress above her heels, Mona viewed Steven's body.

"May I?" she asked, holding the zipper to his body bag. "Thank you, Jesus," she whispered as she zipped until the last notch locked. The weight was finally lifted from her spirit.

Mona drove to the hospital. Hiking her dress over her shoes, she trotted inside. Glad to see the pastor, Mona said, "Thanks for coming on such short notice. Come with me."

Escorting the pastor to Lincoln's room, Mona stood outside Lincoln's door. "Besides the obvious," she said, fingering her veil, then feeling her gown, "I asked you to come here to pray for William Lincoln. I imagine you heard on the news that he was recently shot. He's a war veteran and he's suffering from PTSD. He served ten years in the military and not once was shot. But he has killed. He was never physically wounded while protecting our country, but mentally he'll never be the same. Your words can help mend his broken spirit. Wait out here for a moment."

Slowly, she opened the door. Lincoln laughed when she stepped inside.

"You are so crazy, Mona. I never know what you're going to do. What are you up to?"

"Surprise," she whispered, then smiled. "Before you change your mind, we're getting married today."

He smiled back at her. "This isn't exactly how I saw the wedding going, but I'm not changing my mind. If you want to get married now, let's do it."

Mona pressed her lips to his. "I love you." In that moment, everything seemed perfect.

"Are we marrying ourselves?" he asked, elevating his bed to a sitting position.

"No, silly." Mona opened the door.

The person facing her was not the person she expected to see.

KATHERINE
CHAPTER 68

December 2010

"You are one desperate woman."

Katherine entered Lincoln's room. Mona stepped into the hallway. Came back with a man dressed in a black suit and white shirt. A gold cross dangled atop his black necktie. He held the King James version of the Bible in his hands.

"If you don't mind excusing yourself," Mona said, "we're in the middle of a ceremony."

Katherine shook her head. Looked to Lincoln for a response.

"Give us some privacy," he said. "You should've called first. Besides, I asked you not to come back here without —"

"Without your son. He's here."

Lincoln's eyes widened. "For real."

Mona interrupted, "This won't take long."

"No, getting married can wait a little longer. I want to see my son. Where is he?"

Katherine was happy she arrived in time to stop their wedding. Mona looked ridiculous draped in all white. Was she serious? Tramp.

Mona pleaded, "The pastor may not be able to come back. Lincoln, we need to do this now. She's trying to ruin our wedding on purpose."

Katherine interjected, "You have to know there's a wedding happening in order to plan to sabotage it."

Mona's eyes narrowed in her direction. If they could speak, they'd probably say, "Bitch."

"What? You want to strangle me again? Go ahead. Do it while there's witnesses." Katherine spoke to the pastor. "If she wants to punch me in the face again, she should do it now so I can press charges." She turned to Mona. "You're not so bad when other people are watching, are you?"

Katherine spoke to Lincoln. "You want to see your son or not?"

Lincoln looked at Mona, then at the pastor. "What do you think, Rev?"

"Doesn't matter what I think, young man. But what I know is, *I'm* not performing a ceremony here today. Neither of you are spiritually grounded enough to get married."

That was Katherine's blessing. Lincoln seeing Jeremiah might swing his heart in her direction.

The pastor placed his hand on Lincoln's head, then said, "Lord, I ask that You watch over this young man. He may have done some things not favorable in Your sight, but he has risked his life to protect the freedom and liberties afforded to every man, woman, and child in this country. We will not forsake him. I ask that You protect his mind, give him peace from within. Cast out any and all demons inside of him. Stop all demons that seek to invade his light. Build a shield of love around him. Whatever sins he may have committed, we pray for forgiveness. We pray for his full recovery, in Jesus's name we ask for these blessings. Amen."

Katherine said, "Amen." She was shocked when Mona Lisa said it too.

"Young man, when you do what feels right in your heart, it's never the wrong thing. Mona, tell your mother hello for me." The pastor clenched the Bible to his chest, then left the room.

Soon as the door closed, Mona said, "You can't just spring this on Lincoln like this."

"Do something constructive. How about you go take off that white gown and go bury your husband?"

Slap!

This time Katherine struck back. She snatched Mona's veil over her head, tightened it around her neck. Katherine balled her fingers into a fist and began repeatedly punching Mona in the back of her head. All the rage inside her surfaced, making Katherine want to ram Mona's head into the wall, but she decided not to.

Reporting the news, she understood the fine line between life and death. She was so angry with Mona she could've killed her. But what was the real underlying basis for her hatred? Steven? Mona? Lincoln? Or was she in doubt about the part she'd played in all that had happened?

Lincoln yelled, "Stop it! Didn't either of you hear the prayer? Stop it right now!"

Jeremiah opened the door. "Mommy! Mommy!"

Katherine shoved Mona to the floor, then slammed her veil on top of her. Heaving, she reached for her child. "Everything is okay, baby."

Lincoln shook his head. "Jeremiah?"

"Mommy, who's that?"

Katherine looked at Mona scraping herself from the floor. "Leave, now."

Mona sat in the chair beside Lincoln's bed. "We're not done."

Katherine exhaled. Lincoln's door opened. Two officers in uniform walked in.

Katherine recognized Detective Davenport. The other officer she'd seen but didn't know. "We apologize for the disturbance, officers. Everything is okay."

Detective Davenport said, "Mona Lisa Ellington-Cunningham?"

Mona remained silent.

"You're under arrest for the suspicion of murdering Davis Singletary. You have the right to remain silent . . ."

Now Katherine wished Mona hadn't known about her relationship with Steven. She could hardly breathe, wondering if Detective Davenport was going to call her name next. Katherine prayed her decision to accept Steven's gifts didn't involve her in whatever he and Mona had done.

Mona's hands were cuffed behind her back. She glanced at Lincoln. "I've never killed a soul. Promise me you won't break our engagement."

Katherine awaited his response.

When Lincoln said, "I promise," to Mona, Katherine knew her engagement to him was officially over.

MONA
CHAPTER 69

December 2010

What a disastrous difference a day made.

Suddenly she wished Steven were alive. That no-good, low-down bastard got off easy. Mona had an idea he'd kept the clothes from Calvin's murder, but now she knew for sure. Not only had he hid them, they were in her car, the car her parents had given her when she was in high school. But that wasn't nearly as shocking as his leaving Davis's body in her Bakersfield home.

Quietly she sat on the bus with the other women. Instead of marrying Lincoln, she was in transit to CCWF — Central California Women's Facility, the only California women's prison with a death row.

Praying her sentencing didn't warrant the death penalty, Mona had to prove she didn't kill Davis. But Shawna Forde received the death penalty for orchestrating a home invasion that ended in two murders. Shawna hadn't pulled the trigger, but the jury found her guilty. Listening to Marion Jones share her story on *The Mo'Nique Show* was frightening. She'd spent forty-five plus days in solitary confinement for defending herself. Mona's crime was marrying the wrong man, and the only woman that could help prove her innocence wasn't her mother, it was Mama V.

Mona was speechless as Detective Davenport had said, "We've got proof."

Proof? Based upon Steven's confession, the detective concluded she was guilty of murder?

She had demanded an attorney but quickly discovered she couldn't afford one. Her assets, frozen. Steven's assets, frozen. Hopefully Lincoln would find a way to help her get out of prison.

"Oh, shit. The video." They had to have found it.

Guards escorted her and the other women off the bus; she scanned her surroundings. "This can't be my life." They led her to the intake area. Was she really being processed into prison?

"I told you I'm innocent," Mona Lisa cried. "I can prove it."

Her naked body stood cold.

The manly looking woman said, "Open your mouth."

Mona wanted to bite her fingers as the woman probed under her tongue, underneath her upper and lower lips. Mona's lips trembled. Tears streamed down her cheeks.

"Bend over and spread your cheeks," the manly looking woman said. "Let them tell it, every person in here is innocent."

Mona's ass was spread wide. The woman's gloves slid over her anus, slipped into her vagina, roamed, slid up to her anus, probed. "Put this on," she said, handing her a prison uniform that would become her daily wardrobe.

"My engagement rings. What are they going to do with them?" Mona asked.

"You're cute. We have twice the number of inmates we should, so you'll probably get several rings while you're in here. They won't look the same, but it's the thought that counts, right?"

This shit was a joke to her. Mona was serious. She was no longer a name; she was a number. Another woman called out her number, then said, "Come with me."

She knew she'd be back in California. But she'd imagined it would've been to move her things out of the house she was renting and bring permanent closure to the years spent with Steven.

"My engagement rings, what are they going to do with them?" Mona asked the woman behind her, the same as she'd asked the intake person.

"You do realize you're in for murder. An engagement ring is the least of your worries. Wait until you meet your cellmate. My suggestion, never sleep."

"Then why are you putting me with her?" Mona asked.

"We're overcrowded. Almost double our capacity. Be happy you have a bed. Here you are," she said.

Another person unlocked the cell. Before Mona stepped inside, her cellmate blocked her entrance, then said, "Bitch, you don't wanna come in here."

Determined to clear her name, appeal her case, get her money back from the government, and get revenge on Katherine, Mona had to survive. She had to stay out of trouble.

The guard shoved Mona inside the cell. The metal door closed behind her. The woman in the cell stood an inch from Mona's face. "You won't last a day in here. I hate cellmates. I hate sharing. And I fucking hate kids. Don't post any damn pictures in here. Keep your mouth shut, so I don't have to shut it for you."

"You —"

Wham! Mona's head hit the wall.

Her cellmate whispered, "Say something else, bitch. I dare you."

Mona touched the side of her face. Blood streamed down her fingers. She stared at her cellmate. *Do I kick her ass or shut up?*

Wham! Mona's head hit the wall again.

"That should help you make up your mind. Either way you gon' shut the fuck up. I'm Bambi Bartholomew, bitch, and until I get out of this hellhole, I run this block."

Wham! Mona slammed Bambi's head into the same wall three times.

"I'm not looking for trouble," Mona said. "But you need to know, I'm nobody's bitch."

KATHERINE
CHAPTER 70

December 2010

"Good morning to you, America, I'm Katherine Clinton. At the top of the news is great news. I'm standing in front of the prison waiting for Sarah McKenny's release this morning. It's wonderful when justice is served. In the background are Sarah's family and friends anxiously waiting for her. We'll give you a breaking update when Sarah comes out."

The day ended with Katherine giving thanks for not being an accomplice to whatever Steven was plotting. She hadn't walked in Mona's shoes and wasn't celebrating that Mona was behind bars but felt Mona deserved to do time.

On her way home, Katherine stopped by Steven's parents' house, knocked on the door. His mother greeted her.

"Come on in, Katherine," his mother said. "Buttercup really is dead. I still can't believe it." Mrs. Cunningham wept.

Mr. Cunningham consoled her. "We don't believe our son killed those people. Steven wasn't a murderer. And although he's gone, we're going to fight to the end to prove he was innocent."

Katherine wasn't there to discuss whether Steven was innocent or guilty. She knew he was guilty.

"Can you help us?" Mrs. Cunningham asked in between weeping. "We'll pay you."

"No, ma'am. I can't get involved in this. I don't mean any disrespect, but I have a son to take care of by myself. Which brings me to the reason I'm here," she said, still standing in their living room. "I'm pregnant with Steven's baby."

Mrs. Cunningham's face lit up. "Are you sure it's from our Steven?"

Taking a deep breath, Katherine said, "I'm positive. But I'm not keeping it."

"I don't understand," Mr. Cunningham said.

"Why would you tell us this, then tell us you're having an abortion? You can't kill Steven's baby." Mrs. Cunningham's voice grew stronger. "We won't let you."

Katherine sighed heavily. There was no way she wanted to break her promise to her mother. She couldn't afford to be a single mom with a second child. God may never forgive her if she aborted the baby. But either way, she had to make a decision.

Mr. Cunningham hugged his wife, then asked Katherine, "What are you thinking, child?"

"My options are, I could put the baby up for adoption. I could relinquish my parental rights and give the baby to you guys to raise. Or I can terminate the pregnancy."

Katherine also worried that she'd lose Lincoln forever if she had Steven's baby. Lincoln wouldn't care if she put the baby up for adoption. He wouldn't see her the same if she had an abortion. With Mona Lisa behind bars, Katherine had one last chance to win Lincoln back. But had she blown that opportunity by telling the Cunninghams? She was sure they'd tell everyone, including her mother.

"We'd like for you to have the baby and give the baby to us," Mrs. Cunningham said.

Mr. Cunningham asked, "What would you like to do?"

This was by far the most difficult decision Katherine had to make. She thought about her options, looked at Steven's parents for a long time wishing she hadn't come to their house. But she was there. Her pregnancy was real.

Katherine opened the door, took one last look at their sad yet anxious faces, then answered, "I'm not sure."

Whatever decision she made, either way, her life would never be the same.

Cheating Is Never the Real Reason for a Breakup

Let me say that no relationship breakup is because of cheating. Irreconcilable differences are the primary reasons relationships — marriages included — end. Far too often breakups are bitter and backstabbing. In most instances, your irreconcilable differences are preexisting. Basically, we all have baggage.

Whether you've never been monogamous, you're a pathological liar, you're a user, you have self-esteem issues, you're sexually inhibited, you're bisexual, you're insecure, you've been abused, you're abusive and have anger management problems, or whatever your flaws are, it's a fact that most people harbor these detrimental toxins within them long before meeting their mate.

You're not honest enough or brave enough to tell your potential partner the truth about yourself. You don't dump your baggage in the middle of the floor. Your life is not an open book, and in some cases you won't even crack the spine on your own life story. You suppress your emotions. Yet you sit at the table with a long list of expectations for your partner, who is more than likely sitting on their book of lies to boost their own ego.

Now you have two people pretending they're in love when in fact neither of you know what love is. What you become is emotionally codependent. You need someone to care about you, so you say, "I love you," expecting them to regurgitate the same. If they don't, you'd rather they lie to make you feel better about yourself?

Stop lying to yourself. Covering up your truth is the demise of your relationship. People want others to accept them for who they are, but most people aren't who they claim to be.

If you know someone has lied to you, don't ignore the lie. Yes, it's imperative to forgive, but don't be a fool about it. Yes, everybody plays the fool sometimes, but don't marry the fool thinking they're going to change. Accept people for who they are. But the only way you can honestly do that is to keep it 100 with who you are.

Marriage does not entitle you to control your spouse. You have no right to tell an adult what they can or cannot do. You reserve that right in your parent–child relationship. But please don't have children outside of your marriage and complicate things for the child. If the child was born prior to marriage, that's great. But after you say, "I do," please don't get caught up. That's inconsiderate and selfish.

Speaking of selfish, this is the real reason people cheat.

You meet someone. They look, feel, and smell good to you. They flirt. You flirt back. Maybe your partner/spouse doesn't make you feel this way anymore.

You subscribe to "eating ain't cheating" or what "he/she doesn't know won't hurt 'em." Maybe your spouse has stopped sexing you for any number of reasons, to punish you, or they're too tired, they've lost their libido and don't know how to get it back, or they've lost interest in having sex . . . with you.

Whatever the reason, now you feel justified in cheating.

So you hook up with someone. You make a conscious effort. You take off your clothes. You lie down with the other person. You may not have the decency to make sure protection is used. You take the risk. You either penetrate or allow yourself to be penetrated by someone you may barely know. Or perhaps it's an old flame that you fan until you explode with sexual pleasure.

But let's say your partner is smarter than you. They find out about your affair. You're confronted. What now?

They say to you, "How can I ever trust you again?" I'd like to say you've broken your trust with that person, but the fact is you've never had trust in your dysfunctional relationship. Deception isn't trust. Thus, the constant confrontation begins. You try to justify your actions. The anger comes out. You blame the other person. Tears of pain stream down your partner's face. You apologize.

Yet you do it again. Why?

Because you're a selfish liar. You lie with a straight face. Perhaps you straighten up for a moment, but when the opportunity presents itself again, then what? You do it again. You're not man or woman enough to accept who you are, so you lie about what you think the other person wants you to be because you don't want them to leave you. You. My point exactly. . . . You are selfish and inconsiderate.

Now, it's a fact that everybody doesn't cheat. Some people are committed to their relationship irrespective of their challenges. Problem is, opposites do attract, and seldom do two of a kind meet.

Then there's the concern of growing apart. I'd rather look at it as growing together, because when you meet someone you're not honestly on the same page. Oh, sure, it appears that way. Why? Because you gravitate to what you have in common. You highlight your likes. You don't discuss your dislikes. You think you're a match made in heaven.

Perhaps. But if you're in tears before the ink dries on the marriage certificate, consider your relationship a match made on earth, maybe in hell if that's what you allow the other person to put you through. Fire.

As time goes on, what happens when the thing you loved the most about the person is the same shit you can't stand about them later? For example, you start out saying, "Oh, my baby is so smart." You end up saying, "You know what, I can't stand your smart ass."

In parting, I say to you, "Take ownership of who *you* are and you'll have a better relationship. Don't use others for your personal gain and gratification. And equally as important, don't let anyone, I mean anyone, use you."

Better to be a smart-ass than to be a dumb-ass.

Family, Friends, & Fans
From My Heart to Yours

January 1, 2011, 12:22 a.m.

As we ring in the New Year, I'm not at a festive event. I'm not at a gala or a club. I'm sitting at home with my son and his girlfriend, Emaan.

My son, as 2010 ends, kneels in our living room and prays. I watch him. As the New Year rolls in, he kneels at my bed (which is in our living room) and he prays again. I watch him.

The three of us watch the fireworks at the Waterbar's waterfront in San Francisco exploding on television. We are in awe. I think, man-made. It's drizzling outside our ceiling-to-floor window. The rain is God-made. We briefly stand in the window, and we see the fireworks shooting in the air in Oakland.

My son and girlfriend retreat to his bedroom. I sit alone, yet not lonely. I open up my heart. I give thanks for my guardian angels. I wonder what my dad's childhood was like. I wonder why he was physically so close but yet emotionally so far from all of his children. What happened to him?

I wonder what my mom endured. Why the things in this world made her feel she was better off dead. Then I reflected on the moments (as a child) when I believed I was better off dead. The two moments that are most vivid are the times when my great-aunt had my younger brother make a noose. She hung it from a tree in our backyard at 2118 Second Street in New Orleans. The noose was for me.

She put it around my neck and choked me until I couldn't breathe. I cannot, even in this moment, recall why. What did I do as a little girl that was so awful that made her threaten to take my life away? Tears streamed down my face, but I'm not sad. I have too much to be grateful for to be sad.

Then there was the time when all of my friends put together their money, bought cookies, punch, and chips. They did this to celebrate my birthday, September 17, but I can't remember the year. I do vividly remember that everyone was there except me.

My great-aunt wouldn't let me go. So I stood in the door at 2118 Second Street, and I could see my friends across the street celebrating my day. They taught me that the party should go on with or without the guest of honor. I was missed, but they had a great time. I felt honored that day even though I wasn't there. Knowing how much my friends cared made me feel loved.

I then began to give thanks for my great-aunt, for I know not her struggle. But I do know that it takes a hellava woman to rear not one but four children that weren't hers.

I thanked my mother and father, for I know they watch over me all the time. One by one, I visualize their faces and I give thanks. I'm not sad in this moment. When I visualize my dad, my glass that sat in front of me on my coffee table, filled with Godiva chocolate, Baileys Irish Cream, and one ice cube, chimed one time. That moment reminded me of when Whoopi said in *The Color Purple,* "God's here."

I opened my eyes. I gave thanks to my dad for acknowledging his presence. I know he's with me always; my guardian angels are with me always.

I wouldn't change a thing. God made my life, my struggles, this way for a reason. As I bring this note to an end, I realize that I am most grateful for three things: my family, my friends, and my fans. I hold each of you in my heart because your presence reminds me of what is most important in life — people.

I am not alone. You are not alone. Whatever your journey, remember, every road traveled leads to higher ground. And no matter how difficult your journey, always navigate with faith.

And so it is, this note ends on January 1, 2011, at 1:07 a.m.

AND YOU KNOW
WHAT IT'S LIKE TO LOVE

Sparkles in your eyes gleam from your
   soul.
Your fingers dance in their hair.
Your touch rejuvenates the spirit.
You sit in silence and your silence speaks
   volumes.
And you know what it's like to love.
A favorite thing remembered.
You freely give your all.
You reminisce with a smile.
A helping hand extended.
And you know what it's like to love.
Your light shines bright.
You put yourself last.
It is more blessed to give than to receive.
You're taught this and you believe.
You give so much.
You cannot conceive.
You know what it's like to love.
But do you know what it's like to be loved.

DISCUSSION QUESTIONS

1. How would you feel if you found out that the man you were in love with proposed to you and another woman on the same day? What would you do?
2. Do you have family or close friends serving (or who have served) in the military? If so, do any of them suffer with post-traumatic stress disorder? What type of personality did they have before, during, and after serving in the military?
3. Do you believe the saying, "You don't know a person until you live with them?" Do you believe Mona's impromptu decision to marry Steven was more greatly influenced by the fact that she'd known Steven since the second grade, by her desire to leave her mother's house, or by the money he'd spent on her?
4. What would you do if you knew you only had twenty-four hours to live?
5. If you could turn back the hands of time,

change one decision in your life, which decision would that be? You have to choose one thing for discussion purposes. For better or worse, how do you think having made that decision would have impacted your life today?

6. Would you have accepted the material things Katherine accepted from Steven? Do you think Katherine gave herself to Steven because she cared for him or she was impressed with the things he'd done for her and wanted him to do more? Would you have given back the money and the car if you were Katherine? Why?

7. Would you impulsively get married? Why?

8. Do you believe it's possible to truly know everything about a person before marrying them?

9. Do you feel Mona Lisa should've gone to jail for Davis's murder? Was there anything that Mona was involved in that she should have served time for? If so, what sentence should Mona receive? How would you feel if Mona were your daughter?

10. Should underage girls have the right to an abortion without parental consent? How do you think Lincoln would have felt about Mona if he knew Mona had aborted his child?

11. A nice kid like Steven, reared by wonder-

ful parents, was driven in his adult life by greed. Do you think bounty hunters have integrity? Would you marry a bounty hunter?

12. What would you do if you found out that your partner lied to you about something that landed you in prison for life? And they die before you can prove you're innocent?

13. If you could vote to eliminate one paid federal/government holiday and have all the funding for that holiday allocated to helping veterans, would you vote? If so, which paid government holiday do you feel should be eliminated?

ABOUT THE AUTHOR

New York Times bestselling author **Mary B. Morrison** believes that women should shape their own destiny. Born in Aurora, IL, and raised in New Orleans, LA, she took a chance and quit her near six-figure government job to self-publish her first book, *Soulmates Dissipate,* in 2000 and begin her literary career. Mary's books have appeared on numerous bestseller lists, and she's a frequent contributor to *The Michael Baisden Show.* Mary is also actively involved in a variety of philanthropic endeavors, and in 2006 she sponsored the publishing of an anthology written by 33 sixth-graders. In 2010, Mary produced a play based on her novel, *Single Husbands,* which she wrote under her pseudonym, HoneyB. Mary currently resides in Oakland, CA, with her wonderful son, Jesse, who is following in his mother's creative footsteps and pursuing a career in

TV/film. Visit Mary online at www.mary
morrison.com.